The little girl raced into the arms of…Rhys Gannon

What on earth? *Why is* he *here?*

Still holding the phone, Whitney peeked through the curtain and felt a surge of fear. Had he found her out, learned that she was here under false pretenses? Or was he just paying the elderly couple a visit? They were acquaintances, after all.

Rhys swung the child around, and as he did, the hood on her little sweatshirt fell back, exposing a profusion of golden curls. Whitney pressed her forehead against the window, straining to see more.

His whole face lit up. His mouth split into a broad affectionate smile as they all talked back and forth——Rhys, Gretta and Johnny, who ran the inn, and their granddaughter. Then, with the little girl still in his arms, Rhys leaned over and hugged both Gretta and Johnny.

Whitney stared. "Oh…my…God," she whispered. The phone slipped from her fingers and she watched in stunned surprise as the scene played out before her.

It took every ounce of willpower to blunt the excitement of her discovery.

She'd found her nie

Dear Reader,

I've always been fascinated with what makes people tick, and as long as I can remember, always had a passion to write. So it's no wonder I pursued dual degrees, one in behavioral science and another in journalism. Working in both fields has given me an inside view of people's lives and, at times, landed me in the thick of dramatic and intriguing situations. Those experiences have stayed with me—and taught me so much about the healing power of love.

Though born and raised in Minnesota, I've lived in Arizona nearly half my life. I love the diversity of my chosen state and thought it the perfect setting for my first novel, *Her Sister's Secret*.

Just as Arizona is a land of dramatic contrasts, the backgrounds of my characters Whitney Sheffield and Rhys Gannon are dramatically different from one another.

The fictional mountain town of Estrade (which means a high stage or platform) is similar to many of the revived ghost towns in central and northern Arizona, where the Mogollon Rim cuts across the state, dividing mountains from the desert floor. The setting of *Her Sister's Secret* has basis in fact; the rest is the product of my imagination. I must confess that I'm a hopeless romantic, and writing Whitney and Rhys's story allowed me to do what I love most—explore the complexities of human relationships...and write about them.

I hope you'll enjoy the journey to Estrade.

Linda Style

P.S. I would love to hear from you. You can reach me online at lstyle@uswest.net.

HER SISTER'S SECRET
Linda Style

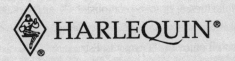

HARLEQUIN®

TORONTO • NEW YORK • LONDON
AMSTERDAM • PARIS • SYDNEY • HAMBURG
STOCKHOLM • ATHENS • TOKYO • MILAN • MADRID
PRAGUE • WARSAW • BUDAPEST • AUCKLAND

ISBN 0-373-70923-4

HER SISTER'S SECRET

Visit us at www.eHarlequin.com

Printed in U.S.A.

To my family—
whose love, support and encouragement spurred me on.

Jay—the wind beneath my wings and the love of my life.
Tim, Todd, Barry and Jason—my sons, heroes one and all.
Courtney and Connor—awesome kidlets who brighten my
days. Margie and Theresa—two remarkable women.
Mildred Lane Torborg—my mother, whose love
knows no bounds.

CHAPTER ONE

MORGAN'S MURDERER stood less than thirty yards away.

Turn around, you lowlife.

Whitney Sheffield raised her camera, squinted into the viewfinder, then clicked off half a dozen frames. Mouth and throat dry, she zoomed the lens, focusing on Rhys Gannon.

The devil himself.

Fear and anger knotted her stomach as she watched the man strut among the ragtag band of motorcyclists— men wearing leather, chains with keys dangling, torn and dirty jeans. Some wore bandannas or Billy Jack hats over long straggly hair.

She glanced around. If she could just find a better position, maybe...

Hidden behind a post in an old bandstand across the road, Whitney found an opening between the heavy pine boughs, then panned the narrow mountain street. She stopped to focus on the motorcycles lined up in front of the Old West storefront like iron horses hitched to a post.

Some of the bikers straddled the low-slung seats or stood slumped against their vehicles; others carried on like a marauding band of outlaws, poking and punching, hooting and shouting loudly enough to be heard in Phoenix.

Come on, come on. Look this way...

Her breath came in quick snatches as she hurriedly

clicked off a few more shots. No good. He wouldn't turn—and she couldn't get closer without being seen.

She studied Gannon through the telephoto lens, and despite the hatred pumping through her veins, her photographer's eye caught his body's graceful symmetry as he strode from one man to another—then stopped in their midst.

That's it! Make that deal…and turn, dammit.

She needed proof. Even though her hands were shaking and her heart battered her ribs, she wasn't going to leave without it.

A man pointed in Whitney's direction. Oh, God! She jerked back behind the pillar and squeezed her eyes shut, praying he hadn't seen her, praying she hadn't made the biggest mistake of her life in coming here alone.

But there'd been no choice. She'd finally found Rhys Gannon, and it didn't take a nuclear physicist to know he could disappear in a photoflash. Time was of the essence.

As a result, she'd jumped headlong into something as far removed from her life as Harlem—and she couldn't remember ever being so scared.

Whitney waited a moment, then hauled in a deep breath and peered around the post. Seeing the bikers' attention was now elsewhere, she sighed in relief, raised the camera and zoomed in.

Gannon had his back to her, but he looked every bit as dangerous as Morgan had said. The ebony hair that curled over the collar of a black leather jacket, the boots and snug-fitting jeans—his appearance affirmed every evil image Whitney had conjured up in the three long months it had taken to find him in this godforsaken place.

Three torturous months filled with despair over Morgan's death. Despair and the uncertainty of ever finding her sister's child.

She continued to track the man, following his lithe arrogant strides. Tall and broad-shouldered, he carried himself with cocksure confidence, the kind found in men who knew full well how to defend themselves.

He sauntered from one biker to another, exchanging high fives with each. One man noisily revved his motor. Then came another blast, and another. Raucous shouts rode the crisp October air, and amid a spate of whoops and hollers, the steel cavalcade spit gravel and peeled out in a cloud of dust and exhaust.

Fearing he'd leave, too, Whitney grabbed her bag, preparing to follow. But when the dust settled, she saw that Gannon had stayed behind. He jammed a hand into his jacket pocket and pulled out a small package.

A jolt of excitement zapped through her. Yes! She readied the camera, but before she got off a shot, he'd stuffed the bundle back in his pocket. He climbed the wooden steps and disappeared into the store.

Rats! Whitney glanced at her watch, then at the sky. Five o'clock and it was already dusk. Well, so what? She gritted her teeth and crossed her arms, staring at the door of the motorcycle shop. She'd wait—no matter how long it took.

And if the bikers returned? She shuddered at the thought and rubbed her chilled hands together.

Whatever it takes, that's what! If she had learned nothing else in thirty years, she'd learned that much. *Just do it* had been her mantra long before a shoe company had appropriated the phrase.

Waiting, she cursed the man who'd brought her here. Rhys Gannon. His name was probably as phony as everything else about him. But whatever he called himself, he was the man she blamed for her sister's death.

No, he hadn't been accused or tried in any court of law, nor had he actually lifted a hand to do the deed. But he was responsible. Rhys Gannon had dragged Morgan into a life of drugs and prostitution to support his own drug habit, and when she'd finally had enough and left, he'd kidnapped their baby to force Morgan to come back.

Tight-jawed and trembling, Whitney clenched her hands. He was to blame, all right, every bit as much as if he'd crammed the pills down Morgan's throat.

He was going to pay for that.

Whitney swallowed hard against a surge of grief and blinked back the sudden tears. Her sorrow fused with a bone-deep ache of guilt. She hadn't been there when her little sister needed her, and nothing she did now could change it.

She sucked in a lungful of air, quelling a flood of regret. It was too late to help Morgan—but not too late to carry out her last request.

Whitney would find SaraJane, the three-year-old niece she'd never seen. She'd find her and gain custody, just as she'd promised Morgan. She would *not* let her sister down again.

She sat down on the dusty wooden bandstand steps to switch lenses, glad for the expertise of her profession—though she could hardly compare snapping pictures of a junkie with photographing the rich and famous.

In the midst of swapping lenses, she caught a shadow of movement and looked up. Gannon stood on the empty wooden boardwalk, legs apart, boots firmly planted, thumbs hooked in his front pockets. Like a sentinel, he surveyed the street from one end to the other.

Then he stared directly at her.

She shrank back, wincing in pain when her spine hit a sharp edge on the pillar. Her breath caught. Had he seen her? Or was he simply looking in her direction?

She should run. She wanted to run. But if she did, he'd see her for sure.

She fumbled with the lens release, cursing her cold stiff fingers as she rammed the new one in place. An engine blast split the air. She jumped, startled nearly out of her skin.

The noise resounded off the mountains like explosions in a war zone. Panicked, Whitney darted another look in Gannon's direction and saw the black-and-chrome machine moving toward her.

Oh, God! Oh, dear God. Her body went taut. The blood pulsed through her veins.

Her hands shook as she shoved the camera into her jacket, caught in the act when the massive motorcycle and its helmeted rider rumbled up beside her. Suppressing a tiny cry, she bolted to her feet. The case tumbled to the grass and landed right beside the man's boot.

"Need help?" he asked over the idling growl of the engine. After a moment he leaned down, picked up the case by the strap and held it out to her.

Her insides whirled like the contents of a blender on high speed, but she couldn't let him know that. Besides, it was silly to be so nervous. Even if he guessed why she was there, what could he possibly do right in the middle of town?

She glanced down the morgue-quiet street. A fresh shiver of fear crawled up her spine. Okay. Okay. She tightened her grip on the camera and steeled her resolve by focusing solely on what she needed to do.

Find SaraJane.

It didn't help.

She'd never felt so utterly out of her element. Pulling on her old college drama training, she flashed the most brilliant smile she could muster and reached for the bag.

"I...don't...know." She drew out the words, stalling for time to think. She brushed back a long strand of hair that the wind had flicked across her face and tucked it into the barrette at the nape of her neck. She nodded toward his machine.

"Your motorcycle. It looks, uh, unusual."

The sleek helmet masked most of Gannon's face, preventing her from seeing his expression. But then he flipped the visor and through the rectangular eye slot she saw crinkles near the corners of his eyes. She hoped that meant he was smiling.

"You interested in bikes?" His voice, a husky baritone, held a hint of amusement. Or was it sarcasm?

Whatever the case, it was obvious that her plan—to get secret photos of him doing a drug deal and then offer him money to give up his parental rights to SaraJane—might be shot all to hell.

"Or maybe you see something else that interests you?" he drawled suggestively.

Exactly the kind of response she'd expect from a man like him. Still, the question rankled. For the life of her, she couldn't come up with an answer—at least none that didn't include *dirtbag sleaze* or *lowlife scum.*

His dark gaze slid to the base of her throat, then drifted upward to her mouth. Her pulse thundered in her ears, whether from fear or anger, she couldn't tell. After what seemed an eternity, his lids slowly raised until his eyes locked with hers.

Cobalt blue and ocean-deep. So deep, she seemed to founder in them like a speechless idiot.

Oh, for crying out loud, Whitney. Say something! Do something! In one swift movement, she put her camera into the bag and zipped it shut.

"Well, yes. I am interested in motorcycles, sort of," she lied, making up her story as she went along. "I'm on an assignment." She studied his vehicle. "An assignment to photograph motorcycles."

Despite the chill in the air, a rush of heat prickled her skin. She waved a hand at his bike. "Photographs. For a book," she clarified.

Silence.

The heat grew in her chest, then worked its way up her neck to her cheeks. But when she saw the cold scrutiny in Gannon's eyes, she felt a moment's panic. Did he know she was lying?

She ignored the thought. SaraJane was all that mattered.

"Yes." She cleared her throat and plunged ahead. "It's a book on motorcycles, and unfortunately, since I'm just starting my research, I don't know much about them." She shrugged and stuck out her hand. "My name is Whitney Sheffield."

She figured it was probably safe to use her real name. Morgan had disowned the family when she ran away at sixteen and had always used an alias; it was the reason Whitney hadn't been able to find her, though, Lord knows, she'd tried often enough. Besides, if Whitney used a fake name, she could easily forget and screw things up.

Finger by finger, Gannon removed one black leather glove while his insolent gaze traveled over her. She struggled to maintain her cool under this blatant assessment, but felt her vulnerability intensify.

Morgan had described Rhys Gannon's arrogant in-your-face attitude to a T, but even so, the vivid description failed to prepare Whitney for such a coarse appraisal.

He reached out, enveloping her hand in his. His skin was hot, his touch firm. Disturbed by the contact, she ducked her head and looked down. Her gaze landed on faded denim stretched tightly over well-muscled thighs straddling the idling bike.

Lord, she could almost feel the raw animal power humming through him—a high-octane sexual aggressiveness of which she was suddenly all too aware.

How could she even have noticed? She couldn't forget, not for a second, that this was a man without conscience.

But then, she'd have to be blind not to see him as he was. She was trained to notice such things. A good photographer had to be aware of her surroundings.

She inhaled a deep breath of crisp pine-scented air, eased her hand from his grip and forced her gaze to meet his. His eyes evaluated and challenged her—then, in the next instant, went all hot and vibrant.

The man radiated attitude. Attitude and steaming masculinity. Yes, even though she could see only his eyes, she could easily understand Morgan's attraction. Her baby sister had always been susceptible to the reckless physical side of life.

And Rhys Gannon might as well have had *DANGEROUS* emblazoned in fire-engine-red neon across his broad chest.

But it was *Morgan* who found that element attractive, not her. Morgan had always been more daring—and more needy.

"Actually, I was passing through Phoenix when I heard that Estrade might be a good place to do some research. I was told Bruce Springsteen came here once with his motorcycle entourage,'' she said, remembering the photo shoot she'd done with the singer.

Gannon laughed, a rich baritone from deep within. ''Lady, you've come to the right place, but you're a couple years too late.''

''What do you mean? Too late for what?''

''Used to be a biker bar here.'' He motioned down the street toward the place where he'd gone inside before. ''It's just a parts shop now.''

''But those riders...?''

''Passing through.''

Whitney frowned, torn between the need to keep him talking so she could get information about her niece and the rush of panic that made her want to run like hell.

''Okay,'' she said. ''Can you tell me something about your motor—I mean, your bike?'' She narrowed her eyes to examine the vehicle more closely.

He glanced at his watch, which Whitney noticed was a high-tech stainless-steel digital, definitely not the kind a typical gang member would wear. Spikes on black leather would be more fitting.

''Nope,'' he said, steering his bike around to head in the other direction. ''I've got an appointment. C'mon round tomorrow morning if you want.'' He paused, adding seconds later, ''I might be back then.'' He gunned the motor.

Right. And I might be Peter Pan. Damn! Damn and double damn. If he left now, what was the likelihood he'd come back tomorrow?

And what would she do in the meantime? Sleep in her car? She hadn't seen a single hotel or motel in the small town.

Frustrated, she let out an audible sigh.

She'd flown in from New York this morning, rented a car, driven three long hours on twisting mountain roads and then waited all afternoon for Gannon to show up at the shop. She'd had a hard time even finding him, and if it wasn't for the name ''Rhys'' on his license plate, she might still be looking.

Lord, she was tired. Her shoulder muscles ached, and from habit, she rolled them to get out the kinks.

''Can you give me a suggestion where I might stay?'' she asked, hoping that if he knew she was staying overnight, he'd feel some compunction to come back.

Gannon watched her with speculative eyes, then reached out a hand. ''Get on,'' he commanded over the engine's noise.

She stiffened and slung the camera bag abruptly over her shoulder, retreating a step.

The last thing in the world she wanted was to get on a motorcycle with a drug-dealing kidnapper.

He nodded toward the road. ''I'll show you where to stay.''

Oddly, his tone sounded understanding. Was he really offering help or was there more to it? Morgan had said he was smooth. She'd also said he was cruel, dangerous and as volatile as nitroglycerin.

Whitney had no reason to doubt it.

His hand remained outstretched.

She pointed to the white sedan she'd rented in Phoenix. ''I have a car. Tell me where the hotel is and I'll drive there,'' she answered, praying she sounded more confident than she felt.

He glanced at the car, then withdrew his hand.

''I'll follow you,'' she added quickly.

''You ever been on a bike before?''

She drew her bottom lip between her teeth and shook her head.

"Afraid?"

Hell, yes! Whitney squared her shoulders. "No," she fired back. "But I don't know you. I don't know anything about you."

He looked down, cracking gloved knuckles, one hand in the other.

Oh, God. She hoped she hadn't blown it. Was he actually being nice? Or was he testing her to see if her story was for real? "I mean, you are a stranger, after all."

Silence. Interminable silence.

"It's almost dark," he said at last, "and the place is hard to find. If you'll get on, I'll show you." He gazed directly into her eyes. "And if you really want to know about motorcycles, you'll need firsthand experience."

Another pause.

"I'll bring you back to your car." He thrust out his hand again. "I promise."

Oh, God! What to do? SaraJane's safety was at stake. If she didn't get on, he could easily disappear and then she'd have to start the search all over again. And maybe, if she went, she could get him to talk enough so she'd know where to look for her niece.

She'd told him she was here on a job, and under any other circumstance, on any other assignment, she'd jump at the chance to go along. He couldn't possibly know why she was here. He probably thought he could make some money if she photographed his bike for the book; guys like Gannon always needed money.

"C'mon, you'll like it," he urged, his tone cajoling, yet firm enough to let her know he didn't want to take no for an answer.

Her heart pounded. Her adrenaline surged. How dangerous could it be? If he believed her story about the book, she should be safe.

Still, ambivalence raged through her. An acrid taste of fear rose in the back of her throat. He could have other motives, and once he got her out of town...

She shivered at the ugly thought. But the image of a golden-haired child flashed before her. A child whose life could well depend on her.

There was no question. She had to do it.

And as long as she kept her cool, she'd be fine. Yes. Fine.

Gritting her teeth, Whitney took his hand. Her stomach rolled. A strange weakness flooded her limbs as she threw one leg over the seat behind him.

The seat was smaller than it looked, and so slick that she slipped up close, her body practically touching his. She inched back, but kept sliding forward. He shifted around, checked her position, then pointed to his helmet.

Was he offering her his helmet? Or asking if she wanted one of her own?

Right now, all she wanted was to get the ride over with ASAP. No sooner had she shaken her head no, than the motorcycle jerked forward, and she threw both arms around his waist to steady herself.

They sped down the switchbacks, heading in the same direction as the gang. When she saw that the town was just a spot on the hillside behind them, reality suddenly hit her. They were completely alone, tearing down a desolate mountain road so fast there was no turning back.

Between gulps of wind, she decided it was better to concentrate on her next step. She'd take mental note of her surroundings and memorize any significant markers—just in case she had to get back to town on her own.

In the waning light of dusk, they sped by emerald trees, with branches jutting from gnarled and twisted trunks of silver gray, dotting the craggy vermillion rock of the canyon.

She clung tightly to Rhys Gannon's solid body. He was strong and sure in his movements, yet flexible enough to anticipate changes in the winding road. As she caught the rhythm and sway of the bike, she molded herself against him for protection from the wind and the threat of falling off, and pressed her cheek flat against the smooth cool leather of his jacket. They spiraled downward, then onto a dirt road that plunged them deeper into the canyon.

The sharp breeze whipped against her face and tore at her hair, loosening it. As she filled her lungs with the heady pine-scented air, a quixotic exhilaration coursed through her. She felt a sudden sense of freedom.

And for a few surrealistic seconds, time was suspended, her mind experiencing nothing but an acute awareness of the moment—and Rhys Gannon. The man she hated. The man whose touch had, just for a moment, made her head spin. The man whose muscles tightened and released with each curve taken. Had they been two other people, she might have enjoyed the sensation, might have delighted in the feel of his muscular power against her body.

But they weren't two other people. And it was dangerous to think like that.

The road leveled out. As they slowed and pulled onto a flat precipice, the intense roar of the motor receded to a deep-throated growl. Gannon eased the bike to the edge of an escarpment overlooking a turbulent rain-swollen river that crashed against piles of rocks and boulders. The thundering crescendo echoed upward between the granite walls.

Inhaling the musky scent of dried leaves and the chill moisture in the air, Whitney glanced around. They were surrounded by dense trees—and completely isolated.

Her throat constricted. She looked back to the angry river below. An instant helpless feeling coursed through her, followed swiftly by self-reprimand. She hated feeling fearful. And she hated feeling helpless even more.

She'd learned early on that fear only generated more fear. Once she'd faced that fact and strengthened herself against it, she no longer felt helpless. For most of her life that philosophy had worked well.

But right now, things were out of her control. And the need to find SaraJane was so great she'd do almost anything.

Her thoughts clamored as she fought to still her runaway emotions. She waited, body rigid, poised for escape while Gannon sat in silence, his long legs stretched out to steady the bike.

What was he contemplating?

Just as she spotted a narrow dirt road, Gannon gestured toward it with a wide sweep of his arm. The road ran across a small wooden bridge that spanned the river and curled up the mountain on the other side.

She squinted. There was a house. A huge house that resembled some of the old homes in the Hamptons. Stifling her relief, she reprimanded herself for having an overactive imagination.

Gannon shifted to face her. "That's it. The only place around here to stay."

"Will I need a reservation? It's getting kind of late."

He laughed, his tone warm, almost cordial, but she

couldn't quite tell over the bike's idling engine. And for the first time since she'd climbed onto the seat, she was conscious of Rhys Gannon's muscular thighs pressing hot against the insides of her own and vibrating with the steady rhythm of the engine.

"Not in Estrade in the fall." He settled himself more snugly against her, then guided the bike toward the road. "Think you can remember how to find the place again?" he asked over his shoulder.

"Sure—if my brains aren't too scrambled from the rough ride," she said, raising her voice to be heard.

"Ms. Sheffield, I doubt you have any idea what a rough ride is." He gunned the engine until the noise exploded and ricocheted through the canyon like fireworks.

The sharp thrust forward jerked her backward. She clamped both arms around his waist as they roared out even faster than before.

He opened the throttle and blasted up the mountain at breakneck speed. Her breath lodged in her throat. They skidded recklessly around the switchbacks, flirted with sheer drop-offs edging the narrow unfenced road, then whizzed within an eyelash of the jagged granite wall on the other side.

The relentless wind clawed at her hair and stung her eyes until they teared. She was terrified—but she'd be damned if she'd let him know it.

Back in town, he roared up to her rental car and jammed on the brakes. The bike spun around in a cloud of dust, then screeched to an abrupt stop. Turning from the waist, Gannon extended a hand to help her off.

She stood for a long moment, propped against the trunk of the car, legs wobbly as gelatin, before she expelled her breath.

When she finally turned to face him, he lifted the visor and asked, "Rough ride?"

Shoving back her snarled hair, Whitney wiped the tears from her eyes. She straightened with as much dignity as she could muster. "Point well-taken."

Again Whitney saw crinkles form in the outer corners of his eyes, but it was hard to tell their nature. She drew in a deep breath. "I have a lot to learn." She tried to disguise her feelings, but anger sharpened her words.

They were playing cat and mouse, and suddenly she wasn't sure who the predator was. She'd started out intending to set him up, and now she wondered if he'd cunningly lured her into some kind of trap she didn't recognize. Or maybe he was trying to scare her off?

Whatever the case, she wasn't going to let him take control.

"I know," he said, gunning the motor in spurts, sidling so close she could feel heat from both the man and his machine. "Maybe your boss ought to get someone else for the job."

Arrogant SOB. She held her stance, drew in another breath and counted to ten. "Not a chance. I've never once bailed on a job," she answered. "And I can't tell you how much I appreciate the riding lesson. I'm looking forward to learning everything I can tomorrow."

His laugh was low and husky. "You still want to hang out with the biker boys? It's not exactly high society, Ms. Sheffield." He placed a hard emphasis on her last name.

Fear shot through her. He *couldn't* know who she was, could he? Morgan had said he wouldn't. And there was little resemblance between her and Morgan since her sister had dyed her hair black and taken on that pale gothic look. Whitney held her breath while he examined her from head to toe.

"And you look like you're real used to the good life." His words dripped with provocation.

"I'm a professional photographer and—" Whitney started to protest.

"Could be dangerous."

Again she heard the challenge in his tone, and again she straightened her spine.

"I've been in dangerous situations before." She forced a tight smile. "I've got a job to do, and whether I do it here or elsewhere, I *will* get it done."

He reached a gloved hand to her face. Whitney caught herself flinching, but resolute, she stood her ground.

Slowly he trailed the back of his hand down her left cheek, stopping just under the tip of her chin to nudge her face upward. All the while he studied her.

His eyes, intense and unreadable, settled on her mouth. If he hadn't had the helmet on, she'd almost think he was planning to kiss her.

Her breathing accelerated. Her heart dropped to her toes. Suddenly her mouth was as dry as the desert. She moistened her lips with the tip of her tongue and, despite the panic rioting within her, remained perfectly still.

"You're very pretty," he said, and still cupping her chin, he rubbed his thumb across her bottom lip, applying just the tiniest bit of pressure—enough to part her lips.

"And, Ms. Sheffield, I'm sure you always get what you want."

CHAPTER TWO

RHYS PACED the sidewalk in front of the store window, stopped to glance down the street and cursed himself for opening his big mouth yesterday. He shouldn't have told her to come back.

So why? Why had he?

He tapped the bike tire with the toe of his boot. He knew damned well why. His idiot ego. And the fact that Ms. High Society intrigued him.

He'd been suspicious when he saw her taking photographs. Hardly a day went by that he wasn't aware someone might try to find SaraJane. But the woman had said she was there to research a book about motorcycles. So he'd pressured her into riding with him to see how far she'd go to get her story—to see if she was telling the truth. He'd goaded her and in general acted like the crude bastard he was.

Yeah, he'd said and done plenty to scare her off, and maybe he'd succeeded. Nothing to worry about. She probably wouldn't show. Or would she?

She was unpredictable, that was for sure. It had more than surprised him when she'd actually gotten on the bike. How naive was she? For all she knew, he could be a rapist. Or worse.

It would've been easy to take advantage, and he'd tried his best to let her know it. But when her pale-blue eyes glistened with that silvery sheen of purpose and she said she'd get her job done here or elsewhere, he didn't doubt it for a minute. Which meant she was probably on the up-and-up, her reasons for being there legit. Yet despite the controlled demeanor, he'd sensed her insecurity. It was a subtle thing, but he'd felt it, knew it was there.

Oh, yeah, he knew.

He'd felt her hand quiver when he took it in his to assist her. And he'd felt her stiffen when he'd touched her cheek. Man, that woman was drawn tighter than a guitar string.

Rightly so, if she planned on venturing into the biker subculture.

But regardless of Ms. Whitney Sheffield's apprehensions, she was determined, he had to give her that.

He grinned, remembering her false bravado when she'd nearly toppled off the bike. Yeah, she had moxie. He liked that in a woman. Especially in bed.

Not that it made a difference. It hadn't taken him a split second to realize she was a lot like Stephanie, his spoiled-rotten ex-wife—the kind of woman whose ancestors came over on the *Mayflower*. The kind whose parents would do anything to keep their daughter away from someone like him.

He'd been the proverbial bad boy from the wrong side of the tracks. And he'd never been allowed to forget it. Not in school and not in his short-lived marriage. He'd been blinded by Stephanie's style and class. Blinded by the challenge.

Yeah, he'd pegged Whitney Sheffield immediately, with her cool manner and understated elegance. He recognized the expensive cut of her clothing, knew too well the breathy cultured voice with its traces of East Coast finishing school.

Whitney Sheffield was a replica of his ex and most of the other women in his former life. But his infatuation with high-class women was over.

Because he now knew that infatuation for what it was. He'd always wanted what he couldn't have, and *they* only wanted to play with fire—for a while. After that they wanted him to be one of them. With Stephanie, he'd even been fool enough to try.

No way. He wasn't going down that road again.

But damn, when he'd looked into Whitney Sheffield's eyes, he'd felt that same primal reaction.

THE EMERALD JUNIPERS and red rock of the canyon blurred into one long multicolored streak as Whitney stomped on the accelerator, her thoughts focused on today's meeting with Gannon. Last night she'd easily found the inn, registered, then gone directly to her room to work out her plan of action.

But now, as she rounded the corner into Estrade, the same doubts she'd had the night before returned to plague her. What if Gannon wouldn't cooperate? What then? What if he didn't come back?

She really needed an alternative plan, but without more information, she couldn't do much. Until Albert's PI work produced something new, it would be one step at a time.

She'd decided to follow through with the book idea in the hope that Gannon would spend some time with her talking about motorcycles. She'd offer to pay him if necessary. Once she'd persuaded him to trust her, she'd try to get an interview at his home, where the baby might be. Better yet, if she could hang around, she might catch him dealing drugs and get photos of it, after all.

But, Lord, where would a man like that live? How

would he care for a three-year-old child? According to Morgan, he lived hand-to-mouth, making money by selling drugs, pimping and theft. She'd warned that although he could charm the socks off most women, he was evil, dangerous and potentially violent.

Whitney inhaled deeply at the thought, but somehow couldn't get enough air into her lungs. The altitude. That was it. Estrade was more than a mile high. Still, she had other reasons for feeling breathless.

She steered the car into a parking space in front of the store. For the first time, she noticed the name above the front window—Journey. Appropriate, since it was a place that catered to road people. She glanced at her watch. If Gannon had specified a time, she wouldn't have had to come early and wait. Now she could sit here all day and he might never show.

It wasn't quite nine, yet a dark-green Jeep was parked a few feet away on her right, and on the other side stood a motorcycle that looked like something out of *Easy Rider*. Other than that, the street was dead quiet and as vacant as the night before.

Whitney saw movement inside the store and decided it must be open. After locking her car, she entered the place and glanced toward the back, where two men were talking. One, a paunchy older man, had his back to her and the other, a bespectacled business type, moved around behind him.

Unable to believe that Gannon would actually show up, she fingered the price tag on a black jacket hanging next to her. The pervasive scent of leather saturated the air.

Her dad's cars had always smelled like that, except for the Rolls that had been in the family for years. *The one with a bar in it.* A knot formed in her stomach at the unwelcome thought, and she shook off the painful memory.

Several Harley-Davidson motorcycles were lined up for display near the windows, while the interior housed racks of accessories, motorcycle parts, leather jackets, chaps, caps, vests, gloves, books and even videos. All good reasons for bikers to gather here.

But in Gannon's case, the shop was, no doubt, a place for drug contacts. Yet that was the weird part. Why would Gannon agree to meet her here and possibly jeopardize his cover?

Her spirits sagged even more. He wasn't going to come. She'd been naive to think he would. What made her think someone like him could be counted on for anything?

She trailed a finger across the satiny lacquered tank of the Harley next to her. The sun glinted off the sleek chrome and steel, making the smooth surface warm to the touch.

Instinctively she framed photos in her mind. A close-up, a tire angle, the contoured black seat with a man astride—or a man and a woman. Like yesterday.

Her muscles tensed. *Don't even think it!*

She made a rectangle with her fingers and squinted through the opening, visualizing the subject as she always did before she even took the first photograph.

When she turned, she saw the men at the back still deep in discussion, so she pictured the older guy on the bike. He wore heavy engineer's boots and floppy black leather chaps over blue jeans. An oversize black leather jacket completed the ensemble. She suppressed a chuckle at the image of this man on the powerful bike.

Then she visualized the man behind him straddling the Harley. Her senses jarred at the way he stood and the way his broad shoulders tapered into a narrow waist and hips, the way his dark hair curled slightly over the collar of his white polo shirt.

Recognition hit just as he removed his wire-rimmed glasses.

Gannon.

She caught her breath, and in that same moment, he caught her gaze. At a distance, without the motorcycle, without the jacket and helmet, he didn't even look like the same man, and he certainly seemed less threatening. She waved a greeting.

He nodded back, gesturing that he'd be right with her. Her stomach lurched as if she'd just descended in an elevator at rocket speed.

Morgan had told her Rhys Gannon was a chameleon, changing his persona to suit his purpose. On the very day Morgan had died, she'd said he was so convincing that no one would doubt his sincerity. Morgan had trusted him because she'd been in love.

But Whitney wasn't Morgan. And she'd stopped believing in love a long time ago. She squared her shoulders. A change of clothes didn't change the person.

"Good morning," Rhys said from across the room after the other man left. Leaning one shoulder against the doorjamb to what looked like an office, he didn't come forward to greet her. Instead, he watched her, his heavy-lidded gaze sweeping over her, dark lashes at half-mast. It was a smoldering look he made no attempt to disguise.

"Good morning." She walked toward him, vowing not to be unnerved by him or by her reluctance to tear her eyes from his near-perfect physique. For the first time since college, she thought about shooting a nude series.

For the first time in her adult life, she wasn't sure she could maintain her professional manner, her controlled reserve. It was one thing to act confident regardless of the situation, but to do it while lying through her teeth was a different story.

But then, the only thing she really had to lie about was why she was there. After all, she *was* a photographer, and she *was* going to photograph motorcycles.

"You found your way back to the inn?" he asked.

He looked older than she'd expected and she couldn't tell from his expression whether he liked the fact that she'd returned today or considered her an intrusion.

"I did. The owners weren't there, but a very nice woman who said she was filling in for the night gave me a room."

"Sleep well?"

Whitney nodded. "Uh-huh." She'd been so tired she'd crashed within seconds after she'd hit the bed. This morning she'd gotten up early, dressed and left without seeing a soul.

"I didn't know if you'd come—or when." She extended her hand. "As I said last night, my name is Whitney Sheffield."

"Rhys. Rhys Gannon." He clasped her hand in a firm handshake, his earlier provocative look replaced by an engaging smile that dimpled his right cheek. He released her hand after holding on just a little too long for her comfort.

She cast about for something to say. Something that wouldn't sound as though she was probing for personal information.

"Rhys. Yes, I saw the name on your license plate. Welsh, isn't it?"

He arched a dark eyebrow and laughed. His deep

voice held a note of playfulness. "It's a family thing. My father has the same name."

She stepped forward, next to a display rack and pulled out a book titled *Touring Arizona on Your Harley*. She riffled the pages, then glanced casually at the blurb on the back cover, wondering where the heck the store owner was. And why did Gannon look as if *he* was running the place?

"Well, it's a nice name. I like it." She lifted her gaze to meet his. "I suppose you'll pass the name on to your children, too." She put the book back where she'd found it, cringing at the pathetic segue.

Somehow she had to get him to talk about SaraJane. "Well, I guess it wouldn't be a very good name for a girl, though, would it?" She drummed up a coy smile.

From the way his back went ramrod-straight, she figured she'd hit a nerve. "You said you're photographing motorcycles," he said coolly. "How can I help?"

He folded bronzed arms over his broad chest, signaling the end of any small talk. Whitney noticed how the short sleeves of his shirt revealed well-defined biceps, reminding her how rock-hard his stomach muscles had felt under her fingers.

Heat rose to her cheeks.

She cleared her throat.

"Well, like I said, I'm doing a book—a coffee-table book on motorcycles. Mostly photographs."

Jeez, it all sounded reasonable last night when she'd planned what to say, but now she wasn't so sure.

He nodded for her to continue.

"Because I haven't delved into the research end of it yet, I really don't know much about them." She paused. "Not that I need to know a whole lot to take photographs, but I always find the more I know about my subject, the more interesting the photos are. And last night, as I mulled it over, the possibilities seemed endless.''

She pushed a loose strand of hair from her face. When he didn't respond, she continued telling him about her ideas, ideas she'd used before on other books. And amazingly, while she talked, her own interest took flight.

She paced a few steps in one direction, then back again, hands waving in tandem with her words.

''I could go with a historical perspective or maybe concentrate on one particular kind of motorcycle—or include the old with the new! I could do the people who ride, who they are, where they ride, what kind of groups they belong to, the clothing they wear—''

She came to an abrupt halt when she noticed his amused look. ''Well, there are several options,'' she concluded.

''Guess you don't have it all worked out yet. Who did you say this book is for?''

''Uh, actually, it's still in the beginning stages. That's why I'm not entirely clear on the focus. I proposed the book to my editor and now I'm starting the research,'' she lied. ''And I came here because I'd heard in Phoenix that Estrade is a popular stop for bikers.''

She shrugged, raising her hands palms up. That part was sort of true, although it was the guy at the gas station outside town who'd told her. ''Coming here was rather a spur-of-the-moment decision.''

''So you've done other books?''

She nodded. ''Four to be exact. One on the children of Belfast, another about the rooftops of Paris, and—'' She stopped. It was obvious he didn't recognize her name. Which was no big surprise. She'd been shown in major galleries in New York and abroad, her work regularly featured in a couple of national magazines, but her name wasn't exactly a household word. Her fifteen minutes of fame had come several years ago when *People* magazine had done an article about her.

Certainly no one in Estrade, Arizona, would've heard of her or her work. "The books aren't anything you'd know about," she answered modestly.

Rhys's dark eyebrows snapped together. "Yeah? Guess we're too primitive out here in the boonies, huh? We couldn't know all those important things that go on in the big world out there."

She winced at the sarcasm in his voice. She'd obviously insulted his intelligence, and it was rapidly becoming apparent that intelligence wasn't one of his deficits. In fact, she was taken aback by his whole manner. Today he didn't seem at all like the creep Morgan had described.

She studied the faint lines on his face. She'd done enough portraits to be a pretty good judge of age. Even if he'd done a lot of hard living and looked older than his chronological age, he had to have at least fifteen years on Morgan. Which would make him somewhere around thirty-five, minimum.

And now, with his quick self-protective response, she sensed a chink in his armor. Yesterday he'd even helped her find a place to stay. Perhaps he wasn't as devious as Morgan had said.

On instinct, Whitney reached out, her fingertips grazing his forearm. "I only meant that the books may not have been distributed so far from New York."

Rhys looked at the hand still touching his arm; his eyes slowly moved upward until they locked with hers.

"So you're a famous author?"

A smidgen of pride surfaced. She smiled up at him. "No. But I am known in some areas for my photography." She dug in her leather backpack, found a business card and handed it to him.

He eyed the card. "Another Annie Leibovitz?"

"No—the *only* Whitney Sheffield," she shot back, raising her chin in mock self-aggrandizement, hiding her surprise at his knowledge. No, her name wasn't as recognizable as her peer's, but she did have her own unique style, which some people liked equally well, maybe even preferred.

"Well, what can I do to help you, the only Whitney Sheffield?" He gave a dazzling white smile, and they laughed together, a guarded rapport settling between them as he resumed his stance leaning against the doorjamb. His gaze drifted beyond her to the front of the store.

Whitney glanced in the same direction and saw two people dismounting a motorcycle. Rats! Just when she had him talking. Afraid their conversation was about to be interrupted, she asked, "Can we go somewhere to talk?"

"Sure," he said, and before she knew it, he'd guided her by the arm through the office door. "Make yourself comfortable. This shouldn't take long." Exiting, he pulled the door, leaving it slightly ajar.

She whirled around, looking from the large picture window opposite the door to a gold-framed poster from an art gallery in Chicago on her right, then to a similar poster on her left. A battered oak desk took up most of the tiny room.

What the hell? Did he work here? Manage the store? Own the place? There was no one else around, so maybe the business *was* his front for selling drugs, just as she'd first suspected. But why, she wondered again, would he jeopardize his cover by bringing a stranger here?

Or was he that sure of himself now because, with Morgan gone, there was no longer a threat? Morgan had said she'd never told anyone about her family, not even Gannon. Whitney just wished Morgan had given *her* more information.

A knot of pain tightened in her chest. Did he know that Morgan was dead? Would he even care?

It took a second before she realized she had to get a grip on her emotions. Otherwise, she'd never accomplish what she came here to do.

She listened for voices, but the hum of conversation was too far away, so she edged closer to the desk. She craned her neck to read the upside-down writing on the papers—to no avail.

Spotting a small bronze picture frame on her left, she reached for it, her stomach fluttering nervously. Just as her fingers touched metal, the door flew open. She yanked her hand back, nerves snapping like rubber bands.

Rhys stood in the doorway.

"Okay, that's done," he said as he barreled past her and rounded the desk. He motioned for her to sit as he dropped into a pockmarked brown leather recliner. His masculine presence loomed large in the room.

"Have a seat," he urged, then leaned back, obviously comfortable in his surroundings.

Confused, she searched for words as she sat on the oak chair. "What? What's done?"

"The customer. But with luck there'll be more. Now what can I do for you?"

Whitney focused on Rhys. "You work here?" she asked, stupid as the question was.

Rhys gave an easy hearty laugh—one that was disconcertingly appealing. When the even white smile faded, he lifted his arms and laced his fingers behind his head, his biceps flexing with the movement.

"Yes. What did you think? That I was one of the bikers here yesterday?"

Heat rushed to her cheeks.

When she didn't respond right away, a slow grin spread across his face. He bent forward, pulled a slim brown cigarette from his shirt pocket, tamped it against the desk, but didn't light it. He leaned back in the chair again and waved a tanned hand in her direction.

"It's my shop, so unless another customer comes in, my time is yours."

Whoa. She felt a tiny bit like Alice tumbling into the rabbit hole and finding everything skewed. She was here under false pretenses, and Gannon was ready and willing to help her. He was a drug addict who looked nothing like one—and on top of that, he was the owner of the store.

He seemed intelligent and articulate. Moreover, he wasn't the twenty-year-old punk she'd expected. He had fine character lines that cut through dimpled cheeks and crinkled around penetrating blue eyes—and she couldn't stop thinking he'd make one fantastic photographic subject.

The whole scenario was bizarre.

But if Morgan had told the truth, it was all a ruse. He was a con artist. A shape shifter. A man who could seduce wallpaper if he wanted to.

Whitney stared out the window in the suddenly airless room, reminding herself that a shop, even a respectable shop, could easily be a front for a dealer.

The thought reviled her. How many innocent kids had

ruined their lives so he could own this place? How many had he used? How many had overdosed and died like Morgan?

She felt as though her lungs had collapsed and she couldn't draw a full breath. It was as though the oxygen had somehow been sucked from the room.

She fumbled in her backpack until she found a pen and notebook, then stared at the back of the bronze-framed photograph.

She had to ask.

CHAPTER THREE

RHYS STARED across his desk into Whitney Sheffield's translucent blue eyes—the most determined eyes he'd ever seen.

And he was as fascinated today as yesterday.

He recalled her touch, tentative, uneasy. But he liked that. Somehow it made her more real, less the high-society lady. The ice princess.

What he didn't like was the physical reaction he'd had to her yesterday. He could chalk it up to the fact that he'd sworn off women for the past six months, but it was more than that. He'd met his share of desirable women in the past and had no trouble with his self-control.

Not this time. The hormones he'd successfully ignored for months were raging like an adolescent's.

He studied her face. Yeah, right now, Ms. Whitney Sheffield's full pink lips and arresting smile sent his instincts into overdrive. To distract himself, he searched for flaws.

He wasn't too crazy about the way she pulled her long blond hair into that barrette in back. And her features were almost too fine, too perfect. And her smooth skin and the thick dark lashes that rimmed those clear blue eyes were...well...they just *were*.

Flaws? Hell, he couldn't find one.

In addition, her statements about herself and her career held no guile or self-importance. He liked that, too. The lady was convincing, and so was that Hassleblad. That caliber of camera wasn't used for snapshots in a family album.

She'd said she wanted an interview. Well, okay, why not? It might even be fun—if he was careful. He couldn't remember the last time he'd actually had fun with a woman.

"Must be someone special in that picture," Whitney said, waggling her pen toward it.

He glanced at the photo on his desk. "The love of my life—aside from motorcycles—which, I believe, is what you came here to talk about."

The telephone rang. He answered and found it was the bank calling with a question about his loan application. The call served as a stiff reminder that he had no business getting friendly with anyone. He covered the mouthpiece. "I'm sorry. This could take a while. Why don't you grab a bite and come back later?"

She stared blankly at him.

"Say, around three?"

DISMISSED LIKE A DOOR-TO-DOOR SALESMAN! Disgruntled, Whitney kicked a clod of dirt on the road next to her car and watched it explode in a dry puff of dust. She scanned the street.

Okay, Columbo. He's not the only game in this so-called town. Who else can give you information about Gannon?

In five minutes she was strolling down the main street in Estrade, viewing it with a more discerning eye. The air was redolent with the scent of burning wood, and the acrid taste caught in the back of her throat.

The business area was only two blocks long, and the

rest of the road zigzagged upward until it disappeared a short distance later around the side of the mountain. She was struck by the town's eccentric architecture—an odd assortment of buildings that ranged from old tin-roofed mining-camp shacks to fairy-tale gingerbread houses. Several small homes had been converted into restaurants or stores.

Good. She'd have lunch and then hit a shop or two to see what she could uncover from some of the locals.

Tramping up the incline, Whitney made a quick assessment of the town's photographic potential. Above her, decrepit buildings clung to the rocky mountainside, and many bore signs that read Closed for the Season. Others looked abandoned, their windows crisscrossed with crude boards.

Estrade reminded her of an old deserted movie set she'd once visited. Despite that, she decided it was rather picturesque, a statement about another era, another kind of life.

And Mabel's Café, with its handwritten menu taped to the front door, looked as if it had come right out of *The Last Picture Show*.

She stepped up and peered through the yellowed glass on the door. She saw several small square tables with blue-and-white checkered tablecloths in the center of the narrow room. Four or five booths hugged the red used-brick walls on either side, and plants were clustered in corners and dangled overhead from hooks in the copper-tiled ceiling.

Deciding to go in, she reached for the knob and saw another pair of eyes peering at her from the opposite side of the door.

She gave a tiny gasp and flinched sideways, nearly

tumbling onto an iron bench. Steadying herself, she flushed, a little embarrassed.

"Didn't mean ta scare ya, ma'am," an old man said as he opened the door. He smiled, and his eyes disappeared into deep folds in his round leathery face. "Just wanted to tell ya to c'mon in." He extended a gnarled hand to help her up the step and inside.

The man was at least seventy, she figured, and from the looks of his grizzled face and dusty miner's clothing, he'd been around these parts for a long time.

"Can't get better food than Mabel's," he said, sending an affable gaze over her attire. "No matter where yer from."

Well, so much for the jeans and blue denim shirt she'd worn to blend in.

"Thank you. I didn't know if the restaurant was open." She glanced about for a rest room as he led her farther inside.

"Well," the man said, pausing to rub the silvery stubble on his chin, "no place is too busy now that the tourist season's wound down."

She followed him to the back of the café where an opening into the kitchen revealed a robust woman about his age, standing next to a beige enameled stove that looked like one her great grandmother might've used.

"Mabel, whatcha got cookin' for this young lady?"

When the woman turned from the concoction simmering on the stove, Whitney warmed at seeing a familiar face. Mabel, who bore a strong resemblance to former first lady Barbara Bush, was the same woman who'd given her a room at the inn last night. Mabel wiped her hands on her blue gingham apron as she came forward.

"Hello again," Whitney said. "I'm really in need of

a washroom. I mean, first, before I can think about food.''

The couple exchanged glances, then simultaneously cocked heads toward a door that led from the kitchen. Whitney opened it and stepped into a well-used living room that she guessed were the owner's quarters. Mabel was right behind her.

''Over there.'' Mabel pointed to a small door behind a threadbare brown-and-gold-plaid couch. Whitney surveyed the room, suddenly feeling as if she'd been caught in a time warp and catapulted back into the fifties. Wow! The whole town was photographic material.

The elderly woman planted herself on the couch, arms folded across her chest, looking as if she planned on staying for the duration of Whitney's visit to the washroom. And she did.

Heading back to the restaurant with Mabel nipping at her heels, Whitney said, ''I'm going to be here for a day or two. Perhaps you can tell me a little about the town?'' Last night she'd already told Mabel she was a photographer doing research, so her wanting to know more about the community shouldn't come as any big surprise.

''The special's vegetable beef soup,'' the old man piped up from the kitchen as the two women returned. He held the pot lid aloft. ''With barley. And it's mighty good stuff.'' He inhaled with great gusto before setting the lid back on the kettle.

''Charley! I don't need any more of your help today,'' Mabel reprimanded, then affectionately shooed him out of her way. She turned to Whitney. ''What would you like, young lady? As Charley already said—'' she scowled at Charley from under silver brows ''—vegetable beef is the soup of the day. Made it myself.''

Mabel lifted the cast-iron lid and stirred the heavy

broth. The rich beefy aroma wafted through the air and Whitney's stomach growled.

"Grilled cheese sandwich is good to go with it," Mabel added before Whitney could answer.

"Sounds great to me." Whitney claimed a weathered wood stool at the counter and smoothed back a few stray hairs. She'd had no dinner last night and no breakfast this morning. She was incredibly hungry and could probably eat old car tires about now.

"Charley, set the lady up so she can eat," Mabel ordered, winking at Whitney as she took a sandwich wrapped in cellophane from the fridge, then set a battle-scarred griddle on the stove top.

Charley placed a glass of water in front of Whitney.

"And so she can ask her questions," Mabel finished.

Whitney smiled. "I met a man—Rhys Gannon. Can you tell me about him?"

Mabel frowned. "Why?"

"Oh...I'm just curious. I'm doing research on motor-cycles, and since he's in the business...well, I just thought he could help. And if I knew more about him, that might help, too." She played with her water glass. "Does he have a family?"

Mabel flipped the sandwich. "Townsfolk don't cotton to talkin' about their own to outsiders," she said, her eyes fixed on the pan.

O-kaay. So much for questions about Gannon. If she pressed, she might seem to have ulterior motives. "Sure, I understand. I just wondered, that's all."

"In this town, we help each other out and keep our mouths shut. We're family. How 'bout yourself? You got family somewhere?"

Now, that was a question *she* didn't want to answer. "I'm not married," she said evasively, then changed the subject, asking about the town itself. Luckily both Mabel and Charlie were loquacious about the history of Estrade, so she didn't have to elaborate on her own background.

Mabel and Charley weren't married, Whitney learned, but Charley had been hanging around for more than thirty years mining for gold. Whitney guessed the old geezer had been trying to stake a claim on Mabel for a long time, too.

But nothing she'd learned had gotten her any closer to finding SaraJane. After lunch she visited a few shops, hoping to glean whatever information she could. But to her dismay, the people in the stores were as closed-mouthed as Mabel and Charley had been.

If Gannon was the man Morgan had said, he sure had the townspeople fooled. Or maybe they just didn't give a damn.

"AND WHAT WOULD YOU SUGGEST, Mr. Gannon?" Whitney cringed at how stilted her words sounded. She'd explained the book's premise and asked for his suggestions, but he hadn't made a single one. She was losing ground fast and for some strange reason seemed unable to string a sentence together without coming across like a stuffed shirt.

For the life of her, she couldn't recapture their earlier rapport. Something must've happened in the couple of hours she'd been gone, and she felt as if he'd erected an impenetrable wall between them. On top of that, the picture on his desk had disappeared.

Guess he doesn't want to talk about "the love of his life."

Had she come on too strong? Been too pushy?

Then Gannon leaned forward, one hand flat on the

desk. "My friends call me Rhys." His gaze flicked over her. "Call me Rhys."

She shifted in her seat, uncomfortable with the familiarity. But if it helped…

"Rhys," she said without another second's hesitation. "Considering everything I've told you, do you have any recommendations about how I should begin?" She knew what she wanted from the conversation, but she wanted him to suggest it. Nevertheless, she'd do the asking if she had to.

"I mean—" she leaned toward him, eyes meeting his "—I realize I have a lot to learn. Especially now that I know the subject is even broader than I first envisioned. Since I'm at level zero, where do you think is the best place for me to start?"

Rhys was quiet. Thoughtful. An edgy silence hung in the air. He drummed his fingers on a stack of papers, a dull rat-a-tat sound that made her even more nervous.

Whitney watched an odd play of emotions cross his face. Yes, for sure something significant had happened between the phone call this morning and now. And whatever it was had put him off.

"I have all the time in the world," she said. "I mean, this is my job." She brightened. "I'm a quick study. And I'd be really grateful."

Lips thinning, he seemed to stare right through her. "So…you're very quick. I can help you—and I'm sure you can help me out." A suggestive grin emerged. "I might even be able to teach you some things—" he let the sentence hang for a beat "—about motorcycles."

The man was impossible. One minute he was helpful and friendly. The next, he was utterly arrogant.

And he did it on purpose, she could tell. Almost as if he'd recognized that he'd been too nice and then had to find a way to back off. Or maybe he wasn't trying to discourage her at all. Maybe he was *enjoying* her discomfort—and she'd played right into his hands.

Realizing she was still perched on the edge of the chair, she slid back, willing herself to keep her mouth shut. If she told him exactly what she thought of his comments, she'd never get him to talk about her niece.

"I'm sure you could," she answered, reverting to the safety of a professional approach, hoping her voice didn't reveal her uneasiness. "How and when would you like to start?"

He relaxed into the chair. "Let's do it now."

Her pulse quickened. Oh man, oh man, oh man. Now what? Maybe she should just blurt it out, tell him why she was here and offer him money. *And he'll throw you out on your ear.* Maybe do something worse...

"I, ah, I'm not sure..." She crossed her legs and tried to smile ingenuously, which wasn't hard under the circumstances. She was beginning to feel like a tongue-tied teenager.

He waited, watching. "Actually, I feel a little silly. Like I said before, it was pretty much a spur-of-the-moment decision to come to Estrade, and now that I'm here, I don't know exactly what to ask. Maybe the best way is for you to tell me how you got into the motorcycle business, and I'll ask questions as they come up."

She widened her eyes, hoping for something more than sexual innuendo. If she eased into it, interview-style, maybe he'd get comfortable enough to confide in her.

"You want my résumé?" he asked dryly.

Yeah, he'd confide in her about as readily as he would a rattlesnake.

Or was it another tease? Damn. She simply couldn't get a handle on this guy.

"Sure, if you've got a spare," she countered sweetly. "Or maybe you could just wing it."

He stared at her a moment longer, and though she saw he was holding back, he gave her a tiny off-center smile. She forged ahead.

"Last night you said this used to be a bar?"

He blinked a couple times and then, as if he'd finally decided to talk to her, said, "Yep. Before I came here. When I bought the place a year ago, it was a dying parts shop. I restocked, got the word out and gradually business increased. I've got plans for sales and expansion, but that's another story. Mostly I build custom bikes."

"Custom bikes?" Now she was even more confused.

"One of a kind. The shop's out back."

"I'm...I don't understand."

He smiled, this time a full-fledged, blinding-white smile.

"No kidding!"

DRIVING BACK TO THE INN, Whitney decided the time spent with Gannon had been productive, after all. She still didn't know SaraJane's whereabouts, but now she had hope. The man was a business owner; he wasn't about to disappear on a whim. At least, she didn't think so.

Rhys had been aloof during most of their conversation, yet she'd found herself wondering more and more about him. He said he'd worked a lot with motorcycles as a teenager, and that he'd bought the shop to make a midlife career change.

He didn't mention his former occupation—or Morgan, or SaraJane. And when he was telling her about customizing motorcycles and his plans for business expansion, his tone shifted, his expression became animated, and he reminded her of a little boy, gearing up with excitement over a new adventure.

From what she'd seen, Rhys was nothing like the weasel Morgan had described. He seemed quite self-possessed, someone who'd been around the block more than once and who'd put his knowledge to good use.

It was also obvious he was disciplined where his physique was concerned. His body was not that of a drug user. Fine-tuning like that didn't happen by chance.

Lord, it puzzled her. It *all* puzzled her.

And loath though she was to think it, she had to wonder just how truthful her sister had been. Had Morgan been so hurt that she'd become vindictive? Vindictive enough to lie?

Whitney dismissed that idea immediately. Morgan's last thoughts, her only concern, had been for the safety of her little girl. A daughter she hadn't seen in two years—because Gannon had kidnapped her.

Whitney's anger flared just thinking about it. Not only that, she'd bet money there were plenty of drug dealers who didn't look the part.

Fortunately Whitney's ignorance about the motorcycle business had worked in her favor, and after a fairly normal discussion, Rhys had suggested she get firsthand experience by following a biker around or actually working in a shop.

She'd jumped at the chance. "Maybe I could start here."

Initially his expression had been guarded. Then, studying her, he'd passed a tanned finger across his slightly parted lips.

"Maybe." He'd nodded thoughtfully. "Maybe you could."

Once they'd settled it, she'd decided to go back to the inn and get a room for a few days—or longer if necessary. Then she needed to tie up some loose ends from the last shoot and, if she could, reschedule the next two. She couldn't concentrate on getting custody of SaraJane and worry about business at the same time.

Gannon could be hiding the child anywhere—with friends or relatives, out of town, perhaps out of state. It might take a while to even find SaraJane.

She felt a sense of hopelessness each time she imagined the possibilities. Somehow she had to win the man's trust so he'd open up and tell her SaraJane's whereabouts. After that, her next move would depend on what she found.

Caution was the operative word. If he found her out, he could easily send her packing and her niece might be lost to her forever.

She hadn't seen Morgan in four years. Even so, it was difficult for Whitney to fathom that she'd never see her again. There was some consolation in knowing that Morgan would live on through SaraJane. The child was Whitney's only link to her little sister, and she simply had to find her. She couldn't fail Morgan again. She just couldn't.

As she drove, Whitney watched a golden sun melt over the top of the mountain range as trees of orange, crimson and burnt umber set the hillside afire. But the deeper she descended into the canyon, the darker it became.

Watching the evergreens and shrubs thicken, she recalled yesterday's motorcycle ride and how she'd panicked when Gannon stopped on the precipice above the river to show her the inn.

She smiled, remembering how foolish she'd felt when she realized he was earnest in showing her where to stay. Now, craning her neck to see, she saw the well-lit approach, then drove across the bridge. She pulled into the circular driveway and parked in front, under an arch of multicolored ash and maple.

Although the old Victorian inn sat on the side of the mountain, the area was on level ground that covered at least an acre. Above the double-door entry, a fixture splayed warm amber light across the wide veranda, the sign underneath it the only clue that the Estrade Inn was a place where people could stay. It looked more like a bed-and-breakfast than an inn.

She stepped from her car, her senses immediately stimulated by the fresh scent of river flora—a fragrant earthy aroma that evoked memories of the Hudson River behind her childhood home outside Hyde Park. One of the few good memories of a childhood filled with anxiety and terror. The other memories she'd learned to block the second they surfaced.

She closed her eyes for a moment, took a few deep breaths, then rang the bell and waited, absorbing the ambiance. Three white wicker chairs and a love seat with colorful floral-patterned cushions were grouped in a corner on her right. Farther down, a wooden porch swing hung from chains, and next to it were two large rocking chairs and a child's hobbyhorse. The sight of the horse elicited a wistful sigh, reminding her of her purpose.

If she'd known last night that she was going to stay, she would've made reservations for a few days and would also have left her luggage in the room, instead of taking it with her when she went to meet Gannon. The front door swung open and a tall gray-haired man welcomed her into the large reception area.

"Come over here and we'll get you signed in properly, young lady," he said, ambling toward a rosewood library table on one side of the foyer. "And we'll get you a key for the front door. Mabel did the best she could last night, but sometimes she forgets the details."

Whitney followed him to the desk. She hadn't been called "young lady" as many times in her entire life as she had in the past two days. And how did he know who she was and that she'd be coming back?

He slipped on a pair of Ben Franklin glasses and printed something in his book before sliding it toward her. "My name's John. Everyone calls me Johnny. My wife, Gretta, and I run this establishment," he announced proudly, straightening his shoulders.

"Pleased to meet you. I'm Whitney Sheffield," she returned.

"I know. Rhys called to tell us you were coming and that you needed a good room. He said you're a photographer on an assignment."

Well, that took care of any further explanation on her part. She felt relieved, although it bothered her that Gannon had called ahead on her behalf. And the fact that the innkeeper had used Gannon's first name made her wonder just what she was up against.

"My wife isn't here right now," the man apologized, "but she'll be back soon. In the meantime we'll get you set up. You can meet Gretta tomorrow morning at breakfast." He peered over the top of his glasses at her. "Unless you don't get up for breakfast?"

"No, no." Whitney shook her head. "I mean, yes, of course I get up for breakfast. Well, at least coffee,"

Whitney corrected, then gave him her credit card to complete the transaction.

"You can get room service between 6 and 10 a.m.," the innkeeper said on the way up the stairs. "There's a menu in your room. All you have to do is pick up the phone and let us know." He winked, smiling pleasantly, his soft words making her feel more welcome than she had anywhere in a very long time.

Johnny unlocked the door and told her to look around while he brought up her suitcase. Whitney stepped into the spacious suite, but hearing a noise behind her, pivoted around to see a tall woman standing in the doorway. She wore a long black knit dress, cowboy boots and silver-and-turquoise bracelets on both wrists. Her dark hair, artfully highlighted with an equal amount of silver, was precisely cut in a chin-length bob.

"Hello," the woman greeted her warmly, coming forward. "I'm Gretta. I got back a little earlier than expected, so I came up to meet you."

Whitney clasped the woman's outstretched hand and decided instantly that her eyes, an unusual azure color, were her best feature. "Nice to meet you, too. I'm Whitney Sheff—"

"I know. Welcome to Estrade." Still smiling, Gretta brushed a dark thread from Whitney's shoulder, much as a concerned mother might. The woman's warmth filled the room.

"Just hit that red button and you can get right through to either Gretta or me," Johnny said, entering behind his wife. He deposited Whitney's suitcase on the rack. "We can get you anything you need. Hit nine and you can dial out directly."

Once they'd left, Whitney did exactly that.

"Albert, it's Whitney. Got anything new for me?"

"Hey, Whit, I was worried about you. You find the slime?"

"I'm okay, Al, and yes, I did find Gannon. Plans have changed a little, though."

"Changed? How?"

After a brief explanation Whitney asked whether Albert had discovered the child's birth certificate yet.

"Tough one, Whit. No record anywhere in Orange County."

"Damn, I was sure Morgan lived there when she had the baby. What now? Have you tried outside Orange County?" Whitney paused, thinking, pacing. "Maybe you should try a couple of other counties or the neighboring states."

Albert let out an enormous sigh. "It would help, ya know, if we had even an inkling of what alias your sister used, or a social security number, an address—anything. It's impossible to run a trace without at least one fact."

"But can't you just do some kind of Internet check? Isn't all that information available right at your fingertips?"

"Ah," Albert hedged a little. "Sometimes. But even with the big database providers like DBT and IRSC or DATAFAX that most PIs use, you gotta supply some facts to get something back. I've done that using all the information you gave me, but Morgan was using a phony name and apparently never used her social security number to work anywhere. Under those circumstances, it's pretty hard to run a trace or do any kind of background check. Especially when the last verifiable information was from four years ago, when she was only sixteen and living at home."

"But you found Gannon...and Morgan was with him. Can't you just go from th—"

"Whit," Albert interrupted, and after a moment, she heard him take a deep breath. When he spoke again, his voice was even. "I know how you feel. But I have done this before, and believe me, I'm following up on it from every angle I can. Sometimes people use part of their real names, or a relative's, or even assume a dead person's identity. It takes time to check it all out. And I'm following up on Gannon's end, but at this point, it requires footwork, working backward, tracking down people Gannon might've known back then. That all takes time." He stopped for another breath, the frustration in his voice evident. "Ya know?"

Whitney's spirits flagged.

"And I do have other clients—and even a social life—such as it is." He gave a derisive laugh, but when he continued, she heard the understanding in his voice. "I'd love to drop everything and devote every waking minute to finding the kid for you, but it just ain't practical. Ya know?"

"I can give you more money if that'll hel—"

"Whit!" He cut her off. "I can't do that and you know it." After another long pause, and another sigh, he said softly, "Believe me, I'm doing everything I can. I know it's hard, but we'll find her. But...uh, if you'd feel better getting someone else—" He let the sentence hang.

"I'm sorry," Whitney said. "You're right. I know you're doing everything you can." It wasn't Albert's fault that Morgan had given Whitney only a few shreds of information.

Morgan had called Whitney the day before she died, told her Gannon's name, the last address where she'd known him to be, and then launched into all the despicable things he'd done to her. She'd told Whitney

SaraJane's name and age and made her promise to find the child and gain custody. That was it.

Her cousin had been there for her through it all, even when the police told her she might as well forget the whole thing. As far as the LAPD was concerned, the biological father had every right to his own child.

But Albert had found Gannon for her, and she was sure he'd get the birth certificate somehow. Not that finding the birth certificate would be sure proof of anything, either. There was only the off-chance that Morgan might've listed her own name or birthdate or place of birth, which would help prove Whitney's relationship to her niece. But the most important thing was to find out if Morgan had named Gannon as SaraJane's father. If not, the man would have no legal claim on the child. Not without DNA tests—or proof of marriage. According to Whitney's attorney, finding the birth certificate was as much a way to rule out certain things as it was to prove them. Because without it, even if she found SaraJane, Whitney couldn't prove the child was her niece.

"Our best bet is Gannon," her cousin said. "He'd know where the kid was born and where she is now."

"Yeah, I know, Al. That's the plan, but I don't know how much time I'll need. I have to take it slow so he doesn't get suspicious."

"You sure you don't want me to do it?"

Whitney sighed. "Can we not get into that again? I need to do this. Really."

"Okay, okay. Just so you know my feelings about it. I've got some other ways to get the info, like I said, but it'll take some footwork. I'll do what I can, but you be careful. You sure you're gonna be okay?"

"I'm fine, Al," she answered, wishing she could say it with more conviction.

"You don't sound so good."

"I'm fine. Just a little tired." Tired and emotionally drained. "Listen, Al." She pulled the barrette from her hair. "I've got to take care of a few business things before I do anything. If I can't do that by phone, I may fly to La Jolla for a day or two. You can get me there. Call my service or this number—" she read it out "—the instant you get anything, okay? And I'll be in touch."

"You're on. Catch ya later, babe."

"Albert," Whitney said quickly before he hung up.

"Yeah?"

"Thanks. Thanks for everything."

Whitney hung up, squelching her frustration. She knew getting the baby's birth certificate wouldn't be easy, and her impatience was unreasonable.

Morgan had used several names after she'd left home, which was the reason Whitney couldn't find her, though, God knows, she and Albert had tried so many times in the past four years. A huge lump formed in her throat. Yeah, she'd tried, but not hard enough.

She'd failed Morgan. Failed her in every way she'd ever promised to keep her little sister safe.

In the three months since Morgan's death, that failure—that anguish—had lodged sharply and painfully in the deepest part of her. She doubted she'd ever get over it.

Tears welled up, and she wanted more than anything to release the darkness in her soul. But tears would only be a manifestation of her own grief. Morgan was dead and all the tears in the world couldn't bring her back.

Morgan had called Whitney right before she'd overdosed. By the time Whitney reached Morgan, her little sister was dead. A letter asking Whitney to keep the promise she'd made on the phone was Morgan's last wish.

According to Whitney's attorney, the birth certificate was critical in proving Whitney's relationship to the child—that or DNA tests. And it was even more important now, since her plan to catch Gannon in a drug deal, get the transaction on film and buy him off, probably wasn't going to work.

She would have to sue for custody. In that case she needed all the help she could get. Because one of the first things she'd learned was that it wasn't easy to take a child from a natural parent—even when the parent was as unsavory as Gannon was purported to be.

But now, after meeting him, she even wondered about that. Whatever his character, though, Gannon was the key to finding her niece.

Her heart ached whenever she considered the kind of life the poor kid had been subjected to—living with a teenage mother on the run, kidnapped by an alleged drug dealer. She shuddered to think how such early trauma might have affected the child.

Whitney banished the thoughts. She could only try to make it up to SaraJane—give her niece a secure home where she'd know she was loved and wanted, the kind of home Whitney and Morgan had never had.

She'd bought the house in La Jolla as soon as she'd known she'd need a real home for SaraJane. She doubted any judge or court would see either her condo in New York or the apartment she worked from in San Diego as an appropriate and stable environment for a child. And she wasn't leaving it to chance.

She picked up the phone again and punched in her

editor's number. Though it didn't look as if her original plan would pan out, it seemed the hastily hatched book idea just might. It would get her closer to Gannon—and, with luck, her niece.

Impatient, she tapped a finger on the receiver. Tanya's voice mail kicked in. "You've reached Tanya Elliot. Please leave a message."

"Tanya, it's Whitney. Sorry I didn't call before I left New York, but I promise I'll fill you in when we talk. I have a terrific idea to run by you." She paused, thinking. "I'll be gone early in the morning, so call me before eight, Arizona time, or leave a message on my service."

Whitney left the number and hung up. For a moment she stood perfectly still as a feeling of resolve settled within her.

This was going to work out. It just had to!

If she could get Tanya who was not only her editor but her best friend, to agree to the book idea, she'd feel less vulnerable when she faced Gannon again.

A sharp twist of apprehension coiled in the pit of her stomach. Around Gannon her emotions took one erratic turn after another. His presence assailed her sensibilities, filling her with doubt and guilt and a whole lot of other reactions she didn't want to acknowledge.

She closed her eyes and focused on the one thing she needed to do. Because she absolutely had to maintain control. If she didn't, she could lose everything.

The book was the vehicle through which she'd insinuate herself into Rhys Gannon's life. Then, when she found SaraJane, she'd make her move.

If everything went well, Gannon would never know what hit him.

CHAPTER FOUR

RHYS GATHERED gathered the gearshift and a few other parts that had come in for the custom job he was working on, placed them in a box to take out to the workshop and patted his pockets for the keys. It probably wasn't necessary to keep the shop locked in Estrade, but he did, anyway, from force of habit. The equipment was too expensive to take chances.

He grabbed the blueprint from the top of the file cabinet and unrolled the tube. He couldn't suppress a smile of satisfaction. This was a far different career from what he'd been doing for the past twenty years, and far more gratifying.

He picked up a wrench and tossed it from one hand to the other, glancing around the vacant store before he headed out to the shop. Not a customer in sight.

He'd had plans when he bought the business a year ago, not big ones, just plans that went along with his need to change the direction of his life. But since then, with the trial taking up most of his time and money, he'd been unable to get his plans off the ground.

He scoffed. *No point in thinking about what you can't change.* He figured he'd get the money one way or another. He dropped the wrench into the box, picked up the phone and punched autodial.

''Hi, it's me. How's my girl? Oh, she's playing with

her dolls? *All* of them?'' He grinned with genuine plea-sure. At least some things had worked out.

SaraJane was safe and happy. It was the one part of his life that *was* going perfectly. And since it was the most important part, he wasn't about to let anything screw it up.

''No, I didn't call to check up on the photographer. Maybe she'll come back, maybe she won't. Makes no difference to me.''

He drew in a patient breath. ''You're impossible, you know that?'' he said affectionately. ''Besides, I'm forty. I think I can handle my personal life.'' He paused. ''Even if I haven't done a spectacular job of it up to now.''

He listened for a moment. ''Yes, I'll be there at the usual time. See you then.''

He hung up and smiled at the framed photo of SaraJane he'd replaced on the desk. Her golden curls reminded him of the blond woman who'd appeared out of nowhere and now had him thinking about her more often than he wanted.

He didn't need a woman in his life right now. And when, or if, he ever did, it sure wouldn't be a woman like Whitney Sheffield. He'd had enough of her kind to last six lifetimes.

Still, the lady unsettled him, made him wonder if her skin felt as smooth as it looked and how she'd feel naked against his chest, and if that long blond hair would slide through his fingers like silk. Yeah, he'd had a fantasy or two. But hell, he could wonder from here to Alaska, because he wasn't going to do anything about it.

Not that he had to worry. She'd said she had to wind up some business in California, said she'd be back in a day or two, and that was three days ago. She'd probably blown him off without another thought—which wouldn't surprise him. It was typical self-centered born-with-a-silver-spoon-in-her-mouth behavior. Like Stephanie's.

And he hadn't exactly given her a rousing welcome.

He slapped a hand on the box, hefting it with purpose. One effective way to take his mind off Whitney Sheffield—good hard work.

"HELLO?" WHITNEY STEPPED through the wide double doors into the foyer. When no one answered, she fished her room key from her purse. If Gretta and Johnny were around, they'd see the car and know she'd returned. She could get the rest of her luggage later.

She bounded upstairs and swung open the door to her suite. Entering, she tossed her camera bag onto the chair in the sitting room, then walked toward the window. As she did, she caught the scent of fresh flowers and noticed a daisy-filled glass vase on a gate-leg table next to the couch.

Gretta's touch, she figured, stopping to finger the delicate crocheted doily under the vase, registering how everything blended so perfectly with the peach-and-vanilla floral pattern of the sofa and the quilt on the bed. A gentle rap on the door brought her to attention.

"Yes?" she called. "Please come in."

Johnny's cheerful face greeted her. "Welcome back. I came up to see if you need help with your luggage." He stood tall in the doorway, his height and build oddly familiar in the muted light of the hallway.

"Oh, hi. I didn't think either of you were here." Whitney was comforted by the warm welcome. "And yes, I'd appreciate it. There are only two bags." She handed him the car keys. "I travel light."

"Sure, sure. That's what they all say," Johnny quipped before he turned to head down the stairs.

Hearing laughter outside her window, she swiveled around to take a peek, but couldn't see anyone.

"Here you go, young lady." Johnny returned with her bags a minute later and hauled them into the room. He left them near the closet, then hoisted the largest piece onto the luggage rack. Finished, he dusted his hands and began to leave.

Whitney walked him to the door. "Do you have other guests?" She pointed to the window. "I heard people outside."

Johnny's face lit up. "Nope. That's probably our grandchild—we watch her most every day. Can we expect you at dinner tonight?" His salt-and-pepper eyebrows bunched. "Gretta's the best cook in town."

"Funny, that's what Charley said about Mabel's cooking," Whitney joked, adding, "but after the muffins I had the other day, you don't have to convince me of Gretta's culinary expertise. What time did you say? Seven?"

"Yep." He stopped at the door. "If you decide to come, better let Gretta know by six so she can adjust the menu."

Whitney smiled, appreciating the invitation. "Thanks. I think I can say right now that I'll be there."

She'd been in such a hurry driving back from the Phoenix airport she hadn't taken time to eat. Even though she was famished, she needed to hustle over to Rhys's store to see what kind of schedule she could arrange with him. Maybe even shoot a photo or two.

She would photograph Rhys, she knew that. First of all, he'd think it strange if she didn't, since that was supposedly why she'd come to Estrade. And regardless of her negative feelings about the man, he'd make a gorgeous subject. No denying it.

Even without his motorcycle attire, he had a James Dean quality about him, a latent volatility that simmered just beneath the surface. It was, she realized, what made him so interesting. Photographically, of course. And if she could just capture that essence on film...

When she arrived, the sun was low, its coppery light stretched over the weathered-pine storefront, giving it the appearance of an old photograph yellowed with age. Standing in the street, she clicked off several frames from different angles.

In the middle of a setup, Rhys stepped out and leaned one shoulder against the doorjamb. He was dressed in bleached jeans, a black T-shirt and boots.

Perfect.

Her excitement mounted. It always did when she worked on a new project. She moved from side to side, shooting several frames in rapid succession, anxious to capture as much as possible before the light, or Rhys, disappeared.

Without acknowledging her, Rhys drew a cigarillo from his shirt pocket and, lighting it, turned in her direction. *Oh, yes.* Perfect again. Head tipped down, a lock of ebony hair carelessly looped over his forehead, eyes dark and brooding, strong chin. A thin curl of smoke rising from the slender cigarillo.

Absorbed by the image in her viewfinder, she was startled when he looked up at her and nodded.

She lowered the camera and strolled toward him. "Hi."

He studied her, then took another drag.

"The light was so perfect just then," she said, feeling compelled to explain. She walked closer and climbed the stairs. He hadn't moved an inch, just kept staring at her, making her squirm under his scrutiny.

"You always carry that thing?" he asked when she reached his side. His voice was deeper, huskier than she remembered.

"Pretty much. A good photographer is always prepared." She waved a hand toward the setting sun. "It's beautiful." Then she added, "That's not good for you, you know."

He pulled another long drag and, exhaling, stared briefly at the length of burning ash before snuffing it out in the container next to the door.

"I know." He motioned with a wide sweep of his arm while he held the door open.

Almost before she stepped in, the scent of new leather captured her senses. She felt a flurry of anticipation at the prospect of actually learning about the business of motorcycles—and, she hoped, about SaraJane.

How close would she need to get to Gannon so he'd trust her enough to talk about SaraJane? A jolt of anxiety diminished her anticipation. Getting close to Gannon was the last thing she wanted to do.

He followed her in, quickly walking past her to lead the way. "Come on back and we'll talk," he said bluntly.

Trailing him into the office, she sensed a distance in his manner. A fresh panic bubbled up. Had he changed his mind? Had he realized she might pose a threat?

She took one of the paper cups next to the bottled water and, after filling it, sat in the chair facing his desk. Rhys sank into the chair behind it, his eyes shuttered. Leaning back, he fixed his gaze on the desktop.

"I know we talked about the possibility of you working here,'' he said, obviously choosing his words with care.

Damn. She felt a rejection coming. He'd had too much time to think, and now he was going to renege on their agreement. ''Research,'' she interjected. ''Work in exchange for the opportunity to gather information.'' She spoke earnestly in an effort to redirect a conversation that might destroy her plan before it ever got off the ground. ''And the opportunity to learn from an expert.''

His expression didn't change, but the look in his eyes did. And right now she was acutely aware that Rhys's eyes held a combination of caution—and lust—and the effect was nerve-racking.

From a purely photographic perspective, the man had a dangerous sensual appeal, a darkly compelling aura, the kind that made some women weak in the knees. Women like Morgan…

But not Whitney.

Still, she worried that he might suspect her motives. She had to be nice, agreeable, maybe even willing to do things that went against everything she stood for. But if that was what it took to save her niece, so be it.

''I cleared my schedule. Totally. So I'm free to help out.'' Maybe a little guilt would work. ''And I did some research while I was in California,'' she continued. ''I retrieved some information from the Internet and learned a bit about motorcycles. It's amazing stuff,'' she said, resting one elbow on the desk, hoping to engage him in conversation that would keep him from sending her away. ''But there's so much I didn't understand.''

She sent him a college-student-awed-by-her-professor look. ''Can you tell me why one bike would be preferred over another? For example, the one you were riding the other day, why would you ride that when it's obviously not as comfortable as one of the, uh, Big Twins?'' God, she sounded like an idiot.

''Big Twins?'' he asked with a smirk.

She not only sounded like an idiot, she felt like one, too. But she forged ahead. ''Yes, you know…'' She fiddled with the pen on the desk. ''Wouldn't a smaller bike, something like the Sportster, be less comfortable to ride?''

His smile broadened and he slanted a teasing glance at her from under his brows. ''Did you find the ride uncomfortable? I didn't get that impression.''

Instant heat reached her cheeks. She shifted her position, crossed her legs. Why did she get so unnerved by his stupid innuendos?

Regardless, she had to play along. She leaned against the back of the chair, smoothed the sides of her hair, tucked a wayward strand into place and, unflinchingly, returned his look.

''It was a smooth ride,'' she said softly, deliberately, quieting the disturbance that rioted within her. ''At least, the first part was.''

He sent her a knowing smile, and she couldn't help giving him one back. She would *not* let him unnerve her. ''And I enjoyed it very much. Actually, I just wondered why you chose the bike you did.''

Watching him, she noticed that his expression had gradually changed from amused to interested.

''Lots of reasons,'' he finally said. ''Racing is one. It requires a smaller lighter bike.'' He pointed toward the back door. ''Like my Sportster. But that's not the reason I ride it.''

''And your reason is?''

''I collect old bikes. They appreciate in value. But I

also like the quick response I get.'' He grinned. ''A quick response is one of my requirements.''

Again her cheeks flamed—until the look in his eyes made her realize he did it on purpose. He *liked* to unnerve her.

''Really,'' she said tersely. ''I have a feeling I'd prefer the big one.''

His eyebrows shot up, but his hesitation was brief. ''I've got one of those, too.'' He scraped a hand across his chin. ''I can take you for another ride. Then you'll know which you like best.''

Refusing to let him rattle her, Whitney leaned forward again, elbows on the desk, one hand cupping her chin as bits and pieces of research came back to her. ''You own a...fat boy? A HOG?''

Rhys threw back his head in a burst of laughter. ''Yeah, it's a Harley. Most of the bikes I own are Harleys.'' He stood, picked up a magazine from a table near the window and handed it to her. Pointing at the title, he said, ''That's a HOG—Harley Owners' Group—magazine.''

She spared him a speculative glance, waiting for further explanation, or another innuendo, or God only knew what. She hadn't a clue what would spring from this man's mouth next.

''So HOG's an acronym, not the name of a bike. Though some people use it that way.''

He smiled again, that same blinding smile he'd given her before. ''I knew that,'' she deadpanned. ''It was a test...to see how much *you* know.'' She allowed a grin.

''Well,'' he said, presenting a tutorial posture, ''I can see you do need a little guidance.'' With a gesture he indicated that Whitney should pull her chair around next to his, and as he sat back down, he reached behind her and took several books from the shelves. He gazed into her eyes. "Let's start with the basics."

WHITNEY FRESHENED UP for dinner, replacing her denim shirt with a soft navy turtleneck. Her brain was still frazzled from all the information Rhys had heaped on her, but at least they seemed to have arrived at an understanding.

He realized she was serious about her job, and regardless of any sideline he had, it was obvious the man knew his motorcycles. He said he'd been riding since he was fifteen and had dozens in his collection. She'd asked immediately when she could photograph them, but he'd put her off. Which only meant she'd try again.

She glanced around the room. While she'd been gone, her room had been cleaned and the bed turned down. She loved her hosts' attentiveness, loved the way Gretta and Johnny made her feel like part of the family in the short time she'd been at the inn. Perhaps when this was over—

Stop! Just stop it. If she found SaraJane and got custody as planned, she'd probably never return to Estrade.

Voices filtered up from outside, and Whitney padded in stocking feet to the bay window. Once again she couldn't see anyone, since the sound came from below her on the veranda. She sat on the window seat, curled her legs under her and picked up the phone.

She punched in Albert's pager number, anxious to tell him what she'd learned today, in case he could use any of it in his search for SaraJane's birth certificate. She left her number, then called Tanya.

"Hey, Ms. Editor, it's about time you decided to show up for work."

"Yeah? Well, I had another hot date with one of my

many lovers," Tanya said facetiously. "Where are you? And what's so urgent?"

Whitney cringed a little, trying to figure out the best way to broach the subject.

"You mentioned another book," Tanya prompted.

"Motorcycles. A coffee-table book on motorcycles."

"Motor— Uh, excuse me, I think there's something wrong with the phone."

Whitney heard a loud thumping on the other end, as if Tanya was hitting the receiver with her hand.

"There, I hope that's better," her friend said, coming back on the line. "I actually thought I heard you say you wanted to do a book on *motorcycles*."

Whitney laughed out loud. The woman's terse sense of humor, which she claimed was the result of being raised an only child in a multicultural Italian and Jewish family, never failed to amuse Whitney.

"Right. Motorcycles it is," she said, launching into her best sales pitch, describing the concept in the same way she had for Rhys. "And the bottom line is that I still have an enormous amount of research to do even to get a proposal to you. What I really want to know is if the project interests you."

Tanya's silence suggested she liked the idea or was at least considering the possibilities. When she didn't like something, her reaction was immediate.

"Besides, I think it's a good departure from my usual work."

"Any particular reason you picked motorcycles?"

"Not just motorcycles," Whitney said. "Also the people who ride them, where they go, what they do— you know, all that stuff I just said."

"You checked *Books in Print?*" Tanya switched to her editorial mode.

"Yes, but like I said, I still have a ton of research to do." Whitney paused, wondering how much to tell her friend. Tanya knew almost everything about her, and had ever since they were roomies in college. She knew about Morgan and knew that Whitney had hired her cousin to locate her niece, but Whitney wasn't sure she wanted to divulge how the book tied in with it—not just yet.

She didn't want anything to screw up her chances of finding SaraJane. Besides, she *was* excited about the idea. Nothing wrong with dual research, especially if it gave her legitimacy with Rhys.

"I plan to be in Arizona for a while doing research at a motorcycle shop called Journey. The owner's offered to let me hang around for a couple of weeks to research the business."

"You had to go to Arizona to research? There's no places like that in Southern California—where you happen to own a house?"

Obviously, Tanya knew something was up. They were too close for her not to know. Still, Whitney felt she had to keep her information to herself for the moment. "Estrade was recommended, so I checked it out. That's all."

Another pause. "What do you want from me? Carte blanche so you'll have a good reason to hang out with this biker guy?"

"Tanya! It's work. And besides, you know I've never been attracted to the macho type."

Her friend's laughter rippled through the phone line. "Maybe you oughtta consider it. A little macho might do you good."

Whitney gave a derisive laugh of her own. "Yeah, guess I couldn't do any worse than I have in the past, could I?"

So far, she'd had three strikeouts in the love department. No question, she was a lousy judge of character when it came to men, always picking ones who turned out to be interested in her money or the publicity they could gain from the association.

Her relationship with Brock had certainly proved that point. Maybe Tanya was right when she'd joked that Whitney's poor choice in men was her way of avoiding commitment.

"Anyway, it might do *you* some good not to work eighteen hours a day, either," Whitney added.

"Okay, okay. Truce," Tanya said. "Motorcycles it is. When do I get a proposal? And when are you coming back to New York?"

"Soon—so I can sell the condo." Whitney waited for a shriek but got silence.

"I need to do this, Tanya. It's all part of my plan to settle in one place once I get custody of SaraJane."

More silence.

"Jeez, Tanya. Put yourself in my place. I've thought about it a lot. La Jolla's a better place to raise a child than Manhattan." Whitney braced herself for objections. She was one of the few people close to Tanya, and if she moved away, it would affect her friend's life, as well.

Finally Tanya said, "I wouldn't let you get away with a cliché like this—but aren't you putting the cart before the horse here, just a tiny bit? I mean—and I don't want to sound like the little cartoon guy with the black cloud over his head—what if you don't find your niece? Or even worse, what if you do and you can't get custody?"

Whitney took another deep breath. She'd played out every scenario in her head a dozen times. And when push came to shove, she had to move forward. She'd do whatever she needed to get custody of SaraJane. If that meant living in a house in La Jolla, instead of a New York condo, so she'd appear more stable, she'd do it.

"I've got a pretty good lead. And from what my attorney says, custody shouldn't be a problem. All I have to do is show the father's unfit to care for the child, and with this guy's record, that shouldn't be too hard."

"Based on what your sister told you?"

"Sure. And some other things I learned from Albert."

"Albert?"

"The PI. My cousin."

"Oh, yeah. And what if they're wrong? Or even if they're not and you still don't get custody? That can happen, you know." Tanya said softly, "I'm just playing devil's advocate because I don't want you to get your hopes up and then have them come crashing down."

"That's always a possibility," Whitney admitted, knowing Tanya did care about her. She and Albert were probably the only people who really did. "Right now I want to take it one step at a time."

"Good. And you might not want to sell your place here until you're sure about the next step."

Whitney *was* sure. She wanted—no, needed—everything in her life well in place so there'd be no doubt about her ability to care for her niece. Heaven knows, she'd had enough of her own doubts without someone else chiming in.

"Well, you can rest easy. I'm not doing anything immediately. I have other things to take care of, and getting the book off the ground is one of them."

"You know, I just don't get this new fascination with motorcycles," Tanya said on a melodramatic sigh. "You've got all these things going, trying to find your niece and getting custody and all, and then you decide to hang out with a bunch of bikers? You gotta admit, it's kinda out there.''

''It's complicated, Tanya. Too complicated to get into right now. But I promise to fill you in the first chance I get.''

After their conversation Whitney considered what Tanya had said. But at the moment things were moving right along, and her insides jumped with nervous energy at the thought that everything would work out in the end.

All she had to do was stay focused.

Today she'd been so intent on appearing legitimate and asking Rhys research questions that she'd almost forgotten about gleaning any other information from him—until he mentioned he'd lived in Chicago before he'd moved to Estrade a year ago.

He'd also said he'd been married once, but hadn't elaborated. Said he had one child, and after disclosing that, he'd gotten all moody and closed up. Whitney sincerely hoped the marriage he'd mentioned wasn't to Morgan, because if it was, getting custody would be that much more difficult.

She needed indisputable evidence that he was unfit, and after their meeting today, she had new concerns about how difficult it would be to prove. He wasn't a user, that was certain. She'd seen enough substance abuse among her own set of acquaintances to be reasonably sure she'd recognize the condition.

And if he wasn't a user, how would that change things? Okay, maybe he'd kicked the habit and used the business as a cover for the sale of drugs.

Still, the business seemed to be for real, and she had a hard time imagining it wasn't. Just as she had a hard time imagining Rhys as the person Morgan described.

Yes, he was charming. He was attractive. Sexy. In those ways he was everything Morgan had said.

But he was more than that. He was much more complex than Morgan had described, and that thought created a sudden twist of need low in her belly. Another reason to keep her guard up.

Hearing voices outside again, Whitney rested her forehead against the window frame. A child's laughter drifted upward, and she saw what must be Gretta and Johnny's grandchild skip across the yard while they watched from a glider swing.

The phone rang. It was Albert returning her call. After perfunctory greetings, she told him the information she'd gathered. Albert said he'd follow up on her lead and check for the birth certificate in Chicago. Then he began his usual litany about when Whitney might come back to La Jolla.

Hearing the child's laughter again, Whitney parted the lace curtain and watched as the toddler, in a blue hooded sweatshirt, skipped in a circle around Gretta and Johnny. Finally they all held hands doing a ring-around-the-rosy dance, and Whitney felt her heart squeeze thinking about SaraJane, who would be about the same age. She let the curtain fall, wistfully savoring the warm family scene.

"Not for a while," she murmured, but someday she would experience the same happiness as the family dancing in the yard below. No matter how many doubts she'd had about her ability to raise a child, she was certain of one thing: she and SaraJane would be close, just the two of them. Whitney regretted that the little girl wouldn't have grandparents to love her the way Gretta and Johnny loved their grandchild.

But having lived through Sheffield parenting firsthand,

she'd never allow SaraJane's maternal grandparents the opportunity to destroy another life.

"I can't finalize the move to California until I finish what I started, Albert—or not until I'm convinced I've done everything I can from here. Right now, it's too soon to tell."

"Look, Whitney. You're paying me to handle the investigation. Why don't you just let me do it my way?" Albert asked. "It'll be easier on you."

"I'm paying you to get information for me, Albert. And speaking of information, do you have anything more?"

Finding SaraJane, fighting for custody—this was something she needed to do for Morgan, something she needed to do for herself. She knew that even when she did locate her niece, it wasn't likely Rhys would allow her to simply walk off with the child. And there were SaraJane's feelings to consider. How would she react to being taken away by a stranger?

Whitney knew only too well that even abused children still sought love from their parents—at least, until they were old enough to know better.

Yes, there were definitely more things to consider than appeared on the surface, and she wouldn't know the full extent until she found her niece.

Albert sighed heavily into the phone. "Okay. You already know Gannon lived in California before heading for Arizona. Chicago might be a lie. Or maybe he only spent a little while there. What I learned recently from one of his live-ins is that he lived for a year or two with a young girl named Isabelle."

"That's the name Morgan called her favorite doll," Whitney whispered. She closed her eyes. "Go on."

If she was going to win Rhys's trust, she needed to know everything she could about the man.

If Rhys didn't have the baby in Estrade, if he'd left her with friends or relatives or, God forbid, had her adopted, they had to have some clue about where else to look.

By the time Albert finished, Whitney learned that Rhys and Morgan—if the girl named Isabelle was Morgan, which Whitney believed—had lived like nomads, moving from place to place, operating a small-time drug business. She learned that Morgan was a recreational-drug user, but Rhys, as Albert so aptly put it, was "into the stuff big time."

Even though business was good, the profits went to support his habit. When money got tight, he found a couple of johns and made money selling his girlfriend's favors.

Whitney stifled her pain. It was too terrible to imagine. But apparently, to Whitney's relief, when Morgan became pregnant, she stopped using drugs and alcohol altogether. And according to Albert's source, Morgan desperately wanted to live a normal family life and urged Rhys to seek treatment. When he refused, she left him and disappeared.

"I haven't been able to pick up her trail from that point on," Albert said. "Though she must've got in touch with him or he wouldn't have known where to get the baby."

Unable to speak around the lump in her throat, Whitney barely heard Albert's voice droning in the background. Hearing descriptions of Morgan's life with Rhys sickened her, reminded her how she'd let her little sister down. God help her, she was as much to blame as her parents. And she could never make up for it.

"Thanks, Albert," she said. "You've done enough for now." She had other questions, but first needed to sort out what she knew for sure from what she only thought she knew.

Albert had located Rhys because he'd left a forwarding address to General Delivery in Estrade. If Albert had found him, why couldn't Morgan have found him, too? Had Morgan even tried to get her baby back? And why had she kept the child a secret from Whitney until right before she died?

Seeing the headlights of a car, Whitney peeked through the curtains. A forest-green Jeep drove up near where Gretta and Johnny stood with their grandchild. They watched expectantly as the car came to a stop, and when the door opened, the child rushed headlong into the arms of...Rhys Gannon?

What on earth? *Why is he here?* Fear raced through Whitney. Had he found her out? Or was he just paying Gretta and Johnny a visit? They were acquaintances, after all.

Rhys swung the child around, and as he did, the hood on the little sweatshirt fell back, exposing a profusion of golden curls.

Whitney's adrenaline surged. She pressed her forehead against the window, straining to see more.

Rhys's whole face lit up. His mouth split in an affectionate smile as they all talked back and forth. And then, with the little girl still in his arms, Rhys leaned over and hugged both Gretta and Johnny.

"Oh...my...God," Whitney whispered. The phone slipped from her fingers and she watched in stunned silence as the scene played out before her.

"Whitney, you there? Hello? Whitney? Hellloo?"

Her mouth went dry. She couldn't speak and she

couldn't hear over the thundering in her ears as she saw Rhys Gannon gently place the little girl in a car seat in the back of the Jeep. He strapped her in, then kissed the top of her head.

Before Whitney could gather her wits, Rhys shut the back door, climbed into the Jeep and drove off.

"Whitney?" Albert continued. "You there? Whitney?"

CHAPTER FIVE

"CAN I HELP?" Whitney fought the urge to fire off a multitude of questions. It took every ounce of her willpower to blunt the excitement of her discovery.

Both Gretta and Johnny waved her off. "Nope," Johnny said. "Guests aren't allowed to help. You just set yourself somewhere and relax till dinner's ready. Cocktails will be in the parlor."

Whitney stared at her host. No wonder Johnny had looked so familiar. It was obvious. How in the world had she missed it?

If the little girl was Gretta and Johnny's granddaughter, then Rhys was their son. She should've noticed it early on, great observer of people that she was.

Both men were tall, with similar builds, although Johnny didn't possess Rhys's muscularity. And deep lines had settled around Johnny's mouth and eyes. Oddly, they enhanced his strong features and showed he was a happy man. She could see Rhys in another thirty years aging in much the same manner.

In an instant the pieces had fallen into place. And then she had even more questions. Her head began to throb as she tried to sort it all out.

How could such lovely people as Gretta and Johnny have a son with Rhys's reputation? How could parents of their caliber have an offspring who went so bad? God, she would've given her inheritance for such caring parents, and to think that Rhys had done anything hurtful to them was horrifying beyond belief. Her heart went out to them.

But the most important thing was that she'd found her niece. It was, in fact, the *only* thing that mattered.

The thought of SaraJane sent another swift jolt of excitement coursing through her. She'd actually found her niece! The beautiful little girl she'd been watching was SaraJane. Morgan's child. Whitney's own flesh and blood.

Reeling from her discovery, Whitney headed for the sitting room and sat in one of the two matching paisley chairs, sinking deep into the down-filled cushion. *Right here under my nose the whole time.* It boggled her mind.

Just then Johnny entered the room with a man and woman at his side. "Whitney Sheffield, Mr. and Mrs. Blaelow," Johnny announced.

"Carl and Helen," the portly man said as Whitney stood up to shake hands. "Just call us Carl and Helen." The man's grin spread all over his face. Whitney felt an instant letdown, realizing she couldn't ask questions with strangers in the room.

A dull ache began to throb behind her eyes and at the base of her skull. She rubbed the back of her head, still thinking about the complexities of this new situation.

"Nice to meet you both," she responded numbly, and received a dead-fish handshake from Helen and a pumper from Carl.

Johnny excused himself for a moment, and she vaguely heard Carl rattling on about his and Helen's trip.

"Chardonnay?" Johnny entered wielding a large tray of hors d'oeuvres and wine, which he placed on the library table. "Or a merlot?"

"Actually, I think I need to take a couple of aspirin,"

she said, rising. "Maybe I'll skip the hors d'oeuvres and rest for a bit. I'll come back later for dinner."

Climbing the stairs, she knew it wasn't likely she could rest. There were too many questions bombarding her.

She needed answers. Lots of answers. Learning that Gretta and Johnny were Rhys's parents had thrown her for a loop. If Rhys was such an abominable person, why hadn't Gretta and Johnny tried to get custody of Sara-Jane?

If he was the degenerate Morgan made him out to be, why didn't Gretta and Johnny see it? Had he fooled everyone?

Mercifully, the aspirin kicked in and she dropped into a deep sleep not long after her head hit the pillow. The next thing she heard was a soft rapping on her door, and when she finally pried her eyes open, she saw moonlight slanting through the lace curtains.

Groggy, she rolled off the bed and padded to the door without turning on the lamp. Gretta stood in the dimly lit hallway, a silver dinner tray in her hands.

"When you didn't come back, we figured you needed the rest, but you can't go without dinner entirely."

Whitney opened the door wide, inviting her in. "What time is it?" She stretched her arms over her head. "Did I sleep long?"

"It's nine." Gretta set the tray on the table beside the bay window and then, reaching up, turned on the Tiffany-style floor lamp next to it. The light shone through the soft rose-and-green glass shade. Removing the covers from the plates of food, Gretta urged Whitney to sit. "Feeling better?"

Whitney rubbed her temples with two fingers. "Yes, the headache's gone." She was thankful for that and also for the food Gretta had brought up. "I'm starving and it smells wonderful, Gretta. Thank you. I'm sorry I missed dinner. I was looking forward to it."

"There'll be other nights and other dinners," Gretta said matter-of-factly, taking the plates from the tray as she spoke. "The important thing is that you're feeling better. Besides, you didn't miss anything since the food's right here." She sighed. "And, well, let's just say you didn't miss any stimulating conversation."

Whitney watched Gretta shift the table arrangement to accommodate the plates. Her eyes, Whitney noticed, were the same cobalt blue as Rhys's and rimmed with the same dark lashes.

Gretta sent Whitney a concerned look and gently touched her shoulder. "Are you sure you're okay, dear? You look a little pale."

"I'm fine. Really." Whitney motioned for Gretta to sit across from her. "Just tired, I guess." She glanced from her food to Gretta, observing the resemblance to Rhys and trying to see a bit of SaraJane there.

If Rhys was thirty-five or thereabouts, Gretta had to be at least fifty-five, but she did appear a bit older. Even so, she was a handsome woman, and it was evident where Rhys got his good looks.

"I—I saw Rhys pick up your granddaughter tonight."

Gretta beamed at the mention of the child and nodded. "He drops her off in the morning and comes to get her after he closes the shop. It works out well."

"I was surprised to see him." Whitney hedged a little. "When he told me about the inn, he didn't mention your, uh, relationship."

Gretta frowned briefly, then her eyes filled with tenderness. "Well, I can understand that. He's had a lot on his mind. Especially since—" She stopped short. "Well, he's a bit guarded because he's been through so many changes in the past year, and he's trying very hard to hold things together.''

A thin tight smile flitted across Gretta's face, as if she'd said too much, especially to someone she barely knew.

"Your granddaughter is beautiful," Whitney said, desperate for more information.

Gretta rose from her chair. "SaraJane is the light of our lives. Rhys's, too."

"That's easy to see. And she's a lucky little girl to have grandparents like you and Johnny to take care of her. It's hard when parents work." Whitney hoped she'd stay and talk about SaraJane or Rhys, or both.

But the older woman started for the door. "Unfortunately Rhys doesn't have any other option. SaraJane's mother abandoned her when she was an infant." She raised her chin. "But we all try very hard to make up for it. We give her all the love we can."

A hard knot formed in Whitney's stomach. Gretta believed SaraJane was abandoned by her mother? How absurd. Morgan's very last thoughts, her last words, concerned her daughter.

"Abandoned? Are you sure?" Whitney blurted.

The woman's expression questioned Whitney's meaning.

"I mean, it's hard to believe anyone could abandon a helpless child," Whitney added.

Gretta reached for the doorknob. Thoughtful, she rubbed the brass with her thumb, then eased open the door. "It is, isn't it?" She sighed deeply and brought her gaze to Whitney's. "That's something I'll never understand."

"Oh, don't go." Whitney stood. "Have some tea?"

Gretta's expression warmed at the suggestion. "Thank you, dear. I'd love to, but I have to finish preparations for morning." She indicated that Whitney should sit. "You just enjoy your meal—then try to get some more rest. You really don't look well."

Damn tough to do, Whitney thought dejectedly after Gretta left. Leaning forward, elbows on the table, she stabbed a spinach leaf in the center of the stoneware salad bowl with her fork. Rhys had lied to them about SaraJane's mother abandoning her.

But then, what else could he say without incriminating himself? He'd deceived his own parents to get them to do what he wanted. It was despicable. And he was setting them up for a world of hurt. How could he do that to them?

But wasn't she about to do the same? She couldn't take custody of SaraJane and not hurt them in the process. It was obvious, even if she told them about Rhys, that they wouldn't believe it. What parent would?

Gretta had alluded to changes in Rhys's life in the past year. She'd said he was trying to hold things together. But why? What did it all mean?

Was it possible that Rhys had undergone some life-changing metamorphosis, and that he'd actually come here with SaraJane to start a new life? Could the man Morgan had described truly change? If so, how would it affect her own bid to gain custody?

The image of Rhys with SaraJane in his arms formed in Whitney's mind. A loving father who, as Gretta said, considered his daughter the light of his life.

Even as Whitney undressed and went to bed, she couldn't stop thinking of Rhys as he'd looked holding SaraJane. She snuggled under the puffy down-filled comforter, more confused than she'd been in a long time, again welcoming the respite of sleep.

Throughout the night, the dream came in fits and starts, like a photographic collage. Rhys was there, and then Whitney was there and in his arms, and they whirled in slow motion, body to body, gaze to gaze, his face so close, his breath so hot. Teasing, tantalizing, lips closer and closer until his full sensuous mouth connected with hers, and she could feel his hands as they caressed, explored, touching her everywhere. A deep ache of desire throbbed inside, and she begged him to make love to her.

Whitney bolted upright, her heart pounding, her skin feverish and damp with sweat. Dazed, she fought to clear her head.

Rhys Gannon was the man who'd fathered her sister's child, then kidnapped her baby, leaving Morgan sick and alone. Ultimately, that was how Morgan had died. Alone. Without the man she'd once loved. Without her family. Without her child.

A murderer. A kidnapper. How could she think of Rhys in any other way? Even in her dreams.

A thud, like the sound of a car door, brought her fully awake. Oh, jeez. It was morning already.

She darted from the bed to the window, hoping it was Rhys and SaraJane. She couldn't wait to talk to her niece and had already decided not to go to the shop until later, but she needed to do it without arousing suspicion.

She peered outside. Her stomach dropped to her toes. *Rhys.*

She wouldn't approach him now. Instead, she'd wait till he left, then call the shop to let him know she had a few things to do and that she'd be there in an hour or so.

The phone rang, jarring her. Who'd call her so early? Who even knew she was here? Finally, reluctantly, she plucked the receiver from the cradle.

"Still asleep?" Rhys's husky voice was unmistakable.

"No." And why was he calling? Had Gretta told him about their conversation last night? "Is something wrong?"

"Nope," he answered cheerfully. "Just checking to see if you wanted to hitch a ride with me—since we're going to the same place and all." A moment of silence fell before he added, "And we're both coming back to the same place."

Her heart tripped involuntarily at his thoughtfulness. "Thanks. I appreciate the offer, but I have a couple of things to do before I can get there this morning." It wasn't a total lie. She did have things to do. "I'll be there in an hour, how's that?"

"Works for me." Whitney heard a child's giggle in the background. "Wait just a second, angel," she heard Rhys say softly away from the receiver. She clutched the phone, listening.

"Here, punkin face, let me help you get that off." Another pause. "Sorry, Whitney. Yeah, whenever is fine. Just thought I'd check."

She thanked him again for offering and said she'd see him later. When she heard the car pull away, she quickly showered, threw on a pair of jeans and a white cotton T-shirt with a denim shirt over it and dashed downstairs.

Gretta was in the kitchen by the butcher-block island, intent on arranging hot scones in baskets lined with floral-printed linen napkins. Whitney glanced around, searching for SaraJane. Where was she?

Her stomach cramped, her anxiety building. She

couldn't very well start asking questions about the child. Gretta was too smart not to suspect something.

She sauntered toward Gretta. This was a working kitchen, but cozy, the kind photographed for country-home-decorating magazines. Copper pots and pans dangled from hooks overhead, cookbooks lined the shelves next to the refrigerator, and several crockery pitchers with an assortment of wooden spoons and wire whips were strategically placed near the white enameled stove.

The scents of homemade bread and fresh-brewed coffee completed the scene. "Good morning," Gretta said, handing Whitney two brimming baskets.

Whitney automatically took them and started toward the dining room, wondering briefly why Gretta allowed her to help today when she hadn't let her last night. She didn't mind, though; in fact, it felt good to do something.

"I'm glad you're joining us for breakfast," Gretta said as Whitney nudged the swinging door with her hip.

"It smells wonderful," Whitney said. "And you're right—it is a good morning."

Entering the dining room with the scones, Whitney again looked for her niece, her gaze falling on the Blaelows who sat at the table like a pair of matching Buddhas. Damn. She'd forgotten about the Blaelows.

Whitney managed a polite greeting, placed the baskets on the oak table and flew back into the kitchen.

"I'm not so sure about the good-morning part anymore." She cocked her head toward the dining room with a pained expression.

Gretta laughed, eyes sparkling. "Change your mind about breakfast?"

"Nope, not a chance after sampling your cooking last night. I'll be a regular from now on." Whitney leaned over the countertop and whispered, "Not even the Blae-lows will keep me away."

Just then the back door banged open and the little girl bounded in, Johnny right on her heels. "Here, Grammy. We got flowers." Her small arms were filled with a com-bination of fall flowers, reeds and weeds, which she promptly dropped on a side table. She started pushing a chair toward the cupboard, completely oblivious to Whitney's presence.

"Wait a minute, young lady." Johnny held her back. "Where d'you think you're going with that?"

The child's eyes widened as she pointed a chubby finger to an open shelf above the cookbooks. "Grammy's vases are up there now."

"Ah, right you are. Well, you just relax for a minute, young lady, and I'll hand you one. Then we'll put some water in the vase and you can arrange your flowers." He grinned affectionately at his granddaughter.

The child responded with a nod, blond curls bouncing. That was when she noticed Whitney standing next to Gretta.

"SaraJane, honey, this is Miss Sheffield." Gretta crouched to the child's level and gently brushed dried leaves and dirt from the knees of her denim coveralls.

Oh, Lord, the little girl looked so much like Morgan it made Whitney's breath catch. Her pain got all mixed up with an incredible happiness, and her heart seemed to swell. She blinked back the tears that came to her eyes.

"I'd like you to call me Whitney, SaraJane." Her voice was a mere whisper.

The child stared up at Whitney curiously, her cheeks rosy from the brisk morning air.

"I got some flowers." She pointed toward the table

where she'd dumped the bouquet, but kept her gaze on Whitney.

"And they're very beautiful." Whitney bent down to talk to her. She was so tiny, or maybe she just seemed that way to Whitney. She'd never been around children much, except when Morgan was a baby, and a slight panic took hold of her.

Whitney had been ten when Morgan was born, and for the next seven years, she'd protected Morgan from her mother's alcoholic tirades and abusive behavior—being more of a mother to Morgan than Kathryn Sheffield ever was. But that was thirteen years ago, and she hadn't a clue what to do now.

"I'm sure your grandmother appreciates your help, too," Whitney finally said.

SaraJane frowned thoughtfully and pressed her Kewpie-doll lips together. "What's pre-she-ates?"

Oh, God, she was precious. So very precious. Whitney looked to Gretta.

"It means Grammy's happy you helped," Gretta said, coming to Whitney's rescue.

Johnny reached for a vase, and after checking its size against the bouquet SaraJane had picked, he set it on the small table next to the flowers. "There you go, angel. You arrange them and I'll fill it with water when you're done."

SaraJane quickly unzipped her pink corduroy jacket, shrugged it off and dashed to the alcove, where she hung the coat on a low hook. "Wanna help?" She looked up at Whitney before latching onto Whitney's fingers with her tiny hand, urging her forward.

"You can do the big ones 'cause you're big, and I'll do the little ones, 'cause I'm little," SaraJane said, her cheeks dimpling as she directed Whitney to the table.

SaraJane *was* an angel. An absolute angel.

Breakfast with the Blaelows was bearable because SaraJane sat on a booster seat beside Whitney and chattered through the whole meal. When everyone was finished, Whitney gave the departing couple her perfunctory regrets.

The Blaelows related their travel plans, saying after breakfast they were off to Disneyland, at which point SaraJane piped up with, "Poppy's taking *me* there, too." She poked a finger into her mouth and giggled.

For a child who'd been through a couple of years of uncertainty, she seemed completely unscathed, Whitney observed, watching SaraJane's eyes round with excitement. No doubt it was Gretta and Johnny's love and stability that had helped her through it.

"After Christmas," SaraJane finished as she wriggled down from her chair. She skipped into the sitting room and picked up a stuffed bear from the floor. Clutching it to her chest, she plopped into a child-size rocking chair. Then she held the bear at arm's length. "Pooh is going too," she said matter-of-factly, before she brought it to her chest again and squeezed hard. "Aren't you, Pooh Bear?"

In the next instant SaraJane was dragging out toys from a large wicker basket, completely absorbed in her task.

Fascinated, Whitney felt catapulted back in time, as if she were watching her little sister. Her heart ached with the terrible knowledge that Morgan would never see her daughter again.

And SaraJane would never know her mommy.

"Well, it's been nice meeting you, Whitney," Carl Blaelow stuck out his hand. "Good luck on your book.

We'll look forward to seeing it and we'll be sure to tell all our friends about it.'' Helen giggled.

Whitney knew she should leave for the shop, as well. Though it was the last thing she felt like doing, she couldn't stay with SaraJane the whole day, or she'd have everyone wondering.

What she wanted was to pluck the child up and whisk her away. But much as she wanted it, she knew it wasn't reasonable. She'd only just met SaraJane. She had no bond with her and Rhys and the grandparents did. And most importantly, she couldn't even prove a kinship with her niece.

Not yet.

She had to bide her time.

She bade the Blaelows goodbye, went to her room for her cameras and came back down. Just as her foot hit the bottom step, SaraJane appeared. She latched onto Whitney's fingers and pulled her into the sunroom, where she had an assortment of dolls precariously perched on tiny chairs around a play table set with miniature cups and saucers.

''Would you like some tea?'' SaraJane asked, enunciating each word as clearly as a three-year-old could. She proceeded to hoist herself onto one of the chairs, her feet barely touching the floor.

Watching the morning sun glint off her niece's golden hair, Whitney took out her smaller camera and clicked off a couple of frames. ''Can't right now, sweetheart.''

SaraJane seemed oblivious to the camera, going about the business of offering tea to the Raggedy Ann doll sitting across from her.

''Maybe later, when I come back after work.'' Kneeling beside her niece, Whitney fought a desperate urge to pull her close and hug her hard. Instead, she reached out to smooth a springy blond curl from the child's face and squeeze her small hand.

Swallowing painfully, Whitney stood. On the way out she turned and blew SaraJane a kiss. When SaraJane blew a kiss back, as naturally as if they'd been doing it forever, Whitney was sure her heart would burst.

WHITNEY ENTERED THE SHOP and as she turned to close the door, a draft of wind pulled it shut with a bang. At the sound, Rhys's voice boomed from the back office.

"Be with you in a minute."

She picked her way through the aisles, glancing at the unopened boxes on the floor against the wall. A razor knife and price labeler lay on top. Yesterday Rhys had explained some of the jobs she could easily do, and she decided to go ahead.

She set her camera bag on the floor outside the office. Not much she could screw up labeling and stocking shelves. Anxious to get started, she slit open a box with the knife, reached inside and drew out a package of T-shirts.

The shirts, she'd noticed, were displayed on a side wall right above the bins that held the various sizes. Easy enough. She also noticed how precise and neat Rhys kept the store. Everything had its place.

And everything she learned about the man challenged Morgan's description. He'd told her his interest was in building motorcycles, one-of-a-kind custom-made originals. And from the photographs he'd shown her, his work was truly artistic, rather like metal sculpture. Art was a medium to which Whitney could relate.

Rhys was a complicated man. And as much as she tried, she just couldn't reconcile the picture Morgan had painted with what she saw.

"I said no!" Rhys's voice boomed, startling Whitney. "Either he comes through with the money or there's no deal. It's as simple as that."

Whitney clutched the shirt close to her chest and inched nearer to the door.

"No. I don't make second offers. Money is up-front. I'll come through with the goods on this end."

Shocked, Whitney held her breath and strained to hear more. But Rhys's voice quieted, and she couldn't make out the rest of the conversation.

I'll come through with the goods. Did that mean what she thought it did? How could she have forgotten?

How could she have forgotten that she was here to prove Rhys was an unfit parent? To prove he was a drug dealer, or at the very least, that he had unsavory connections—and that *she* should have custody of SaraJane.

She'd forgotten because, until now, until this minute, it had been easy to forget. He'd seemed so different. Yes, he was aloof sometimes, even a little secretive, but then why shouldn't he be? What reason would he have for baring his soul to a total stranger?

According to Gretta, he'd undergone a major life change. If that was true, she couldn't blame him for not wanting to talk about his past. And according to Gretta, he wanted to put it all behind him.

Weren't his actions proof of that? He'd welcomed her to his shop, offered her work, given her his help in researching the book. He'd even found her a place to stay.

And because of it, she'd almost forgotten he was a man capable of despicable acts.

Conflicting thoughts raced through her head. He'd been so gentle and loving with SaraJane. He'd been that way with her, too, patiently explaining, gently teasing when she didn't remember names and types of bikes.

But the conversation she'd just overheard was confrontational, not at all like his earlier behavior, and it gave rise to further suspicion.

Right now she was as confused about Rhys Gannon's character as she was about her sister's truthfulness.

The doubt ate away at her resolve. All she wanted was to grab her niece and flee. But she was caught in a waiting game.

Resigned, she went back to stacking the racks. A few minutes later she noticed Rhys's backlit form in the doorway to his office.

"Well, whaddaya think?" he asked. His mood had done a 180-degree turn from where it had seemed during the conversation she'd just overheard.

She swung around, her pulse beating in her throat. "About what?"

He walked over to stand beside her. "Your new career?" he said with a wide grin. "Think you're gonna find the motorcycle business interesting enough for a book?"

Even though his spirit was playful, his voice suggested she was very obviously not cut out for this line of work.

She squared her shoulders. "Of course. I never realized how interesting it was until I started doing research." She met his gaze, then bent down for another package to place on the rack.

He bent down next to her, reached into the box at the same time, then clamped his hand over hers, holding it there. His eyes were riveted on hers. "You don't have to do this, you know."

Her heart sped up. "Do what?"

"You don't have to work here just to get information. I'd give it to you, anyway."

Oh, God. What information was he talking about? Information for the book—or about SaraJane? Still clutching the package, she rose to her feet. He rose with her.

She punched the grommet and hung the bag on the metal hook in front of her, not noticing whether or not it actually belonged in that spot.

Play dumb. Take his words at face value. "Oh, but I want to. I want to do this. Really. The more I know, the better my photographs will be."

RHYS WAS BAFFLED by her persistence. Though he liked her tenacity, it hurt his pride that she was working for him without pay—even if she didn't need the money.

Not to mention, if she was just doing this as a lark, she could screw up his business more than it already was.

Still, she seemed sincere. The other day she'd listened to his instructions as if he'd recited a soliloquy from *Hamlet.* Then she'd forged ahead, working like a docker, slicing open boxes, removing heavy parts. She hadn't hesitated to pitch in, even though it was a hard dirty job.

He had to admit that she might have been raised among the blue bloods, like Stephanie, but she was different. His ex-wife wouldn't have lifted a finger. Her expertise was in using his money to co-ordinate charity balls and benefits that were really just social events for the rich. The thought galled him. If only he had some of that cash now.

He picked up another packet, bumping shoulders with Whitney on the way down. He had an overwhelming urge to pull her close, to feel her body against his, to release that silky hair and press his face into it.

Forget it, Gannon! She's off-limits.

He took a step back to put some breathing distance

between them. Way off-limits. He stabbed his fingers through his hair.

''Just remember I can't pay you,'' he said bluntly, stupidly, because she didn't need to get paid and he knew it.

But even as he said it, he wanted her to stay. He liked her presence. He liked the feel of her working beside him. He liked waking in the morning excited and revved with anticipation.

He hadn't felt such a rush since he was twenty.

But he wasn't twenty. A lot had happened since then, and there was more to come. Soon he'd be facing the most difficult task of his life. The last thing he needed was more complications—and a woman in his life was definitely a complication.

Then her eyes linked with his. Pale-blue eyes that sent him ambivalent messages. Hot and cold. Fire and ice. She felt the attraction, too. He could tell. And she was damned uneasy about it.

Which he found intriguing. Why would a woman of her age and her background feel nervous about being attracted to someone? Especially someone she far outclassed? In her world she'd probably think nothing of taking the steps necessary to get what she wanted, when she wanted.

But she wasn't in her world and, he guessed, that threw her a little off center. Besides, she wanted something from him—something important enough to overlook her discomfort. Her work. *That's what matters to her.*

She was dead serious about her photography. Her work came first. It was an admirable quality, and one he would do well to keep in mind.

He muttered some cockamamie instructions about the rest of the boxes and then stalked off to the safety of his office.

CHAPTER SIX

"WHAT'S THE PROBLEM?" Whitney asked. "If anybody comes in, I'll help them. If I can't, I'll tell them to come back when you've returned from lunch."

She was logical, he had to admit—and she was stubborn as hell. He'd learned that much about her in the past week.

"Things can happen. Some of the people who come in aren't the most, uh, socially adept. What'll you do if one of the customers comes on to you? How would you handle it?"

He gave her a quick once-over. Yeah, most guys he knew wouldn't mind getting close to a woman like her. It was hard not to notice how her jeans fit that perfectly shaped bottom, or how her lips parted so invitingly when she spoke.

She smoothed the front of her white sweater and shook her head. Her exasperated expression and palms-up gesture told him she considered his question ridiculous.

"The same as I do when one of *my* customers comes on to me. I haven't lived in a vacuum, Rhys. Nothing's going to happen to the store in one hour. Nothing I can't handle. Really."

"Okay, okay," he finally agreed. Because just then he realized it wasn't the shop he was worried about; it was her. And he knew she thought that was absurd.

She was completely capable of taking care of herself, had done it for years, from what she'd told him. He grabbed his bomber jacket from the closet and hurried out the back door. The image of Whitney's zealous smile still lingered as he swung a leg over the Sportster and took off, heading to the inn for lunch.

After a week together they'd fallen into a comfortable working routine, and he looked forward to each day with more enthusiasm than the one before.

Yet he hated the way she'd gotten under his skin. It scared him. Every time he'd thought she was like his ex-wife or some other woman he'd known, she'd proved to be different.

But he wasn't going to kid himself. She was here to do a job, and when it was done she'd leave and he'd be just another reference in her book. He had no illusions about anything further with her, not even when he visualized her long legs wrapped around him, hips moving rhythmically. His blood surged as he indulged in that speculation. Or was it fantasy?

Working with her had truly become exquisite torture. And he found it almost impossible to keep his lust to himself.

Some weird ego thing in him liked the way she got all flustered when she guessed what was on his mind. More and more he began to think about trying to make it happen. If he slept with her, just once, he might get it out of his system.

But she'd be gone in a week or so, anyway, and it'd be back to business as usual. Yeah, two different worlds. That was how things were and how they'd remain. He'd learned that lesson the hard way.

WHITNEY WAITED for a moment to be sure Rhys was gone, then yanked open the top drawer of the filing cabinet.

With only an hour, she had to be quick.

Folders full of business papers. The same in the next drawer, and the third was locked. Nervous and unsure of what she was looking for, she rifled the files, checking names and dates.

Maybe something to indicate where SaraJane was born. Something to show Rhys's past. Something to discredit him.

Guilt needled her as she pulled out a folder labeled "Bank Loan." Rhys had trusted her to mind the store for him and she was repaying that trust by snooping through his files.

She felt sleazy, just as sleazy as she'd imagined him to be.

During the past week he'd bent over backward to teach her about the business. He hadn't revealed himself, even once, to be anything other than a man trying to make a living while raising a child to whom he was devoted.

Whitney tried to assuage her guilt by remembering Morgan's description of how he'd fooled her with his charm. As she held a file in her hand, her resolve weakened. God, she'd feel so violated if someone rummaged through her personal things. Especially if it was someone she trusted.

She stuffed the folder back and slammed the drawer shut. Hands on hips, she scanned the room, irritated with herself for not taking full advantage of the opportunity.

Some Mata Hari she was. How did people like that live with themselves? They had to do it, she supposed. For them, the stakes were high and worth the betrayal.

Wasn't this the same? And wouldn't waiting only pro-

long the outcome—and make it more difficult for everyone involved?

*Just do it, Whitney, you coward. You made a promise.
You can't stop now.* She remembered the other promises
she'd made to Morgan as a child. Promises she'd failed
to keep and because of her failure— Oh, God. She *had*
to follow through.

Quickly she slid open the drawer, got out the file and
scribbled the loan data in her time planner. When she'd
finished, she circled Rhys's desk, then dropped into the
leather chair.

She opened the center drawer. It was tidy with small
compartments for paperclips, rubber bands and pens.
Nothing of interest, until she noticed something shiny
poking out from under a stack of billing statements in
the back. A photograph.

Gently lifting the corner with two fingers, she eased
it from under the pile, careful not to disturb anything.

A photo of SaraJane. Sweet darling SaraJane. All blue
eyes and dimpled cheeks.

She wasn't more than a year old in the picture, but
Whitney could easily tell it was her niece. She flipped
it over; nothing was written there—no date or name. She
started to slip the picture back when the corner caught
on the edge of another photo.

She lifted it out and held it up. The Polaroid colors
were faded, but she knew instantly that the man in the
photo was Rhys. On the back ''Florida'' was printed in
large bold letters.

Her heart warmed at the engaging picture. Rhys's dark
hair was flopped onto his forehead, and one arm was
looped around the shoulders of a small boy who clutched
a fishing pole and a string of fish.

Though Rhys's bare chest and rippled stomach didn't

escape her interest, it was the young boy's face that caught her attention. His eyes. There was something about his eyes...

His sister's son? Yes, that was it. He'd said he had a married sister who lived in Florida with her husband and three children. The photo obviously meant something to him. Perhaps even represented a happier time.

So, it was possible that he really was a man trying to change the direction of his life. Maybe some traumatic experience had thrown him temporarily off-track and now he was trying—

"What do I need to do to get some help?" A gruff male voice sent Whitney's hands flying and her insides into spasm. She looked up to see a customer standing in the office doorway. Quickly she shoved the photograph back and closed the drawer.

A wave of apprehension ran through her as she rose to greet the man. He was tall, at least as tall as Rhys, and had on a long black leather coat, the kind she'd seen on outlaws in old western movies.

He wore heavy black boots with metal around the toes, black leather pants and a black T-shirt. His hair was drawn back into a ponytail and a two-day growth of beard was the same blue-black color as his hair. His eyes were hidden behind mirrored aviator sunglasses.

"I'm sorry," she said, edging nervously toward him. "I didn't hear you come in." She wished like hell he'd take off the sunglasses. "What can I do for you?"

His body filled the doorway, forcing her to stop in front of him. She knew she shouldn't be put off by the way he looked. Rhys had explained that many bikers were simply people who took up riding as a hobby, and for some, the clothes were part of it, much like tennis or golf outfits.

Yeah, right. The thought was no comfort, and her legs felt as if they were going to desert her.

"Is Gannon here?" he asked, a little less insistently. The gruff raspiness in his voice remained. She could tell from the tilt of his head that the eyes behind the mirrored lenses examined her from head to toe.

Ignoring the disconcerting image of herself in the lenses, she secured the barrette at the back of her head.

"He's out," she said, then instantly realized her vulnerability. "For a couple of minutes."

She glanced at the rear door. Stupidly she'd fastened the safety chain after Rhys had left and now she was trapped inside. So she did the only thing she could and stepped forward. "Excuse me. If you'll let me by, I can help you in the shop." She made a parting motion with her hands.

He backed away from the door, surprising her. But she couldn't help noticing the curl of a smile as she walked past him. Unnerved, she whirled around to face him and extended her hand.

"I'm Whitney. What can I do to help you?"

Holding her breath, she waited for his next move. He quickly enclosed her hand in his, then slid his thumb across it until he touched her emerald ring, a keepsake she'd inherited from her grandmother.

"So where's Gannon? When did you say he'd be back?"

Fear shimmied through her. Easing her hand from his, she retreated toward the front door, accidentally snagging a leather jacket and knocking it off the rack next to her. She caught it by the collar, fumbling until she'd slipped the thing back on the hanger and slung it crookedly over the bar.

"Soon. He'll be back soon." Her heart thumped maniacally. "If you want, you can just wait." She gestured toward a chair near the front. "Or there's a coffee shop down the street."

She whirled around, opened the door and stepped over the threshold, holding the door for him to follow. She pointed in the direction of Mabel's Café, and when he walked past her to look, she breathed a sigh of relief.

"Guess I'll come back later," he said, smiling.

She waited until he mounted his bike and roared off. Back inside, she shut the door and sagged against it, then heard the phone ringing in Rhys's office. On her way to answer it, she congratulated herself on handling the situation quite well.

Still, she felt relieved when a little later she heard the rumble of Rhys's bike out back. Ensconced behind his desk, Whitney finished the last phone order with a flourish, feeling a grand sense of accomplishment at completing the task. She'd enjoyed talking to the customers and helping them as much as she could, reading them information from the stock list Rhys had left her.

What Rhys really needed, she decided, was a good catalog with national distribution. Something slick with color photos. That might help with marketing and PR if he wanted to expand the business as he'd said.

Hearing his footsteps, she gathered her paperwork into a neat pile, then jumped up to unlatch the safety chain.

"Everything okay?" Rhys asked, glancing around the office. He unzipped his jacket, shrugged it off and hung it in the small closet next to the door.

"Of course. Everything's fine." She pointed at the stack of papers on the desk. "That's most of it. Four orders, all written up and ready to be shipped." She nodded at the boxes by the window, still irritated that he'd doubted she could handle such a simple task.

He scooped up the papers and fanned the corners. "Hey, this is great. Really great." He set the papers back on the desk and rolled his shoulders as if he needed to loosen up. "Any problems?"

"Problems?" She stepped from behind the desk, dismissing his comment with a casual flip of her hand. "What problems could there be in taking a few orders? It's not exactly rocket science."

"But it's money," he said, then picked up the papers again. "Every little bit helps. Let's see, this one is for—" his eyebrows arched "—two thousand dollars?"

Rhys leaned against the desk, stretched out his arms as if he needed glasses to read the order sheet. "You double-checked the figures?" He studied the paper again, as if he'd read it wrong.

"I'm not even going to respond to that." Whitney pretended to feel insulted.

A smile formed, and with a glint in his eye, he asked, "What did you say to the guy that made him spend this kind of money?"

She shrugged and raised her hands.

He picked up another order. Both eyebrows shot up again. "Whitney, this is great! *Look* at these," he said incredulously.

Still clutching the order forms, he reached out and placed his hands on her upper arms. "You've just sold as much as I made in the entire past month."

Now *she* was amazed. Not at herself, but that he thought it was such a big deal. She hadn't done anything special; she'd merely acted as she would in her own business.

But his words made her feel good, and she absorbed his praise like a kid who'd just gotten all A's on her report card.

Only, that feeling was nothing compared to how her arms were getting all hot under his touch. Suddenly the room seemed crowded—and he was right there within kissing distance. If she took one little step, she could be in his arms, her mouth pressing against his, her body—

Oh, jeez. What on earth was wrong with her?

"So I guess you think things were okay while you were gone?" She couldn't squelch the smirk that emerged on her face.

His gaze held hers, then his features softened. In an instant that seemed to stretch to infinity, her ego soared. She'd not only brought in some money, apparently a lot more than expected, but also managed to allay his fears about her abilities.

Rhys grew still, and the sparkle of excitement that danced in those eyes, only seconds ago switched to smoldering desire. Her insides went all warm and liquid, and Lord, she was glad the man who'd been in earlier had said he'd return.

She was glad, because in the past week her feelings about Rhys had been all over the place, and she wasn't sure how she'd react if he ever made a move on her. She'd wondered more than once how it would feel to be wrapped in his strong capable arms.

But every time she wondered, a free-floating anxiety would follow. She'd never experienced such unbridled lust, never knew she had it in her. And the most confusing thing of all was *why* she felt that way about Rhys Gannon—a man she should despise. A man she *needed* to despise if she was to carry out her plan.

But right now it wasn't hate on her mind.

As if he'd been reading her thoughts, Rhys stared at her mouth and gently stroked both thumbs down her arms. She stiffened, fearful she'd give herself away.

Rhys averted his gaze and dropped his hands. "Guess it's your turn, huh?"

She blinked. "My turn?"

"For lunch. Why don't you go and get a bite?" He pulled out a file drawer, picked up one of the files and held it up to the light, squinting, as though it was hard to read. "And while you're gone, I'll see if I can handle things as well as you did."

Smiling, she swung around and headed for the front door. "If you're lucky, you mean," she said, her walk feeling as springy and light as her words.

MABEL, DRESSED IN JEANS and a sweatshirt with a hand-painted mountain scene on the front, yanked a blue gingham apron off a hook near the stove, stuck her head through the loop, then poured two cups of coffee.

Her eyes narrowed as she set one steaming mug on the counter in front of Whitney and shoved the sugar and creamer toward her.

"You're a little late. Do you still want lunch, dear?"

Whitney smiled.

"Sure. I'll have the usual."

Mabel removed the homemade bread from the oven and thumped out the loaves. She slipped a spatula under one and transferred it to a white marble slab. She spared Whitney a quick glance. "You eat breakfast?"

Whitney nodded. Mabel's mother-hen instincts were right up there with Gretta's. "I had a scone earlier at the inn. That's more than I usually eat in the morning."

"Gretta's a good cook. She used to fill in for me when I needed a day off," Mabel said. "But since she and Johnny opened the inn five years ago, she's been too busy. Good thing, too." Mabel paused and ducked her head into the fridge. A second later she emerged with a stick of butter along with Whitney's sandwich. "Considering."

"Considering?"

"Oh, you know." Mabel smeared the butter across the crusty bread loaves. "All those family problems."

Family problems? Was she talking about Rhys's past? Although Whitney was eager for any new information, she held her questions. She peered into her cup. "Yes, it's hard to imagine," she said, pretending to know what Mabel was talking about. She'd already learned not to pry, because people in Estrade were fiercely loyal to one another.

Mabel tossed the sandwich in the pan, and just as she appeared ready to say more, the sleigh bells on the front door jangled. "Right on time," she said, glancing at her watch. She winked at Whitney and flipped the cheese sandwich. "Afternoon, Charley."

Whitney watched Charley make his way between the chairs and tables, straightening those that were out of place. Rats. Just when Mabel might have given her some information.

"Hello, young lady." Charley patted Whitney's shoulder. Mabel set a cup of coffee in front of him while he eased his body onto the stool next to Whitney.

Breakfast and dinner were rituals for Mabel and Charley, and lunch, too, when things weren't going well at the mine. In the past week, Whitney had learned that Charley usually made just enough money to keep the wolf at bay. But he was certain that one day he was "gonna hit a vein"—he'd known it for more than thirty years.

Whitney suspected it really didn't matter much if he did or not. "Hi, Charley. Any luck out there today?"

Whitney saw Mabel roll her eyes at the question.

Mabel harrumphed. "You think that's why the old goat goes out there?"

Charley ignored the comment and sent Mabel an affectionate grin as he addressed Whitney. "Still workin' on that picture book of yours? Hardly seems a gal like you would enjoy hangin' around a motorcycle shop."

Whitney suppressed a grin. It had surprised her, too. A couple of weeks ago, the last thing she'd have considered was photographing motorcycles—or helping customers in a bike shop.

"Yep, I'm still working on it, Charley. Just barely started, actually. But I've got an excellent teacher."

Mabel put Whitney's plate on the counter, raising a silvery eyebrow as she did. "So just how long is this research gonna take?" Her tone suggested more than research was happening.

The question snapped Whitney to attention. She'd wondered that herself. Wondered how long Rhys would allow her to stay before he'd question her presence. She couldn't drag out the project forever.

In the week since she'd found SaraJane, she'd become close to her. She'd become close to them all. And the longer she spent, the more she regretted what she had to do. "I don't know," Whitney answered. "I wish I did."

"Maybe you'll wanna stay here," Charley said. "Like me." He nodded at Mabel. "Yep, I took a fancy to Ma—"

"Charley, mind your manners," Mabel cut him off, and they bantered back and forth for the rest of Whitney's lunch hour, at times drawing Whitney into the conversation. They were quite the eccentric pair, and Whitney laughed right along with them.

She loved her lunches with Mabel and Charley. Her relationship with them was totally unlike the life she'd been used to. And the strangest part was that it felt so natural. She couldn't help wondering what it might be like to live in such a place permanently.

"Uh-oh," she said, glancing at her watch. "Gotta go." She polished off the rest of her sandwich, paid, then slipped her camera over one shoulder as she prepared to return to the shop. On her way out, Charley caught her sleeve.

"Be careful, Whitney." His eyes twinkled mischievously. "Your boss has been known to steal more than one young lady's heart."

Whitney moved toward the door. "Thanks for the warning, Charley, but I'm here strictly on business." Lord, how she wished she felt the conviction of her words.

Walking back, she applauded herself on how perfectly things had worked out. She'd arranged to be at the shop from ten until four. That way, he could count on her help during those hours, and she could devote the rest of each day to her niece. She wasn't sure if Rhys knew how much time she was spending with SaraJane, or if he'd object.

Her spirits soared whenever she thought about her niece. She marveled at the tiny perfection of SaraJane's features, so much like Morgan's it made Whitney's heart ache. And she loved to hear the child's laughter and giggles, loved to hear her talk.

Whitney had never experienced such overwhelming pleasure at just watching another human being, and she couldn't imagine that her feelings for SaraJane would be any more intense if the child had been born to her. She couldn't help wondering if her own parents had ever had such deep feelings for either Morgan or her.

But thoughts like this were better dismissed. She

couldn't change the past, and she'd do anything and everything to ensure that SaraJane never experienced that kind of hell.

Returning to the store, Whitney noticed the back end of a black motorcycle protruding from the side of the building. She recognized the motorcycle ridden by the man who'd been there earlier.

The outlaw.

She headed for the front door, then stopped. Going in through the back meant she wouldn't disturb them if they were in the store talking business.

Nearing the corner of Rhys's workshop behind the store, she heard raised voices and then, through the window, saw Rhys inside. His back was to her and the other man stood on his right. The windows were slightly open, but she still couldn't make out their words.

Inching closer, she saw the two men engaged in a rigid handshake. They both made some kind of sign, then hugged, first on one side, then the other. Whitney's blood rushed.

She jerked back. The only time she'd seen that kind of behavior between men was in the movies.

It seemed out of place in a little town in the Arizona mountains. But Rhys *was* from Chicago, she remembered. Maybe his connections had followed him. Maybe, no matter where he went, they'd follow him and he'd never be able to make a new life for himself.

At that moment Whitney realized how much she wanted to believe in Rhys, how much she wanted to believe that what Gretta had said was true. But if it was, how would that affect what *she* needed to do?

Which was to gain custody.

Instinctively she raised her camera and clicked off a few frames of the men in conversation. Then, lo and behold, the outlaw handed Rhys a stack of money. She took another photograph.

Immediately after that the door opened a crack. "Next week," the outlaw rasped. "I'll see you then." A strange panic rioted within her, and she knew she'd better disappear before they saw her.

She backed away. She had a horrible feeling she'd just witnessed something illegal, and like it or not, she had it on film.

Another jolt of panic ripped through her. She stepped back and turned to run, but the heel of her boot sank into a crevice between the flagstones, trapping her. Her blood pounded, and she yanked so hard her boot heel came off, still wedged between the stones.

She stared briefly at the heel, made a quick decision to forget it and dashed around the building to the front of the store, hoping that if they saw her, they'd think she'd just come back from lunch. Breathless, she hit the steps two at a time, barreled inside and slammed the door behind her. Just as she did, she saw the outlaw fly around the building on his bike, a sleek black raven with the tails of his long leather coat floating behind like glossy pointed wings.

Hands pressed against the glass on the door, she watched his dramatic departure, her breathing ragged, absorbed in her thoughts.

"How was lunch?" Rhys's voice sounded behind her.

She jumped, feeling caught in the act. Slowly she turned, using every second to gather her composure. Straightening the lapels on her navy blazer, she moistened her lips.

"It was very nice," she said curtly, her face stiff as plaster. Rhys's eyes widened at her response.

"O-kay," he drawled, letting her know that he'd noticed something wasn't right. "Anything I can do?"

"Nope. I'm fine," she said, suddenly angry with him. Just when she'd decided he might be okay—that he really *was* trying to change his life—he did something to raise her suspicions.

"Fine and dandy!" she added, then turned and clomped away, one leg shorter than the other.

She felt Rhys's eyes boring into her back. A second later he strode past her to enter his office, shaking his head and muttering under his breath, "Women!"

WHEN WHITNEY LEFT for the day, Rhys hurried over to the file cabinet to get out the loan application. No way around it—the money Luth had paid him, combined with what he'd saved over the past few months, still wasn't enough.

He'd tapped every source he knew to pay for the trial; he'd even used all the money that had been slated to get the business off the ground. He'd have to go to plan B.

As he stared blindly at the papers in front of him, his thoughts drifted, which they seemed to do every other minute, to the woman who'd so recently swept into his life.

Her business acumen impressed him, his parents thought she was delightful, and SaraJane loved having her around. Hell, so did he. Whitney had been spending a lot of time with SaraJane, and he liked the way the two of them had hit it off. That thought brought a smile to his lips.

He reached for the photo. It wasn't fair that a child so young should be robbed of a normal family life. Still, whatever they had was better than what she would've had with her mother. Abandonment wasn't exactly one of the criteria for Mother of the Year.

He returned the photo to its place on his desk.

Man, he was grateful he had his parents for support. If he could just get the business rolling, they could lead a nice quiet family life in Estrade, regardless of the past. He didn't need lots of money to be happy; he only needed the security of knowing he'd done the right thing—this time.

His worst fear was that someday SaraJane's mother would have a change of heart and come looking for her. He was well aware that something needed to be done about permanent custody. But since no one even knew he had SaraJane, and they still had to get through the appeal, the last thing he wanted was to draw attention to *that* issue. He certainly didn't want social services getting involved. They might put SaraJane in a foster home or, God forbid, return her to her mother.

Everything had to wait until the appeals were exhausted. Everything, including the wild notions that seeped into his brain. Wild notions about Whitney Sheffield.

Thoughts that pitted desire against good sense. He'd gone down that road before, and doing it again wasn't even close to what he had planned for the rest of his life.

CHAPTER SEVEN

"YOU BE THE MOMMY," SaraJane said, directing Whitney to a spot at the small play table. "And I'll be your little girl."

Whitney felt an overwhelming surge of affection as she watched SaraJane place the tiny teacups on their equally tiny saucers. She wore a pink corduroy jumper—a color that had always looked so pretty on Morgan—a white shirt and white tights.

Someday, Whitney thought as she sat in the tot-size chair. *Someday I'll tell you all about your mommy.*

SaraJane skipped to the play stove in the corner of the sunroom and Whitney cleared her throat. "Um...excuse me. Shouldn't *I* be doing the cooking if I'm the mommy?"

SaraJane turned, and standing with one hand on her hip and a tiny spatula in the other, said proudly, "I can do it all by myself." Then she held out the spatula. "But you can help."

She looked like a Dresden doll. Her eyes were large and her blond hair sprayed from a ponytail on the top of her head, golden tendrils spilling around her chubby pink cheeks.

Whitney tried to picture Rhys doing so delicate a task as brushing his daughter's hair and decided he probably left those things to Gretta. Though, somehow, it wouldn't surprise her if Rhys did do it himself.

SaraJane skipped to Whitney's side and tugged her hand, urging her off the chair and toward the stove. "I can show you how to do it," she said, enunciating each word separately.

"Okay. What do I do?" Whitney asked, kneeling next to the little girl.

"First," SaraJane said, pressing her lips together, "you gotta have these." She pushed a square pot holder into each of Whitney's hands, then concentrating heavily, arranged them to cover Whitney's palms. It amused Whitney just to watch her.

"Then you gotta open the oven door and take the cookies out." Her expression grew serious. "But you gotta be very careful 'cause it's hot." She dimpled. "Put them right here." She patted the tabletop next to the stove. "Then you take the spatula and scoop the cookies off an' put them on the plate."

SaraJane clapped her hands and giggled impishly. "And then—" she drew the words out "—we eat them." Her bubbly laughter sparkled through the room.

Whitney peeked in the window of the miniature oven door before she opened it. "Hmmm, real cookies?"

SaraJane pursed her lips. A frown creased her smooth forehead in a way that sent a pang directly to Whitney's heart. At times the little girl reminded Whitney so much of Morgan as a child it was utterly painful to watch.

"Well, Grammy helped, too," SaraJane said, ducking her chin.

Whitney burst into laughter. *Sweet innocence.* So much like her mother before life and its adversities destroyed her. "That's wonderful!" Whitney exclaimed, reaching to open the oven and remove the cookies. "We all helped. That's called teamwork."

When SaraJane grabbed another spatula and joined

Whitney scooping the cookies off the sheet, Whitney couldn't help adding, ''And I think we make a terrific team.''

Whitney brushed cookie crumbs from her black velour shirt and leggings and watched SaraJane carry the small plastic plate to the table, taking slow deliberate steps so she wouldn't spill anything.

Just as carefully, SaraJane set the plate on the table, then proudly looked up at Whitney. ''See, I told you I could do it all by myself.'' As SaraJane spoke, her gaze lifted beyond Whitney to the doorway. Her face lit with recognition.

''Poppy, Poppy!'' she squealed, completely forgetting the tea party. She flew at Rhys, who leaned casually against the doorjamb, watching them.

Rhys whisked the little girl into his arms and planted a big kiss on her cheek. ''Are you two spoiling your appetites before dinner?'' he asked sternly.

Whitney couldn't help noticing the differences between them. SaraJane's hair was soft and golden, her complexion the proverbial peaches-and-cream. Rhys's hair was thick and black as midnight, his skin, olive, and while both had blue eyes, Rhys's were much darker.

''I want to eat here at Grammy's.''

Rhys drew back. ''You mean you're tired of my cooking?'' He chuckled and tucked a finger under SaraJane's chin.

''Grammy's food is gooder. I want to eat at Grammy's.'' The child wriggled to get down and Rhys gently obliged, smiling as she skipped back to the tea-party table. His eyes caught Whitney's.

''Can't say I blame her. My cooking stinks and even I know it.'' He shook his head. ''But to be told by a three-year-old—now that really hurts.''

His playfulness threw Whitney off guard, and when SaraJane came back and ordered them both to sit at the table and eat cookies, Whitney obeyed. Rhys followed suit. As they did so, SaraJane ran out of the room calling, "Grammy, Grammy, we're gonna eat here!"

Several silent moments passed. Rhys and Whitney shifted uncomfortably in their seats. Finally Whitney plucked a cookie from the plate and bit off a chunk, more than she wanted. Anything to take her mind off Rhys's presence and the sense of intimacy she felt sitting here with him.

Rhys gave Whitney a quirky grin, then leaned against the back of the pint-size chair, an arm slung over the one next to him, and in a remarkably good Bogart imitation said, "Sweetheart, I think we've just been had." His expression was amused. "I don't think she's coming back."

Surprised in mid-swallow by his droll humor—another side of Rhys Whitney hadn't expected—she suppressed her laughter. Cookie crumbs lodged in her windpipe. She coughed, delicately at first, then spasmodically.

She suddenly couldn't breathe. Within a millisecond, Rhys had leaped to his feet, rounded the table and hoisted her from the chair, ready to administer the Heimlich maneuver.

"Wait," Whitney gasped, then coughed to clear her throat. She raised an arm. "I'm okay. Really."

But she knew her words weren't entirely convincing. Because as she stood there with Rhys's arms wrapped around her ribcage, feeling his taut muscles molded against her, her legs started to quiver. His nearness left her senses reeling.

His head rested against hers, and his warm breath

fanned her cheek. She felt the tension in his arms under her breasts and unconsciously relaxed against him. An unequivocal shiver of wanting rippled through her.

"You sure?" He breathed the words next to her ear.

It was useless to deny the excitement pulsating within her. She couldn't have torn herself away if she wanted.

"I'm an expert at this," he said softly. And at that moment she had no doubts whatsoever that he told the truth.

"I'M GONNA HELP Grammy with the cake," SaraJane announced with authority after dinner as she slid from her booster seat at the long dining table. Johnny had excused himself moments before to help in the kitchen, leaving Whitney and Rhys to stare uneasily at each other across the massive expanse of oak.

All through the meal she'd been preoccupied with thoughts of Rhys and how wonderful it felt to have his arms around her. How many times since she'd come to Estrade had she wondered what that would be like? Now she knew—and, God help her, she was as sure as daylight would come that Rhys did, too.

Her body had betrayed her and she might as well have stamped "NAKED LUST" across her forehead.

His eyes locked with hers. His expression was pensive, yet filled with invitation. Was he weighing the same thoughts? *Of course he is.* She could practically feel the sexual energy coming at her.

She adjusted her barrette, then snatched up her glass, gulping down the cool water, hoping it might douse her internal fire. She *couldn't* be attracted to him. She *couldn't* actually like him. Because if she did... Well, there were just too many reasons why she couldn't. Shouldn't.

And just as many why she did.

Rhys and his parents had welcomed her into their lives with barely a question asked. And every time she saw Rhys with SaraJane, she saw nothing but love and tenderness in his eyes—and every time she wondered if Morgan might have lied.

But what about Albert's findings, and that biker who'd given Rhys a bundle of money? What was that all about? Reminded that she hadn't heard from Albert for a while, she resolved to call him later, even though she realized that no contact meant no new information. And he did have other cases to attend to; she had to remember that.

There was only one thing she knew for sure. If Rhys was a drug dealer, that was unforgivable. A man who destroyed innocent lives without remorse was the most despicable of all.

Yet she'd seen no concrete proof, no proof of a single thing Morgan had said. Whatever the truth, it was her sister's secret, and she'd taken it with her.

Whitney lowered her water glass, deliberately avoiding his gaze.

"I'm going to be gone for a few days," Rhys said. "You might want to take a break, too."

Take a break? She stared blankly. What did he mean?

"I've got to go to Phoenix on business, and as long as I'm there, I thought I'd take in a bike show, talk to other dealers, make a few contacts." He plucked a ripe olive from the bowl in front of him. "Pop's going to mind the shop, so you could take a breather and do whatever photographers do when they've got some spare time."

He was leaving? Going away? Panic infused Whitney. "What about SaraJane? Are you taking her along?"

"Mom'll look after her," Rhys answered as if Whitney had every right to know his plans. He smiled reassuringly. "No need to worry."

Did he want her to leave, too? Was he suggesting that? Why? "Oh, sorry. I didn't mean to imply—"

Rhys cut her off with the wave of a hand. "It's okay. Really."

Whitney regrouped. "Oh. Well, I don't need to go anywhere. I guess I can just stay here. What was that you said about a show?"

"Bike show. Biggest thing this side of Daytona and Sturgis."

Her bewildered expression apparently clued him in that she had no idea what he was talking about.

"The two biggest annual motorcycle events in the nation. Daytona Beach in March—that's the traditional kickoff for the racing season—and Sturgis, South Dakota, in August. Both are major bikers' rallies. People come from everywhere. Thousands." He paused, blinking thoughtfully.

"Come to think of it, you oughtta go to some of those rallies for photographs if you want the real biker scene. The thing in Phoenix is different, more like an auto or home show where vendors come in and set up their booths. But interesting, too."

He studied her, then his eyes lit as if inspiration had just struck. "You could go with me." Leaning forward, he said, "Yeah. It'd be an experience for you. Lots of local color for your photographs."

Whitney's pulse raced. At that moment any resolve she'd had about remaining detached evaporated.

"Sounds wonderful!" she gushed, then caught herself. Shoot, the least she could do was maintain some semblance of professionalism. "I mean, it does sound like a wonderful opportunity for some in-depth research.''

After giving her the general information, Rhys said he could get her a room at the same hotel. That way, she could follow him around, meet the dealers and wholesalers and learn about the business from another perspective.

''If you're interested in getting that involved, that is.'' He gave her another quick grin and reached out an arm, catching SaraJane on the fly from the kitchen. He swept her up onto his lap.

''Hey, kiddo. Did you help Grammy with that dessert? I don't see anything coming out.'' SaraJane snuggled into his chest for a hug, then abruptly sat up, swinging her tiny pink-and-white tennis shoes back and forth.

''Maybe I should go and see about dessert, too,'' Whitney offered, rising, her mind filled with the potential implied by this trip with Rhys. It could be an unparalleled opportunity to get information—nearly three hours in the car each way. She'd be sure to find out where SaraJane had been born—and then get Albert on it.

Except that, right now, watching SaraJane on her father's lap, seeing the love light in his eyes, the unadulterated affection, she wasn't sure she wanted to discover anything that might destroy the picture.

Gretta returned with dessert—a light lemon cake— before Whitney could help, and Johnny came back from the foyer. SaraJane wriggled off Rhys's lap and scooted back onto her booster seat with Johnny's help. Rhys gave Whitney a conspiratorial smile.

''Think about it. I'm leaving on Thursday.''

WHITNEY DEBATED her wardrobe options for the trip to Phoenix. Three days altogether. Definitely not a black-tie affair, Rhys had said teasingly when she'd accepted his invitation and asked what to take along in the way of clothes.

Tossing a couple of pairs of jeans and leggings into her bag, she decided they'd just have to do, especially since it was all she'd brought to Estrade—and there weren't any stores in town to buy more.

A shiver of anticipation coursed through her. SaraJane would be safe with her grandparents, giving Whitney the opportunity to ask Rhys some leading questions. Not only that, she could photograph to her heart's content.

Filled with excitement, she had to remind herself of her goal. She rationalized the emotions she was feeling about this whole Estrade experience. Besides getting to know her niece, she'd be working on a book, which meant taking photographs. It was her livelihood, what she enjoyed doing. Nothing wrong with that.

She surveyed her load—one suitcase and her cameras. That was it. Oh, there was another thing. She plucked up the time planner she'd been using as a diary to chronicle her daily conversations with Rhys. Anything he said might give another clue about where SaraJane was born so she could set Albert on the right course.

During the time Whitney and Rhys had spent together at the shop, Rhys had opened up a little. He'd told Whitney that his parents had worked all their lives to save enough money to move from the city and that they'd come to Estrade more than twenty years ago because Johnny had visited the ghost town once and knew that property in the area was inexpensive. Rhys had revealed the fact that he'd worked in Chicago after college, but kept the rest of his past to himself.

She'd spoken to Albert as often as possible, trying to

put the pieces together. Albert was due to get the vital stat information from Chicago any day now, and maybe that would help. There were gaps in Rhys's life between Chicago and Los Angeles, then Los Angeles and Estrade. Gaps neither she nor Albert could figure out. Something important seemed to be missing—and whatever that something was, it could be the key to gaining custody of SaraJane. But whether it was or wasn't, she felt an utterly compelling need to know.

Again and again, she ran through the chronological sequence and always came up with something different. Rhys had grown up in Chicago, graduated from college and earned an MBA, but she had no idea where or when. She guessed that because of his age, he'd graduated sometime in the early eighties.

His marriage, she had to assume, took place in Chicago, because that was where he'd lived and worked until he left for Los Angeles. Albert's findings had him in L.A. about four years ago, and the bank-loan application indicated he'd last worked in Chicago five years ago. The application, she'd discovered, was incomplete, and his activities during the period were visibly missing.

As much as she wanted to ignore it, she knew Rhys was hiding something. And because of that, Morgan's words kept pounding in her brain. *He'll say and do anything to get what he wants. And it doesn't matter who he hurts in the process.*

And the fact that her own judgment had failed her in the past made her even more cautious. She couldn't allow it to happen again. Not when her niece's future was at stake.

She closed her time planner with a clap, then crossed to the window, where she knelt on the padded seat and parted the curtain to see if Rhys had arrived yet. A moment later, she saw him pull into the drive.

After parking, he opened the back door and tenderly drew a blanket around his sleepy-eyed little girl. He zipped up her jacket and tightened the hood before he gathered her in his arms to come in.

How ironic. From everything she'd seen and learned about Rhys's character so far, proving him unfit was the last thing she'd be able to do. Sometimes she even questioned whether it would be the *right* thing to do.

In the end, she'd still need to prove to a court that SaraJane would be better off with her.

It was a question she asked herself all the time. She'd failed the one person she cared about most. What made her think she'd do anything differently with SaraJane?

She had no qualifications for motherhood. No experience. And she certainly had no close-knit family to offer love and support. All she had was her own overwhelming love for her sister's child, and a promise to keep.

Slowly she released the curtain, resolving not to worry about any of this right now. The time she'd spent with SaraJane was precious and she wanted it to continue.

For the moment she needed to be content with the status quo, although sometimes she feared she was *too* content. It was then that she allowed her thoughts to drift to what it might be like to stay on in Estrade with Rhys and SaraJane.

A major fantasy, that. And it had the added appeal of conveniently resolving an ugly situation. If she could somehow forget about Rhys's past and what he'd done to Morgan—

No! She blotted out the thought. It really was a fantasy. One that was all mixed up with a young girl's hopes and dreams—and she'd learned long ago how unrealistic those hopes and dreams were.

Self-pity was unproductive and dreams were futile.

On that note, she locked her suitcase and hoisted the camera bag over her shoulder. Loaded down with gear, she had one hand free to open the door. A sharp rap sounded on the other side.

She reached for the knob, opening the door as Rhys shoved it from the other side, knocking her off balance. He caught her in one arm before she toppled over.

His eyes locked with hers. His grip around her shoulder tightened. A flash of awareness passed between them.

As if suddenly realizing their position, he said, "Sorry," and abruptly released her. "I came up to see if I could help." He thrust out a hand for the suitcase. "I'll carry that."

She handed him the bag, acutely aware her arm still tingled where he'd touched her. Good heavens, she felt like a teenager whenever he was around!

Worse yet, she liked the feeling. She liked the way her stomach lurched when he was close, the way her heart raced until she had to catch her breath, the way his masculine scent sent the blood rushing through her veins.

The way she felt when she thought about Rhys was the way she'd always imagined being in love would feel. But until now, that had never happened for her. And now that she felt it, whatever "it" was, she was baffled. Truly baffled.

Because he was the wrong person. The whole situation was wrong *and* contrary to her better judgment.

The only answer was that it was physical. A simple physical response. That had to be it.

RHYS DESCENDED the stairs two at a time. He must've been crazy to invite her along. It was like passing a gourmet meal under a starving man's nose and telling him he couldn't eat.

And the worst part was, he'd done it to himself.

Fortunately Whitney was cool and in control—as always.

On the outside.

Yeah, but he saw that banked fire—sizzling, so combustible, so ready to burst into flame. And man, oh, man, he couldn't deny he wanted to be the one to ignite it.

But he knew better. He'd tried before and all it had gotten him was an ulcer and a divorce. Hell, as if once wasn't enough he'd even tried it again, although he'd been smart enough not to get married a second time. And he'd learned from that experience.

He'd learned he couldn't be something he wasn't. It was as plain as that. The old adage about making silk stockings out of pig's hair, or whatever that saying was, more than applied to him.

Downstairs he put Whitney's things into the Jeep, with her cameras close at hand. If he knew anything at all about the woman, it was that she never missed a photo opportunity. Her camera was like an appendage.

Finished, Rhys bounded inside for breakfast with Whitney and SaraJane. As he entered the sunroom, he saw the two of them with their heads close together in quiet conspiracy.

Watching them made him feel warm inside. Anyone might think they were mother and daughter, so warm was their rapport.

His stomach bottomed out and for one anxious moment, he wondered if he was doing the right thing. SaraJane was bonding with Whitney. Which couldn't be good in the long run. Soon Whitney'd go back to her jet-set life and forget all about them.

SaraJane had been abandoned once. He couldn't let it happen again. Still, he wanted his little girl to have all the love she deserved—even if only for a brief while.

Rhys waved them into the kitchen, smiling proudly as SaraJane placed her tiny fingers in Whitney's hand. It was odd, but he liked the fact that SaraJane and Whitney resembled each other.

He'd decided quite some time ago that Whitney's beauty was a bonus, the frosting on a very substantial cake. If SaraJane grew up to be half as pretty and half as smart, she'd be one lucky little girl.

"YOU'LL LOVE IT. I guarantee you'll think it's the most beautiful bike you've ever seen. One of a kind." Rhys wheeled the Jeep into a gas station to fill up. "When it's done, you can photograph to your heart's content."

"But wouldn't it be good to get some photos of the work in progress?" According to Rhys, the motorcycle he was building would be the quintessential custom vehicle. But he refused to let her see it until he'd completed it.

"Even then, I'd need to talk with the buyer before I gave any kind of go-ahead for photographs."

Whitney leaned over to poke her head out the window on the driver's side while Rhys pumped the gas. "I don't understand. Why would you need to talk to anyone? It's your business. It's your inventory until it's done, isn't it?"

The wind caught Rhys's dark hair, giving him a tousled little-boy look. He raised the collar on his leather jacket and cast an indulgent look in her direction.

"Maybe you can operate a photography business that

way," he said dryly. "But if I didn't get money up front, I'd be working at too much of a risk. The potential buyer might never show."

He stuffed the pump back into its slot, waited for the receipt to pop out and slid into the driver's seat again. "Frames, engines, parts, whatever, have to be ordered. It's expensive, and I don't have the extra bucks lying around to do it. A custom bike can go for thirty grand or more."

Checking the mirrors, he headed onto the Black Canyon Highway, the road from Estrade to Phoenix. Whitney remembered it from her previous drive. First the winding mountains and then a long stretch of desert, lots of rock and saguaro cactus.

"Usually I receive half the payment on signing the contract and the remainder at completion. In this instance," he said, "the buyer paid the total cost on signing." His lips thinned.

"Money is the real reason for this trip." He engaged the cruise control and leaned back. "I have an appointment with the bank tomorrow morning." He glanced at her. "So you'll be on your own for a while with all those biker dudes," he teased.

Whitney knew from his taut expression that his concerns went deep, that his attempt to lighten the mood must be for her benefit. From what he'd said earlier, he'd had more than enough money when he bought the business, but then it had disappeared for some mysterious reason. And he hadn't shared that reason with her.

Responding to his need to keep the conversation light, she said casually, "I think I'll be able to hold my own. I've really come a long way, you know." She gave a flippant wave of her hand. "In fact, I've found that I'm rather attracted to the dangerous type."

Rhys stole another glance at Whitney, then brought his focus back to the road. She was joking, right?

He cleared his throat. He didn't have a retort, only a hard knot in his gut at the idea that what she said might actually be true. Or was there more to it than that?

Yeah, okay. It bothered the hell out of him that she might be attracted to anyone—anyone other than him. The realization set him on edge.

"Rhys!" Whitney reached across his chest for the wheel. "You're swerving." Her face only inches from his, she asked, "Is something wrong?"

He tightened his grip on the steering wheel. She was much too close, close enough for him to smell fresh mint toothpaste and strawberry shampoo.

Need bunched in his groin. Wrong? What could possibly be wrong? Except that what he really wanted to do was bury his face in that long hair and run his hand between those firm thighs. And he'd wanted to check out the scents that he knew would linger in that warm place.

Liver and onions, old man. Think night crawlers. Maybe bats. He ground his teeth. He wasn't going to pull off the road and ravish her, but damn, the thought that he *wanted* to almost never left his mind.

"Not to change the subject from your recently acquired attraction for the Hell's Angels," he said in a cool voice, "but could we discuss the plan of action for the next few days? You know, like food, shelter, the basic necessities of life?"

A grin spread across Whitney's face. "I thought I was being very basic."

Another jolt to his groin. He was hard in an instant.

"Anything I can do to help you out?" Teasing, he

sent her a lewd look. "I'd be more than happy to oblige."

Her cheeks grew pink. "Uh, back to the food and shelter part. What did you have in mind?"

Rhys laughed. He'd figured it might be a damn-long weekend with Whitney there—and now he was sure of it. He changed the subject, and for the rest of the trip, he made sure they talked about other things. Boring things. Because he couldn't stop wanting her.

By the time they reached the hotel, they'd set a tentative plan for the next few days. They'd get settled, meet in the lounge at seven-thirty, then have dinner at one of local salsa restaurants. In the morning he'd go about his bank business and she'd attend conference events, shop, relax or whatever.

A solid plan. One that would keep his mind occupied. He just hoped to hell he could stick to it.

THE RIDE TO PHOENIX had gone too quickly. Rhys had regaled her with motorcycle stories galore, and then he'd insisted they play a word game his parents had always played when he and his sister were children.

Before she knew it, they were parked in front of the Cimarron Hotel in downtown Phoenix. Rhys glanced at her.

"The hotel might not be exactly what you're used to. But it connects with the convention center. And it's cheap."

"Seems fine to me," Whitney said, giving the place a once-over. "Besides, I'm here to take photographs."

Rhys nodded thoughtfully. "Right."

They checked in, and once she got to her room, Whitney looked around. It was clean, but small. Really small. Claustrophobic.

Suddenly she went clammy as an old anxiety gripped her. Quickly she headed for the window and yanked the drapes aside, immediately relieved because it made the room seem larger, more open. Her breathing eased.

She pulled back the bedcover, then threw herself on top—for about two seconds. She sprang up, got a drink and turned on the television. Nervous energy jangled through her like electricity, and she felt as if she'd had six cups of espresso.

What was she so keyed up about? Was it being here with Rhys? She refused to dwell on that thought.

It took less than a minute to unpack and only a fraction longer to call Albert. "Albert, it's me." She ran a wet washcloth over her sweaty arms while she stalked back and forth with the phone between her shoulder and ear. "What's happening?"

"Not much. Just got in and—"

"Albert, I mean what's happening with the search? Any luck? Anything at all?"

"Wait a sec. I'll be right back," he said.

She heard the sound of ice clinking in a glass.

"There," he said. "Just needed a relaxer after a day of hard work."

"Okay. Now can you please tell me if you found anything new on the birth certificate."

"Well, yeah. It's odd, Whitney. Very odd."

"Albert," she said sharply, her patience wearing thin. "Please. Just the facts."

Albert sighed dramatically and Whitney knew he was annoyed. He loved to draw things out, even the smallest event. "I have to tell you, Whitney. It's very odd," he repeated. "I didn't find your niece's birth certificate but I did find Gannon's."

She released an exasperated breath. Big deal. What

did that prove? She already knew who Rhys's parents were; it didn't have any bearing on the situation.

"And?"

"Two of them," Albert said.

"Two? Two of what?"

"Two birth certificates for Rhys Gannon."

CHAPTER EIGHT

"WHAT...? I DON'T UNDERSTAND, Albert. Are you telling me there are *two* people with Rhys's name?"

"Exactly."

"Well, so? There's probably someone around with my name, too. What's the point?" Waiting for an answer, she heard him clear his throat.

"Hell, I dunno, Whit. I couldn't get the information on the other guy, though, because I didn't have the parents' names or the date of birth."

"I don't know what difference it makes. I know absolutely that SaraJane is my sister's daughter. There's no question about that. No question whatsoever!"

Whitney paced the room, hugging the phone to her ear. Stopping at the window, she regarded the mountains encircling the city. SaraJane was safe with her grandparents, safe in Estrade.

That's it! The thought of Gretta and Johnny sparked an answer. "The other one is probably his father's. Rhys told me he was named after his father. Johnny is probably his dad's middle name or something."

It didn't really matter. She'd found her sister's daughter, and that was what she'd set out to do. Albert was supposed to find her niece's birth certificate. Not see how many people had the same name as Rhys.

She sensed Albert's frustration. Still, she felt a moment's irritation. SaraJane's birth certificate was the critical document they needed for the next step in her plan—to prove Whitney's relationship to the child.

"Weren't you pursuing some other avenues, as well?"

"Yeah." He raised his voice a little. "I'm running some other background checks. I'll let you know what I find."

"Okay. Listen, I'll get back to you later." Whitney dropped the subject, trying to suppress her annoyance. She felt that Albert was going around in circles and that they'd never get the information they needed.

THE NEXT MORNING Whitney awakened early, still as tense as she'd been the night before. She and Rhys had decided over dinner that they'd go their separate ways in the morning and then get together for lunch. Rhys had a 9 a.m. appointment at the bank; Whitney would see the exhibits and take photographs.

They'd talked mostly business during dinner, and she'd been extra-careful not to let her guard down. Because around Rhys, she felt vulnerable in so many ways. After talking with Albert, she'd realized she didn't want to hear anything bad about Rhys. And she didn't want anyone hurt.

In the short time she'd been in Estrade, she'd come to understand what it felt like to belong somewhere. She felt the Gannons' family bond, even if she wasn't truly a part of it.

It was the same with SaraJane—the little girl had become a part of her.

Last night she'd realized how badly she wanted Rhys to get the financing he needed, how much she hoped he'd succeed, how much she wished his past with Morgan would go away.

Worse yet, she wanted *him*. No, it wasn't rational. It had nothing to do with logic and reason. It had to do with gut feelings and need and emotions that had been locked away for years.

Lord, it was too much to think about. She showered and dressed quickly in jeans and the black leather vest Rhys had snatched off a rack for her on their way out of the shop.

"In case you want to blend in," he'd said with a wicked grin. "Or break out for a while."

She wasn't sure what he'd meant, except that maybe she was just too proper for his kind of crowd. Much as she hated to admit it, she knew he was right. He seemed to know her better than she knew herself.

Armed with her cameras, lenses and film, she headed to the convention center, intending to photograph anything and everything about motorcycles. Last night she'd been utterly fascinated watching the melange of people who strolled in and out of the restaurant. Today she planned to take advantage of the local color, capturing whatever she could on film.

And for the rest of the morning, that was exactly what she did.

Finally, when she noticed it was almost time to meet Rhys, she slipped into the showroom to wait.

As she stood at the door scanning the bright colors and gleaming metal, her excitement mounted, she felt like a kid who'd just been given an all-day pass to Disneyland.

Motorcycles of every shape and form, old and new, filled the huge coliseum. A cacophony of engine noise bounced off the domed ceiling as dealers demonstrated their wares.

The energy around her was contagious, and she took

photo after photo. In addition to the dealer exhibits, there were motorcycles of all kinds—the classics, choppers, futuristic customs and manufacturers' test vehicles.

They were there in abundance. And so were the faithful throng. A photographer's paradise.

Intent on her work, Whitney panned through the crowds—until she landed on a pair of ebony eyes studying her from across the room. Her blood froze in her veins. It was the man who'd come to Rhys's shop last week.

Even without the mirrored sunglasses, she recognized him immediately. She lowered the camera. He looked different standing there among the crowd. He looked...well, normal.

How odd. Two weeks ago she'd been skittish, almost fearful, not only of him, but of Rhys and this whole bikers' world. Now she might not have even picked him out if his gaze hadn't met hers through the lens.

The mirrored aviator sunglasses hung on the neck of his black T-shirt; his raven-dark hair was still drawn into a ponytail. But he was minus the long leather coat, and without it, his appearance wasn't nearly as intimidating.

She raised the camera again. When his image zoomed in without any action on her part, she smiled sheepishly at the man standing directly in front of her.

"Hello again," she said.

"Hello." He had sharp features, and his complexion was ruddy, as if he'd had an adolescent bout with acne. "Rhys asked me to find you and give you a message."

"Rhys?"

He nodded almost imperceptibly. "He says he's sorry, but he can't meet you for lunch. His business took longer than he expected, and he has some loose ends to tie up.

So he asked me to take his place, show you around and answer questions.''

Words failed her. She didn't want a replacement to show her around. She wanted Rhys.

"If you want me to," he added. He shifted his weight to stand with feet apart, arms crossed over his chest. "Rhys said he'd call later, arrange to join you for dinner."

"Oh, I'm sorry," she finally answered, shaking her head. "I guess I'm just surprised that he sent someone in his place."

"Sorry to disappoint you," he said dryly. "But I think you'll find me as knowledgeable as Rhys. After all, I taught him everything he knows about motorcycles."

That piqued her interest. Had this man known Rhys for a long time? Would he be able to fill in the blanks?

"Another expert—how lucky can one woman get." She gave him her best smile and stuck out a hand. "Whitney Sheffield."

"I remember," he said, smiling. "Luther Castelagno. Call me Luth." He returned the handshake, saying that Rhys had told him about the book and that he was at her service. "Rhys made it perfectly clear what my duties are—and what they aren't."

His dark eyes conveyed a meaning she didn't want to acknowledge. Good grief, what did Rhys think she'd do? She'd only been kidding before.

As the two of them toured the building, she discovered that Luth and Rhys had been childhood friends in Chicago and that Luth's family had owned a custom "chopper" shop, which was how Rhys had learned the business.

Surprisingly, she found Luth as charming as Rhys, and it was easy to picture the two of them together as boys, though she couldn't imagine Rhys as the skinny runt Luth had described.

"He's my buddy," Luth said when they stopped for sandwiches at a small take-out place set up just outside the convention room. "Smart, good-looking, successful—everything I'm not."

He grinned sardonically, but his words were filled with admiration, and Whitney sensed the strong bond between the two men.

"He is all that, isn't he," Whitney returned. "He's been incredibly helpful to me," she said, extolling Rhys's attributes herself. "And he's so good with SaraJane."

Luth raised a brow. Then eyed her with approval. "I think when people like each other, they should say so. And," he added, "I think maybe you like him as much as he likes you."

Whitney swallowed the last bite of her lunch and gave a strangled cough. But when they returned to the floor to finish their tour, she felt elated, too. In the past two weeks she'd tried not to read anything into Rhys's actions—although she did know he'd have no problem with a one-night stand. Or a two-week stand, or however long she was in Estrade.

But there was no question that he'd ever be interested in anything more. He'd made that abundantly clear—in more ways than one.

She had to admit, though, knowing that Rhys liked her made her feel...wonderful. Later, as they stood by the elevator doors, Luth said seemingly out of the blue, "It's been good for him having you around to take his mind off the kid."

Whitney did a double take.

"Well...maybe. But from what I've seen, SaraJane is

an angel. I can't imagine Rhys needing a break from *her.*''

Luth nodded. Just then the elevator doors flew open, and he placed a hand on her elbow to guide her in. ''Oh, right. SaraJane *is* an angel,'' he said. ''I meant the boy.''

The doors slid noiselessly shut as he waved her off, saying, ''Thanks for a nice afternoon. See you at dinner.''

Stunned, Whitney stood with her mouth agape. *The boy?*

''What floor?''

''Oh…uh, five,'' Whitney said, only vaguely aware of the two women next to her.

''Howd'ya get that one interested?'' one said, chomping a wad of gum in Whitney's ear and laughing with a snort.

Whitney shifted her stance. The two women, in slinky form-fitting dresses with cutouts in strategic places, were already dressed for the banquet this evening. Their comments and laughter dissipated as she stepped from the elevator and dashed blindly down the hall to her room, slamming the door behind her. Luth's words still clanged in her head.

The boy. Did he mean Rhys had a son?

Rhys had never mentioned anything about a son.

Flinging off her vest and white turtleneck sweater, she dropped onto the edge of the bed, unable to dislodge the thought. That must be what Luth had meant. Good Lord, why had Rhys never mentioned it?

Gretta and Johnny hadn't breathed a word, either. What was the big secret? Frowning, trying to make sense of it, she yanked off her boots, then stripped off her jeans. *The photo.* She remembered—maybe ''the boy'' was his sister's son, Rhys's nephew. And maybe Rhys was concerned for some reason. That made sense.

Well, maybe she'd just ask him about it. That was what she'd do tonight. She'd just come right out and ask him.

She glanced at the clock. Of course, it was possible Rhys wouldn't make dinner, either, since he'd canceled the afternoon's plans. Maybe she'd better call him to find out.

Going to the phone, she noticed the red message light flashing. She pressed the button and heard Rhys's voice.

"Sorry about this afternoon," he said. "Meet you in the bar at six and we'll have a drink before the banquet. Ciao."

At the sound of his sexy voice, a familiar desire curled in her stomach. She pushed the message button again and listened, melting a little more with each word.

As the message ended for the second time, she checked the time again. Not even five-thirty; she had more than half an hour. After a desperately needed shower, she rummaged through her suitcase. Not much of a decision here.

Disgruntled, she tossed most of the clothing aside. Why hadn't she taken a look at the stores in the hotel lobby earlier today? Because she hated the chore of clothes shopping, that was why. That was one of the reasons a plain classic style suited her best—it saved time to do other, more important things.

Now, however, she wished she'd been a little more interested. She pulled out the only halfway-dressy outfit she'd brought, a black Lycra-knit tunic top with a white underblouse and matching leggings. She dressed quickly, finishing the ensemble with black suede slip-ons with two-inch heels. Brushing her hair smooth and back from her face, she secured it with a black velvet ribbon and took one last glance in the mirror.

She frowned at her image. Compared to the women in the elevator, she looked like a schoolmarm.

Lord, now she was reduced to comparing herself to motorcycle molls. She'd never worried about what she wore, not even to the most fashionable restaurants. Why was she so concerned now?

She snatched up her purse and flung open the door, stopping in her tracks as a group of laughing people made their way past. All the women were dressed in daring little sexy outfits. Even the men, some of whom she recognized from earlier at the show, wore their finery. It wasn't black-tie, but they were definitely more dressed up than she was.

And to her dismay, Rhys stood at the end of the hall with Luth and a woman who was wearing an outfit Cher might have envied. The silver lamé dress clung to the woman's body like a second skin, outlining every taut curvy muscle.

And Rhys had never looked sexier. Dressed in a casual black suit with a collarless white shirt, a black-and-silver belt, his hair combed straight back, he looked movie-star dangerous.

Rooted to the spot, Whitney watched as Rhys and Luth exchanged some papers, a handshake and then headed in different directions. The woman went with Luth, but not before Whitney noticed Rhys's appreciative glance as she walked away.

She felt a sharp pang of envy. On second thought, maybe she'd stay in. Maybe she'd just not show up, like Rhys had done earlier. She closed the door and stood with her back against it for a second before stalking to the mirror where she stared at her image with disgust.

She didn't look like a schoolmarm at all. She looked like an old-fashioned nun, covered from ankle to neck in black and white. Irritated with herself, she tugged on the white underblouse, which, like the cuffs, was loosely attached with a series of basting stitches inside a neckline that plunged to a low V.

But not too low, she decided, studying the outfit from all angles. At midthigh, the top wasn't any shorter than the minidresses she'd seen on some of the women outside, and since it was Lycra, it clung to her body and wasn't likely to ride up.

She turned, scrutinizing her backside. In her world, she didn't care what other people liked or disliked, but for some reason, tonight, in this Mardi Gras atmosphere, she wanted to fit in. She wanted Rhys to look at her the way he'd looked at Luth's friend.

And frankly, she was damn tired of always being correct, always doing what was expected—always playing it safe. Maybe she ought to break out, as Rhys had said earlier.

Without another thought, she yanked off the collar and cuffs, peeled off the leggings and removed the bow from her hair, allowing the long strands to drift around her shoulders. She marched into the bathroom, moistened her fingers under the faucet and brushed them through the sides of her hair, lifting it slightly from her face. A touch of gloss over her usual pink matte lipstick, a dab of blush on her cheeks, and she was ready to go.

She slid into her shoes, got her purse and headed for the door. This time she wouldn't look back—because if she did, she might not get out the door at all.

RHYS STARED into the stubby glass of scotch and soda on the bar in front of him. Listening to the pianist's rendition of *Strangers in the Night* further added to his melancholy. He'd met Luth for a few minutes, then arrived at Smoky Joe's, the hotel bar, early to wait for Whitney, hoping to forget about the morning meeting at the bank.

His loan application had been soundly rejected. He didn't generally wallow in self-pity, but right now he wasn't sure he gave a damn. This past year had been the hardest of his life, and not getting the loan felt as though his last hope had been ripped away.

The thought set his teeth on edge which was precisely why he'd skipped lunch with Whitney and asked Luth to take his place today. No reason to spoil her exuberance with his dark mood. It didn't keep him from thinking about her, though—despite the fact that there could never be anything serious between them.

He didn't want serious. He couldn't afford serious. At least not with a woman like her. He wasn't in her league—wasn't even within pitching distance.

That acknowledgment didn't stop his fantasies. Her mouth meeting his, her lithe body, naked and molded against his own, his fingers softly exploring while his tongue traced a path to that most sensitive place…

Damn! He shoved the glass away. Hell, he didn't need a drink. What he needed was a cold shower.

On second thought, he reached for the glass, picked it up and tipped it from one side to the other, swirling the amber liquid over the cubes of ice. Deciding, he tossed it back. One drink would be it.

He needed all his faculties if he planned to spend any time with Whitney. Because if he let his guard down, the intensity of his hunger for her could easily eclipse all rational thought.

As he stared into the empty glass, his senses prickled.

He felt her presence. He felt it as powerfully as if she'd actually touched him.

Slowly, he raised his head.

She stood in the doorway, haloed by the light behind her. Pale blond hair floated over her shoulders, and her face was partially hidden in shadow like a surrealistic photograph. His pulse raced—and his groin tightened.

Two business suits next to him were well into their drinks, and one of them remarked, "Hey, look at that! You wanna flip, see who can score?"

Furious, Rhys started toward her. "Forget it, pal. She's with me."

"Hey, lucky guy," one of the suits said, elbowing the other.

Rhys bristled. If that jerk said another word, he'd give him a knuckle sandwich. Rhys glared at him and continued toward Whitney.

"Right on time," he said, glancing at his watch. Her disarming smile lit the room and cut through his unexpected anger—anger that felt suspiciously like jealousy. He took her arm and directed her to a booth as far away from the two jerks at the bar as possible.

When she sat, he settled on the other side, safely across from her. The waitress scurried up to take their order.

"Nothing for me, thanks," Whitney said.

He hesitated. He'd had one and that was enough. Still, he felt a bit disoriented and ordered another.

"You don't drink?" He fished a twenty from his pocket and laid it on the table for the waitress.

Whitney's eyes held a hint of apprehension. "Sometimes." She paused, running her tongue over her bottom lip. "Sometimes I have a glass of wine."

She lowered her eyes. The subject made her uncomfortable, he could tell. Or was it something else?

"Well, we don't have to stay here. I just figured it would be a good spot to meet and make some decisions about tomorrow."

Her uneasiness seemed to communicate itself to him, and he found it an effort to make conversation. Relieved when the waitress returned, he said, "Really, we can go somewhere else."

"No." She shook her head. "I'm fine. In fact, I think I'll have a diet cola." The waitress nodded and left again.

Rhys leaned back in an attempt to relax. "I'm sorry about lunch. I hope you didn't mind."

He saw her stiffen. "I had a lovely afternoon. Your friend was charming, and very knowledgeable."

Her body language belied her words, and the strange look on her face made him wonder just what had happened when she was with Luth. When he'd asked his friend to go in his place, it occurred to him that if Luth didn't know better, he'd probably make a move on her. So he'd warned Luth in advance that she wasn't his type.

It never occurred to him she might like Luther in that way. A primitive possessiveness coursed through him. He shifted in his seat, watching the waitress return with her drink.

Hell, he hadn't been holding himself back for *that*. "I guess that means you had a good time?"

Whitney leaned forward, both elbows on the table, and parting her lips, she brought her mouth to the straw, slowly sipping as she looked up at him.

"A wonderful time," she finally said. "Of course I was disappointed that you couldn't make it, but Luth was great." She paused. "He said you were busy."

Her words were so cool icicles could've formed on them. Did that mean she was upset he hadn't shown up? It was an interesting thought. One he liked.

"I wasn't busy. I wouldn't have been very good company, so I sent Luth, instead."

He twirled the swizzle stick and suspected he saw a glint of hurt in her eyes. He could tell her about the bank, but he didn't know what difference that would make.

Their lives were so different they might as well be from different planets. More importantly, he knew all too well what happened when planets collided.

Despite that, he felt compelled to explain. "I was kind of depressed after getting a rejection from the bank. Like I said, I would've been lousy company."

Her eyes softened, and she reached across the table, placing a hand over his. "I'm sorry, Rhys. How awful for you."

He stiffened. His chest felt tight. "No big deal. There are other banks." He picked up his drink. He didn't want her pity.

"Let's talk about your day," he said. "Did you get what you needed for the book?"

She pressed her lips to the straw for another sip. "Some, but not nearly enough. I definitely need more skin."

"Skin?"

"Yeah, you know—people."

She smiled, the slowest sexiest smile he'd ever seen, then said huskily, "Photographer's slang." Her mouth went to the straw again.

"You two ready?" Luth's familiar voice brought Rhys to attention, but it was all he could do to drag his eyes from Whitney's. Luth and his girlfriend stood next to the booth.

"Dinner's on, buddy! Let's move it." Luth looked from Rhys to Whitney and smiled. "Hello again."

Luth rarely smiled. And damned if Rhys didn't have that primitive feeling again. Possessive. Territorial.

Ridiculous.

"Your date looks pretty hot," Luth said to Rhys, giving Whitney a thumbs-up.

"We'll be right behind you." Rhys stood and offered his arm to Whitney, guiding her with a hand at the small of her back as the four of them walked toward the banquet room.

When they sat at one of the round tables for dinner, Rhys watched Whitney's face light with excitement. She reminded him of a little kid, ready to open a surprise package. He liked that about her, he realized. He liked a lot of things about her.

He liked her spontaneity, her sensitivity, her acceptance. She was different from the women he'd known in his other life. Never once had he felt she was looking for a thrill or the excitement of the forbidden. He'd never once heard her complain, never once heard her bad-mouth anyone. And he even had the feeling she liked being with him—the *real* him. Yeah, he liked that about her, too.

His chest filled with warmth. Being around her made it easy to forget his troubles—and the differences between them.

"I wish I'd brought my camera," she finally said, moving toward him. "But that would seem rather rude, wouldn't it?"

"We'll get it later."

He breathed in her soft sensual fragrance as he spoke, suddenly engulfed by a deep and very recognizable need. A need that came from the expected places, but also from a place he hadn't expected—his heart.

CHAPTER NINE

WHITNEY SKIRTED the tables and chairs on her way to the ladies' room during a program break. She'd wanted to ask Rhys about the boy Luth had mentioned. She'd wanted to ask him while they were in the bar, but there'd been too many people around. Granted, he might tell her it was none of her business; if he'd wanted her to know, he would've said something already.

Why did it matter? Even if Luth wasn't talking about Rhys's nephew, even if Rhys had ten children by ten other women, what difference did it make?

She knew the answer to that. It mattered to her because *Rhys* mattered to her. If he had another child, she wanted to know. She wanted to know everything about him...and about that child. Was this boy from his former marriage? Or from another relationship like the one he'd had with Morgan? If the boy lived with his mother, surely Rhys would have visitation rights, wouldn't he?

Maybe that second birth certificate really meant he had a son and the boy was named after him. And maybe the boy was sick or mentally handicapped, or the mother had taken him away. There could be half a dozen reasons no one talked about it.

Why did she have to think the worst? Why didn't she just give Rhys the benefit of the doubt? There could be a logical explanation for all of it, and sooner or later she'd find out.

Finishing up, she wiped her hands and reminded herself of Brock—one of the reasons she couldn't take things at face value. Her ex-fiancé's betrayal simply underscored that she was a lousy judge of character when it came to men. She absolutely had to remember that.

When she entered the ballroom, she saw Rhys at the table, looking in her direction. He waved and her heart skidded.

In that split second she realized she'd never ever been so intrigued by a man. Never been so enticed—so blatantly enticed that whenever she was around him, she experienced that slow inexorable pull on her innermost self. And, God help her, despite all her questions about him, she found the feeling exciting and wonderful and completely enthralling.

Making her way toward him, she grimly told herself that it didn't matter what she felt, because he didn't know who she was and why she was there. And once he learned the truth, he'd never want to set eyes on her again. Unless there was some way to explain...

When she'd almost reached the table, Rhys got up and quickly redirected her toward a door on the other side.

"What? Where're we going?" she sputtered. Rhys placed a finger over her lips and continued tugging her by the hand.

"Just be patient and follow me," he said softly, edging around a corner in the long hallway.

"Rhys," she said, "what are we doing?"

"Checking out the entries."

"What entries? What are you talking about?"

"They're all here." He motioned to a door at the end of the hallway, and as they approached it, he removed a key from his pocket. "Got it from a friend," he whispered.

Opening the door a crack, he slipped inside, drawing her with him. When he shut the door, blackness enveloped them, and she clutched his arm.

"Rhys, what's this about? Where are the lights?" He pulled her flush against him, so close it sent her insides into spasm.

"Hold on a sec. Don't move or you might hit something."

His left arm circled her waist and he searched for the lights with the other hand.

"The lights are…"

She felt him reaching, his body moving against hers.

"…right here somewhere," he said.

Her face was nestled on his shoulder, and she breathed in his freshly showered soapy scent.

"There."

She heard the click and the room was suddenly full of light. But he didn't release her. She blinked. He tucked in his chin to look at her. "Your eyes will adjust in a second. Then you can turn around."

Conscious of their intimate position, she, too, bent her head to look at him, and her mouth came dangerously close to his. So close, his warm breath fanned her lips.

Her pulse raced. She wanted to kiss him—to touch her mouth to his. No denying it. She *had* to pull away. She had to pull away.

But she couldn't. Not if her life depended on it.

His sultry gaze met hers, and when she finally spoke, she heard the need in her voice, low and breathy. "Will I like what I see?"

His eyes were riveted on her mouth. "I hope so," he murmured. "I know I do."

Melting inside, she pressed against him, and as she

felt his arousal, hot impulses fired within her. His lips
hovered over hers.

"You better turn around and take a look, or we'll
never make it back for the ceremony," he said, grinning
as if he didn't give a damn whether they did or not.

Reluctantly, she peeled herself away and turned.

"Wow!" was all she could say. She stared wide-eyed
at the roomful of custom bikes.

"I thought you might want to get some work done
before the place gets packed."

She turned, studying him. *How thoughtful.* "You
mean, if I had a camera." She started toward the first
row of gleaming machines, sectioned off by a gold satin
cord.

"Yeah, I know." He smiled sheepishly. "We'll get it
later and come back," he said, enclosing her hand in his.
"Right now, we should have dinner."

Still holding her hand, Rhys led her back to the ballroom, not letting go until they reached the table.

"I wondered if you two were going to make it in
time," Luth said, a knowing expression on his face.
"Thought maybe something better came up."

Whitney felt her cheeks heat. She didn't respond to
Luther's provocation, but she couldn't ignore it, either.

RHYS HELD THE CHAIR for Whitney, then sat between
her and Luth, anxious to rid himself of the desire that
had almost gotten the best of him. He leaned back in his
chair, able to see both the stage and Whitney's profile.

"Bets?" Luth poked him in the ribs with an elbow
and waved a hand in front of Rhys's eyes. "You with
us, buddy, or is that glazed look permanent?"

"Yeah." Rhys bolted to attention. "What's up?"

"Bets. You know, our annual bet on which bike is

going to win.'' Luth gave him a puzzled frown. ''The
bikes you just went to look at?'' He sent Rhys another
sidelong glance and slapped fifty bucks on the table.

''Sure,'' Rhys said absently and reached into his
pocket for some bills to cover the bet. What was fifty
bucks when he needed thousands? And if he didn't bet,
Luth would wonder why.

''C'mon.'' Luth tapped the table. ''Right here. The
ladies will guard the stash.'' He produced a pen from
his shirt pocket and shoved it at Rhys, along with a
napkin.

''Here's mine,'' he said, pointing to his napkin.
''Write down your number and prepare to lose.'' Luth
eyed Rhys. ''Can't decide?'' His dark eyes darted to
Whitney and back to Rhys again. ''Or were you too busy
to get the number?''

Rhys scribbled something on his napkin, folded it in
half and handed it to Luth's date, Lee Ann. Luth was
right. He'd been too preoccupied to think about anything
but Whitney. Fortunately he remembered his favorite
number from earlier that day.

The rest of the ceremony dragged. Like it or not, he
couldn't take his mind off the woman beside him. She
was the remedy for what ailed him. Thanks to her, he'd
even forgotten this morning's disappointment at the
bank.

He'd had a setback, but now that he'd had time to
think, he realized it was only that. A setback. There were
other ways to get the money.

In the meantime he'd had enough of self-deprivation.
He was here with a beautiful woman whose company he
enjoyed immensely.

''C'mon, Rhys,'' Whitney urged when the program
ended. ''Let's go get my camera.''

Stopping outside Whitney's room, Rhys took the key from her and opened the door. She flipped on the light, tossed her purse onto the blue upholstered side chair and kicked off her shoes.

"Want a drink while I get my things together?"

He glanced around. They were alone. And he wanted her. "Sure. What's the special?"

He watched her walk to the small refrigerator, open it, then hold up a tiny bottle. "What's your preference?" she asked.

Did he just imagine that her voice was low and throaty? And how would she react if he told her his real preference? *You and me, naked on the bed—making love.*

"Scotch is fine." The last thing he should have right now was a drink. He shouldn't be here, either, but he *wanted* to be. A lot.

He'd discovered that being with her, whatever his mood, was infinitely better than being alone. Actually, it was more than that; he craved being with her, savored every moment—when she came to the shop each day, when she came back from lunch, when she joined his family for dinner.

For some time now, he'd struggled against his feelings. Because if he got that close, he'd want more than a one-night stand. A strange feeling for him. Strange, indeed.

He barely knew anything about her. She'd been engaged, she'd told him. It hadn't worked out, and he sensed she'd been hurt by it. It bothered him to think about her caring that much for another man.

Which was pretty damn ridiculous.

The one thing he knew with certainty was that she'd leave when she was finished with this project. She'd be off somewhere on another photo shoot, maybe even out of the country.

But this minute, right here and now, none of that made an iota of difference. It didn't change his pounding desire or his incessant need to have her, regardless of the cost.

When she handed him the drink, his gaze caught hers and held. Her pupils dilated as if in invitation.

Slowly, deliberately, he slipped his fingers over hers as he accepted the glass. His breathing quickened.

"I'll get my cameras," she said softly.

Following her as she headed into the bedroom, he stood in the doorway and rested one shoulder against the frame. "Need some help?"

She turned, waved a hand toward the dresser. "You can get me that box of film." Her words were a near whisper.

He walked to her side and set the glass on the dresser behind her, then closed his hand around the box of film. He breathed deeply, absorbing her intoxicating scent. He wanted her. *He wanted her.*

She leaned closer, eyes smoky, lips moist and parted, alluring, inviting. He set the box in her palm, covering her hand with his.

Her skin was hot, his desire insistent. He closed the gap and the next thing he knew, his lips claimed hers. And when she made a low moaning sound and melted against him, his heart hammered like a piston in his chest.

He should stop. He knew better. But instead, he opened his mouth, increasing the pressure, immersed in the desire that flowed between them, his tongue searching, finding hers. She clutched him more tightly, locking her arms around him.

His passion flamed, and when she pressed against him, he lost all reason. He urged her toward the bed, sliding both hands underneath the dress, not surprised that her skin felt as smooth as he'd imagined.

He buried his face in her hair and in the crook of her neck, drinking in her sweet sweet scent. He was a drowning man, and loving it every time he went under.

Whitney moaned again, softly uttering his name. She molded her body against his, yielding to his touch. Her breathing quickened. "You feel good, Rhys. So good." Her words were breathy and ragged.

His need became a sweet agony, and he knew he couldn't stop. He wanted, needed, all of her.

He watched in awe as she drew back and began to unbuckle his belt. As impatient as she, he shook off the jacket, letting it fall to the floor. Her hands slid up his chest, fingers tearing at the buttons on his shirt, and then her mouth came down hot against his chest. Overwhelmed by urgency, Rhys pulled her dress off, taking a moment to revel in her beauty.

He drew back the covers, and she eased to the pillow, her hair spilling around her. Her lips were moist and full from his kisses, and he was drawn back to them again and again.

He kissed her deeply, sensuously, unfastened her bra and discarded it. She deftly removed her panty hose as he trailed kisses down her neck to her small firm breasts. Needing to touch her as intimately as he could, he slipped one hand between her thighs, and when his fingers grazed her warm moist center, she arched her back and raised her hips, increasing the pressure.

He stroked slow and deep, wanting to give her pleasure. Wanting to make her his, if only for just this night. Another low moan nearly sent him over the edge. Dragging himself away, he stood, and in seconds, he'd undressed.

"Oh, wait," she said, her breathing heavy, her eyes on his naked body. "Do you have anything with you?"

Damn! Why hadn't he thought ahead? He couldn't make love to her without protection, and although he remembered he had a condom in his wallet, it was so old it would probably disintegrate on contact.

He watched her chest rise and fall, her nipples peak. Hell, it would have to do. He nodded, fumbling for his wallet.

She held out a hand and whispered, "Let me help."

Seconds later, he eased into her, penetrating slowly. She was hot and silky and more wonderful than he'd imagined. She wrapped her legs around him, drawing him in, deeper and deeper, and then she began rocking rhythmically, sensuously, sending him to the brink.

His emotions soared, the sensations so intense a ragged groan tore from his throat as he fought to hold off. Her passion was as great as his, and as much as he needed release, he couldn't—not yet.

His heart hammering, he shifted position so she was straddling him and he could see her face. He reached up with both hands, and she shivered as he traced his fingers over her breasts and down her flat stomach.

He reveled in watching her, especially when he splayed his hands over her hips and she began moving again, rocking rhythmically until her eyes closed and her head tipped back.

His blood pounded, his excitement spiraled and soared, and when he felt her involuntary spasms around him, he exploded. And in that dizzying rush, he felt her shudder again and again.

Spent, she melted against him, bringing her head to

rest against his shoulder. He wrapped his arms around her and buried his face in her hair. They lay like that for a long time, it seemed, neither initiating a separation.

She'd been with him all the way, and he'd succumbed, physically and emotionally, and he felt... God, he didn't know what he felt.

All he really knew was that he'd never experienced anything like it, and he wanted to stay close to her, locked together like lovers.

"You sleeping?" he whispered.

She shook her head.

She was so quiet he wondered what she was feeling. Not that it mattered, he reminded himself, because she'd be on her way as soon as she'd finished her project.

They moved onto their sides, spooned together. Okay, so she'd leave. What was wrong with that? Hell, it was the kind of relationship men fantasized about. A beautiful woman who wanted nothing but sex.

Purely physical. No strings attached. Most men would give up Super Bowl tickets for a relationship like that.

Then why did it bother him? He'd wanted to make love with her—*needed* it. He just hadn't expected to be this deeply affected by it.

When he heard the smooth deep breathing of sleep, he rolled off the bed, careful not to wake her. The light from the entry was still on and provided just enough illumination for him to retrieve his clothing.

Quietly, he pulled on his pants, gathered his clothes and stood in the doorway for a moment, unable to suppress the wry smile that formed on his lips.

Women don't go to sleep afterward. Men do.

MOONLIGHT FELL on Whitney's face from the arched window above the balcony doors. She blinked under the soft light, then stretched like a lazy cat, enveloped in a cocoon of satisfaction. In that twilight of awareness, she tried to slip back into her beautiful dream, tried to retain the warm feeling of being wanted, needed—and loved.

As she awoke a little more, she realized it wasn't a dream at all. With one hand, she searched the bed next to her. Cold sheets and an empty mattress. She turned.

Gone.

She rolled onto the other pillow and buried her face in it. Rhys's clean soapy scent lingered in the fabric, and she wanted to make love with him all over again. She glanced at the floor. His clothes were gone, too.

They'd made love, she'd fallen asleep and he'd left. That was all there was to it.

Like hell!

A deep knowing settled within her. He'd made love to her. *Really* made love to her. Passionate and tender. Totally. Thoroughly. And she'd relished every delicious minute.

He'd taken her to heights she'd never been. He'd taken her out of herself and beyond all reason. She'd been bold, aggressive, holding nothing back. A rush of embarrassment ran through her. She'd wanted him, all of him. And she'd wanted to please him as much as he pleased her.

Their passion sated, she'd drifted into a deep sleep where her dreams were filled with light and love and a soul-fulfilling happiness. Whatever he'd been before she met him, she knew he was not the man her sister had said he was. And she knew her life would never be the same.

She cared about Rhys—for better or worse. It was true. And she hoped he cared, too. If even just a little.

She closed her eyes and clutched the pillow more

tightly, retracing each and every move. She remembered how he'd looked at her, his pupils dilated, his expression a combination of lust and longing.

She'd felt wanted, desired, and for the first time in her life, she'd even felt loved.

But what did it all mean? One evening together didn't translate to anything beyond that. Still, remembering the passion, the tenderness in his eyes, the ways in which he touched her, so gently, almost reverently sometimes, it *had* to mean more—didn't it?

She could almost imagine— *No! Don't think about it.* Because even if she and Rhys could somehow work things out between them—and with SaraJane—wouldn't she just be living with constant fear again? Love, she knew, could be snatched away in an instant. She'd learned that by the time she was five, and the fear of it had dominated her childhood. Gradually, she'd also learned that if you didn't care, it didn't hurt so much. Sure, as an adult she'd had relationships, but she'd never allowed herself to need someone's love so much she'd fear losing it.

She'd filled the internal void with her career, expressing her emotions through her photographs, letting her needs and desires emerge through light and shadow, shape and texture. And although she longed for a taste of what she'd once imagined real love to be, she knew that if she opened her heart now, she'd only be making herself vulnerable—and she'd be right back where she'd started.

Willing sleep to take her away, she knew she couldn't live that way again. She just couldn't.

THE PHONE RANG just as Whitney left the shower.

She felt her nerves jump, hoping it was Rhys. "Hello."

"Hi. Hope I didn't wake you."

His voice sounded brusque. "No. You didn't. I just finished showering."

There was a long silence before he finally said, "If you plan to get some shots of the bikes, you'll have to do it soon. In another hour the showroom will be jammed."

"Okay. I can be ready in fifteen minutes."

"How long d'you think it'll take to get the pictures you need? We've got to check out by eleven."

She bristled. His tone was sharp, confusing her. Okay—she hadn't expected hearts and flowers, but she hadn't expected a cold shoulder, either. They were both adults. They should be able to move on from last night.

If he needed space, she could respect that. She could step back and remove herself from the encounter just as easily as he could. "I'll make it quick," she said, adding a little coolness to her own words. "I can get what I need in maybe forty-five minutes to an hour."

Whitney glanced at the clock. They had four hours before checkout. What was his rush?

"Fine. That'll work. Meet me in the coffee shop when you're done. Say nine-thirty?"

She hitched up the towel. Guess that meant he wasn't going to join her while she photographed.

"We'll grab breakfast and head out."

"Sure. See you then." Whitney let the phone slide through her fingers, and after hanging up, she hurried to the bathroom to dry her hair.

She might blame his behavior on morning crankiness if she hadn't known better. But every morning she'd seen him so far, he'd been eager, energetic and, well, happy. Perhaps the loan thing was getting to him again or—

Or he'd found her out. God, that couldn't be it. Could it?

She clutched the blow-dryer and, bending at the waist, started on her hair. No, nothing had happened, she assured herself. How could he have found out anything?

But that worry made her decide she needed to tell him the truth. Because after last night, it would be impossible to continue the charade. And she hated feeling like such a fraud.

Whatever the outcome, she had to do it. If she could just find a way to tell him so he might understand. If he knew she'd believed him to be a drug dealer, he'd *have* to understand—wouldn't he?

She tensed every time she thought about it. He'd believed her, trusted her and she'd repaid his trust with lies. Pulling on a pair of jeans, she remembered her promise to Morgan, yet, her mind kept returning to the fact that he was fine and honest, loving and gentle. He was a good father and had sacrificed his own needs to make a life for his daughter.

Maybe something had happened and he'd gotten off track for a little while, but that still didn't explain all the things Morgan had said about him. The only thing that made any sense was that Morgan had lied. But why?

She felt a pain in her chest as she mulled that over. Still, she knew that Morgan's reasons, whatever they'd been, no longer mattered. Once Rhys knew who she was and why she was there, he'd send her away. And if she told him now, before they left for Estrade, it would be one very long ride home—if he didn't simply kick her out of the car first. Yes, she had to tell him, but it would have to wait, at least until they got closer to home.

After getting the photos she wanted, she met Rhys at the coffee shop. "Hi," she smiled, still feeling the rush of success. She always felt that way when her shoot went well.

"Table's over there." Rhys pointed toward a window where the morning sun glinted off the glasses and silverware.

He was distant, all right. His shoulders were rigid as he strode toward the table; reaching it, he shucked his leather jacket and hung it on the chair.

He wore stonewashed jeans and a white V-necked T-shirt that set off his bronzed skin. His hair was damp and he'd combed it back, except for the few strands that hung forward on his brow. Just looking at him made her breath catch.

She hoped he'd loosen up, but once they were seated, she saw the edginess was still there—churning close to the surface. She saw it in the way a muscle jumped in his jaw, the death grip he had on his coffee mug, the pressure on the knife he used to butter his toast.

Hoping to change his mood, she said, "I'm really pleased. I'm sure the photos will be great. You should've—"

"Whitney," he interrupted, his gaze focused on his coffee mug. "I'm sorry about last night."

"Sorry?"

"Yes, well, I don't exactly know how to put this. I— I'm sorry for taking advantage of the situation."

That was the cause of his mood? He was angry at himself for "taking advantage" of her? Relief flooded through her, and she leaned forward and covered his hand with hers.

"Rhys..." She cleared her throat and started again. "Rhys, you didn't take advantage of the situation any more than I did. And I don't want you to think I have any expectations because of it. I want things to remain the same between us.''

She felt the muscles in his hand tighten before he drew it back to rest on top of the coffee mug. His knuckles went white, his eyes dark and unreadable.

''Okay,'' he finally said. ''It's a deal.'' He pointed his index finger at her like a gun, made a clicking sound and winked. It was the same endearing wink he'd given her many times over the past two weeks, but this time, it didn't ring true.

During the rest of the meal, they made small talk, and afterward, while loading the car, Rhys announced that they were taking the scenic route back.

Whitney was surprised. It was obvious that something still bothered him, yet he was making a conscious effort to change his attitude. To say she was confused was an understatement.

On the road she turned to look at him. He'd exchanged the jacket for a blue denim shirt that made his cobalt eyes seem more intense—if that was possible. His sleeves were rolled to the elbows and she caught herself watching the way his muscles moved and flexed as he gripped the wheel. His hair was still tousled and he had one of those quizzical little-boy expressions on his face.

Oddly, an image of Rhys as he'd looked last night, standing naked near the bed, popped into her mind. She'd never been so fascinated by a man's body before, not even in the art classes she'd taken in France.

''What?'' He glanced at her, as if reading her thoughts. ''What's going on in there?'' He tapped her forehead with a finger, then shifted his focus back to the road.

''Nothing.'' She smirked. ''Nothing at all.''

"Right." He nodded disbelievingly. "So what did you think of Luth?"

Luth? "Oh, uh, Luth... Uh, well, he was the perfect guide," she answered, remembering Luther's attempts to be as accommodating as Rhys had apparently told him to be.

Rhys did a double take, gave her a dimpled grin and said, "As perfect as *moi?*"

Relieved to be back on even ground, Whitney chuckled. She liked his not-so-subtle wit. And she was happy that he seemed himself again. "Well-l-l, let's say on a scale of one to ten, he was a nine."

Whitney saw Rhys's fingers tighten on the wheel.

"And you are definitely a ten," she said without further hesitation. "On the guide scale, that is. Anyway, to answer your question, I like him. He seems genuine, said you'd been friends since childhood."

"Uh-huh." Rhys nodded. "It's been a while." He glanced at Whitney. "Yeah, since fourth grade. We were ten. Thirty years. Man, that's hard to believe."

"Guess you guys have been through a lot together?" Whitney was impressed by such an enduring friendship. In her own life, the only close friend she'd made was Tanya, but she hadn't met her until college.

"Yeah." Rhys nodded again, keeping his eyes on the road. "We've been through some hard times together. He was my hero as a kid and I wanted to be as tough as he was. Remember when I told you I grew up in a run-down area of Chicago?"

He turned briefly to her for confirmation. "Well, I was the neighborhood runt and ripe for being terrorized by one particular bully and his gang. And every day without fail, they found some way to do it. But I was a determined little kid and decided I wouldn't ever let them win without a fight. Each time they jumped me, I fought harder.'' He chuckled derisively. ''Always got the stuffing kicked out of me,'' he said ruefully, ''but I never gave up.

''Then one day, during one of the worst fights ever, this badass kid comes outta nowhere and starts pummeling those jerks right along with me. It was Luth. From that time on, I would've given him my right arm if he needed it. He's a true friend. Been one ever since.''

''He said the same thing about you. In fact, he couldn't say enough about how he'd always wished he had your intelligence, your charm, and...your good looks.''

Rhys scoffed.

''It's true,'' Whitney insisted. ''He said he's learned a lot from you.''

''Yeah. He would say that.'' A melancholy look clouded Rhys's eyes. ''I almost had to leave college because I couldn't pay the tuition once my scholarship came to an end. Luth bailed me out.

''I couldn't tell my parents because they'd just put their life savings together to buy the hardware store in Estrade. It was their dream and I know they would've sacrificed it for me. I couldn't let them do that. Luth knew it, too, and he lent me the money. A few years later, when I was down about the divorce, Luth got me back on track.''

Whitney watched the subtle change in Rhys's mood. Instead of withdrawing as she thought he might, he continued, but she could tell it was taking a toll on him. When he mentioned his divorce, his words were laced with anger and bitterness.

Not unlike her own feelings about her past.

''Five years of marriage down the tubes and nothing

to show for it. My ex took my son and left. She kept him from me and poisoned his mind. When he was nine, she decided on a summer in Europe and sent R.J. to stay with me.''

Whitney felt as if she'd been slapped. *A son. He did have a son.* But she'd been right, too. There was a reason he hadn't mentioned him.

Rhys shook his head and he blew out a burst of air. ''Big mistake. R.J. hated me. She'd lied to him about me for four years and there was nothing I could do to change it.''

Whitney saw bitterness shift to pain as Rhys talked, and her heart went out to him. She guessed that his having a daughter now made up for some of the heartache he'd endured over the loss of his son.

''R.J.? Is that Rhys, Jr.?''

He nodded.

''Does he still live with his mother?''

Rhys shook his head again, eyes darkening. ''Nope. But that's another whole ugly story.''

''I'm sorry, Rhys.'' Whitney reached out to touch his arm.

Surprisingly, Rhys went on, almost as if he had to get it all out. ''R.J. became incorrigible. His mother couldn't handle him. She'd spoiled him, given him everything a kid could want. She gave him too damn much. When he got into trouble with the law one time too many, she washed her hands of him.

''R.J. left home at sixteen—about the same time I left Chicago.'' He gave another derisive laugh. ''I didn't know he'd even gone.'' His knuckles tightened on the steering wheel. ''If I had, I would've done something right then and there.''

Whitney's mind spun. Sixteen? For some reason, she

hadn't thought he'd be that old. And if he'd left home when Rhys left Chicago, that was five years ago. Which would make the kid she quickly calculated—twenty-one now.

Her mouth went dry.

"And have you seen him since?" Whitney asked, hoping she didn't sound as shocked as she felt.

"Two years ago he came looking for help. He needed money and a place to stay with SaraJane. I gave them shelter and as much money as I could spare. Then one day he disappeared, leaving me with the baby."

A place to stay with SaraJane? Leaving him with the baby? Whitney tried to speak. Her lips parted, but nothing came out. Struggling with her confusion, she stammered, "Wh-what then?"

Rhys checked his mirrors, then pulled off the road and into a rest area. "Gotta make a pit stop." He indicated that she should do the same.

With her heart lodged in her throat, Whitney moved like a robot responding mechanically to an order. She went into the washroom. Was Rhys saying SaraJane wasn't his daughter? That she was really his granddaughter—his son's child? She searched her mind, trying to pinpoint any time when Rhys had actually said SaraJane was his daughter.

Oh, God! Panic seized her. If SaraJane was Rhys's son's child, where was his son now? And who had legal custody? Would R.J. return and snatch SaraJane again— maybe while Rhys and Whitney were gone?

She splashed cold water on her face. Maybe she hadn't heard him correctly? Maybe… Oh, dear God…

CHAPTER TEN

RHYS SLID INTO the driver's seat, then reached over to lift her chin with his fingertips. "Sorry to drop all that in your lap. Seems I got on a roll."

He held her gaze, as if he was seeking something there. Turning to face front, he started the car, gave a cursory glance over his left shoulder and pulled onto the highway.

"We'll turn off in a few miles and then you'll see the most spectacular scenery in the state." He threw her a smile, one that seemed forced. "Next to the Grand Canyon, that is."

The tension around his mouth didn't escape her. Talking about his son was obviously painful for him, yet he was still concerned about her enjoyment. But enjoyment was the last thing on Whitney's mind. She had to find out exactly what was going on—and she had to do it now.

"Rhys?" She touched his shoulder. "I'm glad you told me about your son. I had a few misconceptions."

"Misconceptions?"

"I...I thought... No, I take that back. I *assumed* SaraJane was your daughter."

At that, his eyes lit up, and a huge grin split his face.

"I wish," he said emphatically, apparently taken with the idea. Then, like quicksilver, both his expression and tone of voice sobered. "If she were, I wouldn't worry as much as I do about what's going to happen."

"What...what do you mean? What's going to happen?"

"My son is in prison," he said bluntly.

Whitney's heart dropped so hard she thought he'd heard the crash. She stared at him silently, searching for words. "Prison? Oh, Rhys. How terrible."

"After he left SaraJane with me, I didn't hear a thing for six months. That's when I decided to move from Phoenix to Estrade. Mom and Dad had sold the hardware store and bought the inn a few years before, and they offered to help out with SaraJane. I'd been contemplating leaving my position at the Kelper Corporation for several months, for other reasons, and...well, the timing seemed right. I figured Estrade was a better place to raise a kid than Phoenix."

"Phoenix?" Whitney frowned. "When did you move to Phoenix? And wasn't the Kelper Corporation the one indicted in that junk-bond scandal?" Had Rhys been involved in that? Lord, she felt dizzy.

"Yep, it was. If I'd known the whole story..." He shrugged. "I moved from Chicago to Phoenix looking for upward mobility. Took a job as Kelper's chief financial officer. I had no idea what the guy was doing, and when I found out, I took SaraJane and my company pension, bought the shop in Estrade and got the hell out of Phoenix. Then I notified the authorities.

"Later, when it all came out about Kelper, it looked like I'd taken my share and split." He laughed scornfully. "No one could prove anything, though, because it wasn't true, but it's been the bane of my existence. It's what prevented me from getting the bank loan."

Good grief. Whitney felt torn between shock and sympathy. "And R.J.?"

"When we finally heard from R.J., he'd been arrested." Rhys kept his gaze riveted on the road. "For murder—a bank robbery gone bad."

Whitney gasped, but Rhys went on as if he'd opened the floodgates and couldn't stop the torrent.

"When I called R.J.'s mother to ask for her help, she told me to get lost, saying she'd disowned him when he left home. So I hired an attorney to defend him. The jury found him guilty and we appealed the decision."

Rhys stomped on the gas, accelerating to seventy, then seventy-five. "After that, R.J. told me to stay away, said he never wanted to see me again. I guess he figured I'd let him down again. And," he added remorsefully, "he's probably right. I should've done something years ago when it might have made a difference."

"Rhys, I'm so sorry," was all she could utter.

"Forget it. I try to most of the time."

She didn't believe he could forget it. Not for a minute. And seeing his pain, imagining what he'd been through, tore her apart. Along with her empathy for Rhys came a multitude of questions.

Most importantly, who had legal custody of SaraJane? How would this new information affect what she had to do?

The only good thing was that at least his son wasn't a threat—not at the moment, anyway.

Although she still wanted to tell Rhys the truth about why she'd really come to Estrade, this was definitely not the time.

She needed a chance to think, to find out who had custody.

Still, a sense of relief washed over her. It was Rhys,

Jr., who'd lived with Morgan. Rhys's son was the slime—and *he* was SaraJane's father. But he was in jail, just where she wanted him.

Of course! It all made sense.

And she was glad. Oh, God, she was glad!

Because it meant that Rhys and Morgan never had a relationship. Because it meant her sister's secret was not a secret at all. She hadn't lied. She just hadn't given Whitney enough information. Her throat closed and she blinked back the tears in her eyes.

Turning off the main highway and onto a narrower road, Rhys said, "I have to show you something. And you'd better get your camera out."

Camera? The last thing she felt like doing was taking photographs. She had too much to think about. He'd handed her a lot of unexpected facts, and they'd blown her carefully constructed assumptions to hell and gone.

Rounding the next corner, Rhys nudged her arm, drawing her out of her reverie. She looked up. Vermillion monoliths sprang up from the earth like huge red dinosaurs, and the sight took her breath away. Yes, she'd take some pictures here, despite her confused emotions, her concerns, despite everything. She couldn't resist.

"Rhys, it's awesome. Can we stop?" She wrestled with the camera case and dragged out a wide-angle lens.

"Not yet," he said, smiling widely. "It's better as we get closer to Sedona."

"I don't know how it could. It's magnificent. Absolutely the most spectacular scenery I've ever seen," she rambled on. "Except for the Grand Canyon, I mean, although I haven't ever been to the Grand Canyon, but I've seen photographs. And this. Well..."

Words could not describe the emotions tumbling through her. Rhys's revelations, the scenery, her confusion and elation, everything was all jumbled together, and it was all too much—just too, too much.

She opened the window and inhaled deeply of the cedar and pine. Oh, she wanted to sing and dance and shout out her euphoria. "It smells like Christmas," she said, barely able to contain the exuberance that filled her. "It's so beautiful. It's thrilling! I've never seen anything that even comes close."

"I figured you'd like it." Rhys's chest expanded, his expression full of pleasure. He whipped the Jeep around the next corner and took a small road to the top of a scenic overlook and parked.

They got out, and he motioned for her to go ahead and shoot. "Take your time. I'll wait right here." He leaned on a boulder, waving her off. "Go."

Rhys studied Whitney as she assessed the landscape, set up her shot and clicked off the photo. Each time he'd been to Sedona, he'd felt the same awe for the natural beauty surrounding him. Mother nature at its best. And never had he experienced greater delight than at this moment, watching Whitney revel in it.

She saw things in a special way—more deeply than he did. Being with her made him want to see what she saw, feel what she felt. Her enthusiasm bubbled up like fine champagne, and he was intoxicated by it.

She'd gotten to him. Directly to his heart. He watched her as she stood atop a rock, surveying the possibilities. Then she lowered her camera and reached behind her head to remove the clasp holding her hair in place. She shook her hair out and let the wind take it.

He remembered how she'd looked with her hair feathered across the pillow, how she'd opened so completely to him. His breathing deepened and the familiar tightening in his groin gave him pause.

He'd thought that making love with her would be the end of it. Instead, last night had merely whetted his appetite. Right now, he had an overwhelming need for her—a need that went beyond the physical. Far beyond.

She liked him, he knew that. She liked SaraJane, he knew that, too. And *he* liked the fact that she'd believed SaraJane was his child. As he'd told her, he wished it was true.

But it wasn't. He wasn't SaraJane's father—any more than he was the kind of man to be involved with a woman like Whitney Sheffield. Regardless of his former successes, he had none of it now.

He had no money, a business on the verge of bankruptcy, a son in prison for murder and enough legal costs to match the national debt. So why, exactly, had he told her about R.J.?

He never talked about R.J.—to anyone. But maybe, somewhere in the back of his mind, he thought that if she knew the worst and still stuck around, then maybe…

He shook his head. He couldn't afford to think that way.

He figured that eventually she'd leave. Maybe, subconsciously, he was trying to hasten her departure. Maybe he just wanted to make it easier on himself. Because if she knew everything about him, she'd run the other way so fast he'd be a blur on the horizon.

His son was a constant burden on his heart and never far from his mind. He had no business inviting anyone else, never mind this woman, into the mess his life had become.

After the trial, R.J. had fired the attorney and told Rhys not to visit him anymore. But he'd vowed he would never abandon his son again. Even though R.J. might have been guilty of drug dealing at one time, he'd sworn he was clean now and also sworn he wasn't involved in the murder. And a father had to stand by his son, no matter what. So, for the past six months, he'd visited R.J. regularly, whether his son was receptive or not.

After his disappointment at the bank yesterday, he'd driven to the prison in Florence to tell R.J. they might have to use the public defender if he couldn't come up with more money for the new attorney he'd hired. Even if he sold everything he had, he couldn't afford the guy.

When R.J. had come out, he'd sat in the chair on the other side of the window, silent, refusing to talk. Rhys couldn't blame the boy after all he'd been through, so he'd tried to carry on, making casual conversation, hoping to get even a small response. He told R.J. about the business, how SaraJane was doing, and he told him about Whitney.

Whitney was the only topic that sparked R.J.'s interest. Once the ice was broken, they'd talked, and for the first time in months, Rhys had hope. R.J. had opened up to him, wanting to know more about this new woman in his father's life.

It was a good sign. R.J. had never expressed the slightest interest in Rhys's life before. Except when he wanted money.

Rhys brought his attention back to the moment as Whitney approached, snapping photos as she walked toward him. He was glad for the respite from his troubled thoughts. Not that *she* wasn't a pack of trouble, too.

Objectivity was what he needed as far as Whitney was concerned. In his present circumstances, it wasn't smart to get involved again—and it sure as hell didn't make sense to get his guts all tangled up about a woman who'd be gone a week or a month from now. But when had love ever made sense?

The thought jarred him.

Love? When had that entered into it?

"I NEVER REALIZED Arizona had such spectacular scenery," Whitney said breathlessly. "Whew! Guess I'd better start an exercise regimen." She sank against the large rock where Rhys had propped his foot.

"It's the altitude. Stay here long enough and you'll get used to it."

She let out another groan and, inhaling deeply, squinted up at him. He leaned down to rest one hand on his knee. The wind ruffled the loose curls at his neck and the sun cast a golden glow on his well-defined features.

She raised her camera, and he looked directly into the lens. When she hit the motor drive, he smiled, that sexy half smile that made her stomach flutter in response.

"Great shots," she said, lowering the camera. "Really great."

"I'd rather you got the scenery." He grinned almost self-consciously. He reached down to pluck something from her hair, and his fingers grazed her cheek.

She tried to decipher his strange almost tender expression.

"What do you intend to do with those photos? The ones of me, I mean."

She shrugged, meeting his eyes. "Dunno. Dartboard maybe?"

Rhys laughed, extending a hand to help her up. "Better watch it or I won't stop for lunch." His hand rested on her shoulder, guiding her as they walked back to the car. "That is if I decide to let you ride with me."

They drove into the town of Sedona and ate lunch at a Mexican restaurant in a complex called Telaquepaque. Despite her preoccupation with Rhys's revelation, Whitney marveled at it all—the scenery, the Southwestern specialty shops, the art galleries, the color of Rhys's eyes, the shape of his lips...

Afterward, they followed the silver ribbon of Oak Creek through Sedona and the Oak Creek Canyon, stopping frequently so she could take more photographs. The crystal-clear water mirrored red rock and cerulean sky, framed by the slender alabaster trunks of lofty sycamores with leaves that glittered green and gold in the sunlight. Sheer granite cliffs soared beside them as they climbed the switchbacks toward Flagstaff, all the while listening to blues music that was as seductive as the scenery.

The rest of the way home, they talked about music, movies and books, their likes and dislikes. She was again impressed with the wealth of knowledge Rhys possessed, not only about the arts, but about the world in general. His life in Estrade and the motorcycle shop seemed at odds with his former life, yet she couldn't imagine him anywhere else.

If she'd thought it once, she'd thought it a thousand times—the man fascinated her.

Rhys expelled a long breath, glanced over his shoulder at her, then back at the road. "Mind if we make a quick detour before I take you to the inn?"

Whitney shrugged. "You're the driver."

He turned onto an unpaved side road. Clouds of dust plumed behind as they rumbled to a stop in front of a rustic redwood home nestled in a stand of towering pines.

"I need to pick up a couple of things," he said, getting out of the Jeep. He walked around the front and opened her door. "C'mon."

Whitney looked at her cameras and the luggage in back. "Aren't you going to lock the car?"

Rhys struck a patient pose in front of her, thumbs hooked in his front pockets, feet spread. "I live here. There's no one else around for miles." He held out his hand.

Whitney latched on, then followed him along the crushed rock drive to the house. "Make yourself comfortable," he told her after they entered. He pointed out the bathroom on their way to the kitchen.

"Want something to drink?" He peered into the refrigerator.

"Sure," Whitney said, and gazed around, astonished by the size of the house. From the outside, only the first floor was visible and the home looked smaller than it actually was. Now she could see there were several levels.

It was rustic, with beamed vaulted ceilings, pine walls and lots of old oak furniture. But it also had a contemporary flair with vertical blinds covering some of the floor-to-ceiling windows, except for the windows that provided a view of the mountain on the other side.

The place fit him perfectly. Solid, masculine and strong, with deep footings that dug into the side of the mountain. The home spoke of comfort, warmth and permanence, and she wondered if Rhys valued those things, as well.

Of course he did, she decided as she watched him move things around in the refrigerator. Yes, the man she'd come to know would value all those things.

He held up a diet soda, the kind she liked. "Feel free to look around. You probably need to stretch your legs after the ride. I've got to grab some papers." He disappeared through a door off the kitchen.

Apparently they'd come in on an upper level at the back of the house, so when she walked toward the stairwell, she peered down from a balcony overlooking the living room. An enormous copper and iron chandelier hung in the middle of the room, a massive natural-stone fireplace spanned one entire wall and soared upward to the apex, where it met the broad wood beams that cut across the A-frame roof.

As impressed as she was, she was equally confused. This was clearly not the home of a pauper.

She edged around the inside balcony, past a cozy study area, to sliding glass doors that led to a wooden deck. She unlocked one side and stepped out, instantly awed by the sight. Rhys joined her when he returned.

"What a fabulous view, Rhys," she said, her eyes skimming the pines that surrounded them. She looked down. "But aren't you a little afraid SaraJane might tumble over the edge?"

"I've had everything kid-proofed. The doors have locks at the top and alarms I activate when SaraJane's at home. The cabinets are outfitted with locking clamps, the poisonous stuff is high out of reach and locked away—and yes, I still worry."

He leaned against the rail, combing sturdy fingers through his windblown hair. "The house and my motorcycles are the only things I own that aren't mortgaged to the hilt. And holding on to them will ensure SaraJane's future. No matter what happens, she'll always have a home."

Rhys's admission underscored his protectiveness of SaraJane. It moved Whitney, but she still couldn't dismiss her discomfort about his son.

"Rhys, I know I might be out of line asking this, but do you have legal custody of SaraJane?"

He shook his head. "Her mother abandoned her more than two years ago. No one knows SaraJane's here, and with R.J. where he is, it's best to keep it that way for the moment."

A knot formed in Whitney's stomach. "In light of what you just said, what'll you do if your son wins the appeal? I mean, won't he want to have SaraJane with him?"

Rhys's expression went grim. He pinched his eyes shut, and when he opened them, she saw profound sadness.

"It would tear my heart out," he whispered, then banged a fist on the rail. "I'd like it if they stayed here, but I realize it's a selfish desire. I love SaraJane and I love my son. R.J. is innocent—and he's clean now. He should have the chance to be a father to his own daughter, wherever he wants."

"But how can you be sure? I mean about his...his other problems?" she asked, choosing her words cautiously when what she really wanted was to scream and shout that a drug dealer had no rights at all. Even if R.J. wasn't a murderer, the other facts were indisputably true. Albert had discovered that much. But maybe Rhys didn't know everything she did, and seeing his torment, she swallowed her words.

His pain was there on his face. The lines that curved around his mouth seemed a little deeper, and the fire in his eyes had died away. R.J. was his son, after all, and from what he'd said earlier, she guessed Rhys carried a fair amount of guilt over the way he'd turned out.

When Rhys looked at her again, misery flickered in his eyes. "If I thought—" He stopped midsentence.

Still aghast at the idea that R.J. could ever have custody of SaraJane, Whitney couldn't hold back her questions any longer. "You wouldn't stop him from taking her—just because he's her father?"

After a long pause he said, "If I ever thought she was in danger, there'd be no question. But right now, after everything R.J.'s been through, the answer is no."

He gave her a thin smile. "C'mon. We'd better get a move on."

As soon as they arrived at the inn, SaraJane rushed out, calling, "Poppy! Poppy!" Gretta and Johnny followed.

"Hey, punkin." Rhys scooped up the child and swung her around before planting several kisses on her pink cheeks.

SaraJane reveled in his affection and hugged him fiercely around the neck. As Whitney walked toward them, Rhys reached out and drew her into their circle.

They stood together, smiling, hugging and laughing, and a wonderful feeling of completeness settled over Whitney. If only they could stay like this forever.

After a quick dinner and after Rhys and SaraJane had left, she hurriedly said good-night to Gretta and Johnny so she could get to her room to call Albert about Rhys's disclosures. She rubbed her temples with two fingers.

The best and the worst of it all was learning that her judgment about Rhys had been correct. He was exactly what she'd believed him to be. But his words about his son came back to her in a rush. There was no escaping what he'd told her today. And the idea of R.J.'s ever taking custody of SaraJane was more than she could bear. She didn't know what to do—but she sure as hell couldn't let it ride.

After shedding her jacket, Whitney picked up the phone and kneeled on the padded window seat.

Maybe R.J. wouldn't win the appeal. What would happen then? What if he spent the rest of his life in prison?

Would Rhys take SaraJane to the prison to visit her father? Did he do that now? Whitney shuddered at the thought.

And didn't SaraJane have a right to know about her mother and her mother's family? Since Morgan had lied about almost everything, Rhys's family weren't even aware that the Sheffields existed. If Whitney backed off now, SaraJane would never know she had another set of grandparents—such as they were—and an aunt.

And what about Morgan's inheritance? The money Morgan had received at eighteen from their grandparents' estate was still sitting in the bank waiting for her—and it was peanuts compared to what her share would be in later years. SaraJane had a right to that money.

But she'd be damned if she'd let R.J. get his hands on it. Or let Rhys use it to pay for R.J.'s defense.

If Rhys believed his son was entitled to be a father to SaraJane and she told him about the inheritance, wouldn't Rhys then tell R.J., and wouldn't that just add fuel to the fire?

R.J. would never give all that up, even if he remained in prison. Her original plan to pay him off would seem like a pittance in comparison.

Today she'd intended to reason with Rhys, hoping that any feelings they had for each other might allow them to work things out. In her fantasies she'd even envisioned the two of them married and raising SaraJane together.

But she knew now just how much of a fantasy that

was. Rhys's loyalty to his son wouldn't allow it. He was a man who'd stand by his principles—no matter how misdirected those principles might be.

And she had to stand by hers. There was no choice. She'd have to pursue custody as she'd originally intended, only now it should be easier to win—now that she knew SaraJane's father was a convicted murderer and Rhys didn't have custody.

Noticing the flashing message light on the phone, Whitney hit the button and listened. It was Tanya wanting a return call ASAP. Good. Talking with Tanya would help. Because right now she needed a friend.

"Hey, Tanya. Got your message. What's up?"

"It's about time! Where on earth have you been? I was getting ready to call out the National Guard."

"I was in Phoenix. I'll tell you about it later. What's up?"

"I don't know. When I returned home last night, there was a strange message on my machine, and I wasn't sure what to do with it, other than let you know as soon as I could. Anyway, it was a woman, Martha somebody, who said your mother needed you and that you should call immediately."

A cold shiver crawled up Whitney's spine. "Call where?"

Tanya rattled it off. "That's your parents' number, isn't it?"

"Yeah. It sure is." A sudden wave of nausea made it difficult to speak. If something was wrong with her mother, surely her father would've let her know—unless he was too drunk to care.

A stabbing pain jabbed into her ribs, right under her sternum. The same pain that had been her childhood companion.

"Listen," Tanya said. "Find out what it's all about and call me back. Okay?"

Whitney's throat constricted, and she remembered the years of anxiety attacks that an understanding physician had finally diagnosed as the result of living with alcoholic parents. Whitney remembered how she'd finally taken a stand with her mother and been thrown out of the house. At seventeen she was on her own, and she'd taken her small inheritance and fled to Europe, as far away as she could get.

"Sure," she said absently, and hung up. She'd fled, all right—and she'd stayed away. And her baby sister had suffered alone. That was Whitney's burden.

If she hadn't quarreled with her mother and left home, maybe Morgan wouldn't have felt abandoned; maybe Morgan would be alive today.

Make the damned call. The sooner you do it, the sooner it'll be over with. Steeling herself, she entered the number.

Four...five rings. She lost count. Then a man's voice answered, slurred.

"Daddy?"

"Whitney, darlin', iss thaad you?"

"I only have a minute, Dad. Is Mom there?"

"Nooope. Not here." A long pause, then a dull clunk like glass against the receiver. "Gone. Sheez gone. Left." His voice was nearly inaudible.

"Dad, just tell me where Mom is," Whitney said angrily. "I can't talk now."

"Wait, jus a sec...jus hold on, missy," he mumbled. The phone clunked, papers rustled, heavy breathing, more rustling. "Goddit. Goddtha nummer."

Whitney listened. "Repeat it for me, Dad." And before she hung up, she made him say the number three more times to be sure.

She recognized the area code as one in California. Probably some resort spa where her mom could be pampered while she drank herself into oblivion. Hands shaking, she punched in the number and waited.

"Palmetto Clinic."

Oh, no! Not again. When she finally managed to ask questions, she learned that her mother had overdosed on pills and alcohol, whether purposely or by accident, no one could say. They told Whitney where to go if she wanted to be part of her mother's rehab program.

The phone dropped from her hand, and that familiar pain lodged in her midsection. *Oh, Mother.* She pressed her hand to her mouth, hard, battling the tears.

Why now? What good will it do? What good had it ever done?

Clearing her head, she forced herself toward the bathroom, where she turned on the taps and sat on the edge of the claw-footed tub, watching the water creep up like the rising bile in the back of her throat.

One more thing to think about, one more problem to solve. Slowly she pulled off her clothes, hoping the tepid water would wash away her despair.

After her bath, she tried reading in bed, but her sense of hopelessness seemed only to grow—an insidious cloak of darkness wrapping tightly around her. There was no escape.

She hadn't conquered the demons of the past at all, and tonight they rose up, spitting fire and flame.

She crossed her arms over her chest, holding tight, rocking back and forth, longing for the comfort of

Rhys's arms. Wishing she had an ounce of Rhys's strength and determination—and his ability to love.

Lord, how she wished...until she drifted into a fitful sleep and wished no more.

CHAPTER ELEVEN

FEELING THE WARMTH of sunlight on her face, Whitney stretched languidly, then curled on her side. A door slammed somewhere in the distance and she roused herself enough to realize it must be Rhys bringing SaraJane for the day. She'd overslept.

Groggy, she struggled to orient herself. She threw off the sheets and the down comforter, rolled from the bed and stumbled to the window. The Jeep was there, but she didn't see Rhys. He was probably inside, but there wasn't time to get dressed and go downstairs before he left.

Then she saw him in the drive heading toward the Jeep. She tapped on the glass. He looked up, and she tried to raise the window, but it wouldn't budge.

She tugged again. No luck. Waving to keep his attention, she mouthed, "Wait, I need to talk to you."

He shrugged, palms up and she repeated herself, moving her lips very slowly. Finally she motioned for him to come inside.

How was she going to do this and not give anything away? she wondered, swishing a toothbrush in her mouth. She tossed on her robe and flung open the door, ready to charge downstairs to catch him. But he'd reached her door first and she nearly plowed him down in her haste.

"Whoa." He grabbed her arms to avoid the collision.

His gaze dropped to where the robe ended somewhere around the middle of her thighs. "We've got to stop meeting like this," he joked. "But on second thought—" he waggled his eyebrows "—maybe not." He ended with a wicked grin.

She backed away, nervously smoothing the satin lapels and tightening the tie around her waist before she managed a crooked little smile.

"Rhys, I need a minute," she said, shifting uncomfortably from one bare foot to the other. How could she tell him about her mother without revealing too much about herself? Lord, she was so sick of the lies.

Interest sparked in Rhys's eyes as he shut the door behind him. Her pulse quickened and she had a crazy urge to throw herself into his arms.

She turned away, then walked to the couch and sank into the welcoming softness of the cushions; Rhys did the same. "Can we talk for a minute?" she said, clasping her hands together.

"Sure." He sat next to her, his voice sober. "What's up?"

"I need to go to California for a couple of days."

A muscle in his jaw twitched. "Business."

"No. Not business. A family problem."

A look of relief flickered on his face. Then he took her hand, almost as if he sensed she needed his strength. Lord, if he only knew how much she did.

"Anything I can do to help?" His eyes held hers.

She shook her head, touched by the tenderness in his gaze. Knowing she'd crumble if she gave in to her self-pity, she abruptly stood, turned to face the window and folded her arms across her chest.

Within seconds she felt the heat of his body behind her. A painful ache grew in her chest, and she wanted more than anything to lose herself in the comfort of his arms.

"No," she said softly. "No one can do anything. I've tried for years."

He moved a step closer, placed his hands on her upper arms. Weary, she leaned against him. God, she longed to tell him the truth, the whole truth, not just about her mother, but also about Morgan and herself.

But what was the point? What would be gained by telling him she was there to gain custody of SaraJane?

He'd already said he'd fight for his son's rights, no matter what. And once he knew why she'd come to Estrade, once he knew that everything she'd said was a lie, he'd never trust her again.

"It's my mother. An overdose. She's in a treatment center." She made every effort to steady her voice before she continued. "I know it might sound cold, but unless she wants to help herself, treatment won't do a damn bit of good." As Whitney pulled in a deep steadying breath, a lifetime of ugly memories flashed through her head. "We've been through this kind of thing for years."

He gently rubbed her arms. "Pills?"

"And alcohol."

"Anyone with her?"

Whitney shook her head.

"Your father? Where's he?"

A brittle laugh tumbled from her lips. "My father. He's as bad as my mother. I talked to him last night. He didn't have any idea where she went. He probably doesn't even remember I called."

Her anger flared; she moved out of Rhys's reach and stalked across the room. She couldn't let him see her this way. And if he touched her again, she was afraid she'd fall apart. "My father," she repeated. She gave another hollow laugh. "I had him read me the number and he didn't have a clue about anything." She paced, desperate to hide her turmoil.

"I had no idea." Rhys stepped toward her. "Perhaps if your father understood how you feel—"

"Please!" Whitney whirled around, hand raised, interrupting him. "Please. Don't. I've had years of experience with this," she said bitterly. "Alcoholics aren't concerned with anyone's feelings. They're selfish egocentric people whose only thought is—" She stopped abruptly, realizing her vulnerability. *I can't let him see me like this.*

Rhys seemed surprised, even a little hurt at her response. "Sorry," he said and headed for the door. "Sometimes I really put my foot in it."

He opened the door, and for a moment, he stood there, looking irresolute. Then he walked toward her again; he rested his hands on her shoulders and massaged lightly. He traced a fingertip along her jawline and, tilting her chin up, leaned down to brush his lips over hers. Softly, tenderly.

Whitney's need for him was overwhelming.

"We'll miss you," he said, backing toward the stairs. "Call, if you need anything. Anytime. I'll be here." He turned and disappeared into the stairwell.

TANYA MET WHITNEY at LAX, and the two of them drove to the clinic together. "I can't believe you're actually behind the wheel, that you're actually driving a car," Whitney teased. Tanya didn't own a car, didn't want one, didn't need one in New York.

"Self-defense," Tanya lamented. "You can't do anything out here if you don't have a car."

"Didn't Albert pick you up at the airport?"

Tanya nodded. "But I can't have your cousin driving me everywhere."

"You could've used mine."

"Yeah, but your car's expensive, and I'm not exactly Mario Andretti."

Whitney murmured a response. Her thoughts focused on her mother, and she dreaded what she'd find when they arrived. She was grateful her best friend had insisted on flying out here to go with her. Tanya had denied it, saying she needed a break, but Whitney knew Tanya had come simply to be with her.

Spotting the clinic ahead, Whitney felt her heart drop. She was short of breath, starting to panic. She grabbed a paper bag she'd brought along and clamped it over her mouth, breathing deeply, fighting the anxiety, the inevitable chest pains.

Tanya reached across the seat and placed a hand on Whitney's arm. "It's gonna be okay, Whit. Just take it one step at a time."

After another deep breath, Whitney muttered, "Sure." But the truth was, she didn't want to do it at all, much less one excruciatingly painful step at a time. She honestly didn't think she could go through with it, not without sacrificing the emotional stability she'd gained over the past twelve years.

She knew exactly what would happen. Because every time she had contact with her mother, even by phone, it all came back—the tirades, the hateful words spewing from her mother's mouth as though she were possessed.

Whitney had thought she'd exorcized all those demons, and in less than a heartbeat, they were back.

She was a little girl again, standing in front of her

mother, tears streaming, still waiting, wanting more than anything to hear her mommy say she loved her.

That was all she'd wanted. Ever.

"I'll wait," Tanya said after they'd checked in at the clinic's desk. "Maybe get some coffee or do some shopping."

"Here." Whitney handed her the cell phone. "Take this and I'll call when I'm ready."

Tanya took it, hugged Whitney and left. Less than fifteen minutes later Whitney called her back. Ten minutes with her mother and it was all over. She couldn't do it. God help her, she just couldn't.

Driving home, she was silent. She hurt too much to talk, and she was desperate to put some distance between herself and this awful place. She had to forget it, close it out of her mind—like she'd learned to do so many years ago.

When they arrived at Whitney's house in La Jolla, Tanya suggested Whitney take a nap. "Maybe I will," she said, then plodded upstairs. She was tired. More tired than she'd ever been.

Her nerves were frayed. Thinking about everything in her life—her mother, Morgan, Rhys and SaraJane—she felt the weight of responsibilities. Of lies and secrets.

Exhaustion set in. Complete emotional exhaustion. And sleep was a welcome respite.

She slept all afternoon, all night.

When she awoke, Whitney got up from the queen-size four-poster and padded to the window, throwing it open, allowing the chilly Pacific breeze to sharpen her senses.

The early-morning sun glinted off the water. Mmm. She inhaled deeply of the moist salt air and listened to the seagulls squawk. She loved the ocean and the healing effect it had on her.

She rubbed her bare arms. Today was a new day. If she could just manage to think about anything other than the fact that she'd abandoned her mother, she might be okay.

Whitney raked a hand through her hair, not understanding at all.

Why did she feel compelled to help her mother *now?*

Kathryn Sheffield had never given an ounce of love to anyone, least of all her children. And her mother's acceptance no longer mattered to Whitney. She'd conquered that weakness, that need—or so she'd thought until yesterday, when the floodgates were thrown open and every heartbreaking memory came crashing in on her.

Why had yesterday's meeting affected her so much? Nothing had changed. She hadn't expected it to.

She'd always been the one to take over, to fix things, clean up the mess, wipe away Morgan's tears. No one had ever been there for her. Why try again? Was there some little hope—

No! Don't even think it. She couldn't go back. She couldn't face all that heartache and pain.

She wasn't strong enough.

She closed her eyes, wanting to shut it all out, but the thought persisted.

What if this was the one time that might be different—and she turned away?

A soft knock at the door roused her from the feeling of hopelessness. She'd almost forgotten that Tanya was there with her. Glad of her friend's presence, she collected herself. "C'mon in."

"Hey, you're up." Tanya smiled brightly.

Tanya's olive complexion was even more golden from just a few hours in the California sun, and in a white T-shirt and bleached jeans, she looked more like a teenager than a thirtyish New York editor.

"I'm up, but just barely." Whitney walked to the bed and sat on it, cross-legged. "Apparently, beach living agrees with you."

Tanya frowned. "Yeah, but not right this minute, though. You have a visitor."

"Really? This early? Who? No one knows I'm here except my mother. And—" her heart raced "—Rhys."

"Rhys?"

"The motorcycle guy."

"Oh, yeah. Well, someone else knows you're here, and he's downstairs waiting for you to be summoned. If you want, I'll tell him to drop dead."

There was only one person who evoked that kind of response from Tanya. "Brock?"

"In the living, slimy, crawling flesh."

Whitney chuckled at Tanya's animosity. "D'you think you could be a tad more explicit about your feelings?"

Tanya wheeled around. "Sorry. Guess it's none of my business. I just have this foul taste in my mouth about him since he was such a jerk to you. And someday I'll tell you about an experience I had that makes me hate him even more."

Whitney arched an eyebrow. Tanya's dislike for Brock went deeper than she'd imagined. "Tell me now. Before I see him."

Tanya wrinkled her nose. "You sure? It's ugly. And you've got enough on your plate."

"Spit it out," Whitney said. Nothing could be worse than what she'd been through recently.

"Okay. If you're sure..." Looking skeptical, Tanya blurted, "This happened last March. I saw Brock checking into the Plaza with two women while you were still engaged to him. And he asked me to join them."

Whitney drew back and, after a moment, exhaled long and hard. "Whew. I don't know if I'm happy to know that or not. Certainly validates my decision to dump him."

"I wanted to tell you before, but there wasn't any point because you found out what a creep he was, anyway. But now that the jerk is sniffing around again..." She hesitated. "Well, I just thought you should know, in case he makes a move on you."

Whitney recoiled. "Tanya! Puh-leeze. Give me a little credit." She rose from the bed and headed for the bathroom. "I'm not *that* needy. Or that stupid."

At least not where Brock's concerned.

Tanya followed her into the bathroom. Whitney loaded her toothbrush, then leaned against the sink. "Listen, I'm going to take a shower. If it's something important and he wants to wait out on the deck until I'm done, tell him he can. I'll make it totally clear to him that he's an unwelcome intrusion in my life."

Tanya grinned. "I'll be more than happy to relay the message."

Forty-five minutes later, Whitney stepped onto the deck. "Hello, Brock." She smoothed the front of her white cotton sweater. "What do you want?"

Brock wiped a desultory look from his face and got up from the redwood chair. He smiled, his usual polished smile, perfected so that the corners of his eyes didn't crinkle. His blond hair had obviously been lightened, and his perennial tan reminded her of a third-rate movie star. She'd never felt quite so repelled by the man as she did right now.

"Whitney, darlin'," he murmured, arms open as if he expected a hug. He stopped short, seeing her arms folded tightly across her chest.

"How did you know I was here?"

He waved a wrist toward a chair, indicating that they should sit at the patio table. "Aren't you going to offer me a drink? I got kinda dry waiting out here like a delivery boy." He pulled out a chair for her and one for himself and sat. "Did you get my flowers?"

Whitney glared. If looks were daggers, he'd already be dead. She'd never realized more than she did right this minute how sick she was of people like Brock in her life. People she'd lived among for far too many years.

"Cut to the chase, Brock. What do you want? And don't hand me any of your lies about still being in love. I've had enough of your deceit to last a lifetime."

Brock's eyes flew open in surprise. He cleared his throat. "We've become very common these days, haven't we?"

"*We've* become nothing! Spit it out or quit wasting my time."

Crossing his legs, Brock went on, all the while brushing at the trousers of his beige linen suit. "Well, I can't say I'm surprised. I suppose when one becomes a motorcycle groupie, that sort of thing is bound to rub off."

Adrenaline pumped into Whitney's veins. She scowled at him. How did Brock know anything about her current work? "Like I said, cut to the chase."

Ignoring her comment, he twisted a thread on his lapel. "Whitney darlin', I sent you the flowers hoping to show you how wrong I was. I wanted to talk to you. To explain.''

He stood, then sauntered to the edge of the deck, hands in the pockets of his loose-fitting pants. He stared out at the ocean and shrugged. ''But I can see you don't want to listen. You should've waited, you know. I did have an explanation.''

Whitney expelled a long-held breath and got to her feet, too. ''You can't explain being in bed with another woman two days before our wedding.'' Not to mention what Tanya had told her. ''And even if you could, I don't want to hear it.'' She moved to usher him out. ''You're a jerk, and if that's all you came here for, then you better leave. I'm busy.''

Brock's expression twisted into an ugly knot of contempt. ''Busy doing what?'' he spat out. ''Busy running back to the mountains and your greaser friend? Does he know why you're there?''

She caught her breath.

''Oh, got your attention now?'' He smirked. ''I mean, does your biker friend know you intend to take your sister's brat with you? Does he know all that?''

She winced but said nothing. Of course Brock knew about SaraJane and the plan to gain custody. They'd been engaged when she'd finally found Morgan. But how did he find out that it had anything to do with Rhys?

''I didn't think so,'' Brock said. ''Anyway, since you aren't interested in my explanations, I'll make a deal with you, instead.''

Whitney's anger mounted steadily.

''Yes,'' Brock continued. ''And it'll only cost you what it takes to produce my film.''

When she still didn't speak, he said, ''You finance the film and I'll stay away from your motorcycle man. You know, darlin', the film I'd planned to do after we were married.'' His lips thinned. ''And I can see you're just so overwhelmed with my generosity you need a little time to think about it.''

He crossed to the sliding door. Just then, Tanya yanked it open from the other side. ''I'll call you tomorrow night, Whitney...darlin'.''

Whitney's fury erupted, but the voice that came out was dangerously quiet. ''Get out. Get out of my house.''

Brock feigned a look of hurt, but on the way out, he gave her a triumphant sneer. ''Shall we say about eight?'' And then he was gone.

Whitney gripped the back of the chair so tightly she broke a fingernail. But if she didn't hang on, she was sure her legs would buckle.

''You did the right thing,'' Tanya said, rushing outside. ''Whatever you said, it ended the right way.''

Whitney lowered herself into the chair, feeling as if she'd been punched in the stomach. The pain in her chest yesterday was nothing compared to the despair she felt right now. ''I've got to tell him,'' she whispered. ''Today.''

''Tell who? What?''

''Darlin' Brock wants money,'' she said flatly. Whitney closed her eyes and tipped her head back.

Tanya came over and sat on a chair facing Whitney. ''And you told him to drop dead. Good for you.''

''He wants money to keep quiet about my sister's baby.''

Tanya stared at her, apparently confused by what Whitney had just said. Tanya already knew most of the story, although she didn't know that Rhys wasn't the baby's father and that his son was in prison.

Unable to keep it to herself any longer, Whitney

blurted out the whole story. At first Tanya registered surprise that Whitney had waited so long and, in fact, hadn't even started custody proceedings.

Then studying her friend's face, Tanya said, "Uh-oh. There's more going on here, huh? Boy, am I dense." She slapped a hand to her forehead, then leaned forward in her chair, elbows on her knees, eyes focused in a tell-me-the-truth look. "Are you in love with him?"

"Tanya, I can't let Rhys hear the truth from Brock. I've got to tell him." Whitney buried her face in her hands. Finally she raised her head. "I should've told him a long time ago." She sighed and bit the soft skin on the inside of her lip.

"Does he love you?" Tanya tried again.

"He'll hate me. So will Gretta and Johnny."

Tanya wrinkled her nose. "Gretta and Johnny?"

"The grandparents. They'll die if I take SaraJane away. They'll all be crushed, brokenhearted. God help me. I don't know how I can do this." She sobered. "But I have to."

Though she'd tried her damnedest to come up with a viable solution, Whitney knew what the result would be—and she knew, without a doubt, that Rhys would never forgive her.

"But if you love each other," Tanya said, reducing the problem to its basics, "why don't you just get married and raise the kid together. That's the best solution possible. The two of you could get custody, adopt the baby and live happily ever after."

Whitney looked incredulously at her friend. "Happily ever after? Are you serious?"

Tanya took a breath. "You'll never know what could happen if you never take the chance."

Whitney let out a tiny helpless laugh. Coming from

Tanya—the last person in the world to take a chance on anything personal—that was a joke. Not to mention that Rhys would find her lies or, rather, omissions unforgivable. And even if he somehow had it in him to understand her reasons, he wouldn't take the child away from his son.

Rhys didn't know the whole truth about R.J. Neither did Gretta and Johnny. Or if they did, they didn't believe it.

"You're scared," Tanya said. "Scared to let yourself care."

Whitney frowned at Tanya. "That's ridiculous." *But true.* She was scared to death. The thought of loving someone terrified her. Especially *this* someone.

It meant opening herself up, being vulnerable. It meant she risked being hurt. And it meant she risked hurting Rhys.

Right now the only thing she knew for sure was that she had to tell Rhys the truth—before he found out from someone else. She owed him that much.

And she'd have to live with the consequences.

SARAJANE FLEW INTO Whitney's arms the second she stepped from the car. Whitney knelt, hugging her niece hard, knowing there might only be a few more times like this—for a while, anyway. Once she talked to Rhys, he would ask her to leave, and she wouldn't see SaraJane again until a court decided who should have custody.

Whitney pressed a kiss to SaraJane's forehead. "I'm surprised you're still up, pumpkin."

"We got flowers for you." SaraJane's chubby cheeks dimpled. "Me and Poppy bought them from the store 'cause it's too cold outside to grow anymore."

Whitney's regret multiplied as she stood up, cradling

SaraJane in her arms. She held her a little longer, inhaling deeply. SaraJane smelled little-girl-sweet, like cookies and milk, and fresh air and grass.

Rhys stood apart from them, his handsome craggy face beaming, his eyes soft with understanding. The way he looked at her made Whitney shake inside with excitement—and dread.

Gretta waved from the kitchen window and Johnny came up to stand in the doorway behind Rhys.

"Welcome back." Rhys wrapped an arm around both Whitney and SaraJane, directing them into the house through the back door. "We didn't expect you so soon. Guess that's a sign everything went well, huh?"

Before Whitney could answer, Gretta said, "I've made tea and scones," and with Johnny's help, she carried the things to the table. Whitney planted another kiss on SaraJane's forehead and set her down. Rhys took Whitney's coat and hung it in the closet with the rest of the family's.

His gaze followed SaraJane as she led Whitney by the hand, showing her the finger painting she'd done yesterday and the new dress Poppy had bought for her doll, Miss Agatha.

"And we put more daisies in your room," SaraJane said proudly.

Gretta asked for them all to sit for tea. "Come on over here, young lady, and let Whitney catch her breath. My Lord, the child acts as if you were gone for weeks."

Whitney grinned, squeezing SaraJane's small hand in hers before the little girl skipped off into the sunroom to play with her toys. Rhys offered a chair next to him, and she felt an immediate sensation of coming home. They were happy to see her, glad she was back, and they wanted nothing from her.

They'd opened their hearts and accepted her as if she was family. Such a simple welcome, and maybe... maybe she could pretend to be part of it for just a little while longer—until she was alone with Rhys. Because she couldn't tell him now. Not in front of his family.

For another hour, they took turns catching up on the local news. No one asked why she'd gone to California, but Whitney figured they all knew. She hadn't sworn Rhys to secrecy, and it would be perfectly normal for him to share the information with his parents.

That was the kind of support they gave each other, and now they were there for her, too. Lord, how she appreciated it, more than they would ever know.

When they finished their tea, it was nearing SaraJane's bedtime. Rhys gathered up her things and, just as he was leaving, pulled a piece of paper from his pocket. "I forgot. Someone called for you. He called me at the shop today and left this number. Said you'd know what it was about."

Whitney clamped trembling fingers over the note. She didn't need to look at the number to know whose it was. No one but Brock would call the shop for her.

She mustered a tentative smile. "Right." And before she could turn away, Rhys placed a fingertip under her chin as he searched her eyes.

"Everything okay?"

No. Everything's not okay! She wanted a family like the one she'd been part of tonight. She wanted not to see the look in Rhys's eyes when she told him she'd lied to him. She wanted not to hurt him or Gretta or Johnny. She wanted her mother and father not to be alcoholics— and she wanted Morgan to still be alive.

She wanted Rhys to love her as she loved him at this moment.

"Sure. Everything's fine."

His eyes probed. She stepped back, averting her gaze. It would only take a second for her to lose all control.

"Sweetheart," Whitney said to SaraJane as she bent down to the small arms clutching her around the knees. "Better button up. It's getting colder and colder out there."

"Pretty soon it will snow. Will you make a snowman with me when it gets re-e-e-eally cold?"

Whitney ruffled Sara's hair. "Sure. Anything your little heart desires."

After Rhys and SaraJane had left, Whitney thanked Gretta and Johnny for the welcome and went upstairs. That welcome was almost too much to bear. In another day or two, they'd all know why she'd come—and they'd hate her.

She closed the door behind her and leaned against it. Would SaraJane hate her, too? If she was successful in gaining custody, how would the child react to leaving Rhys and not seeing him or her grandparents everyday?

She just had to hope things worked out. Children adjusted quickly, she knew, and Gretta and Johnny...well, they'd never feel the same about Whitney, but they'd adjust, too. She'd make sure they saw SaraJane every chance they could.

But it was Rhys who worried her the most.

He'd be hurt the most. He'd trusted her, enough to welcome her into his family and into SaraJane's life. What made it even worse was knowing that he'd had a child taken away from him before, a child with whom he'd never been able to make a connection afterward.

She flung herself across the bed. Even if things

worked out between Rhys and her, there was still the matter of custody. Rhys was *not* SaraJane's legal guardian.

R.J. was SaraJane's father. Morgan was gone, and if R.J. was released from jail, he'd have every right to SaraJane and any money Morgan's little girl would eventually receive from the family estate.

The fact that Rhys believed R.J. innocent didn't change his son's character. R.J. had used Morgan and then used the baby.

Who knows what he'd do if he found out SaraJane was an heir to the Sheffield money? No, she needed to continue her efforts to gain custody, and with R.J. in jail for murder, it ought to be easy. Regardless of the effect it had on her personally. Or on Rhys.

Regardless of whether her heart shattered into a million pieces in the process.

CHAPTER TWELVE

WHITNEY ROUNDED the corner into Estrade in time to catch the sunrise. The pale glow of dawn rose up to crown the peaks of the distant mountain range, and she watched for the inevitable wall of sunshine to break and spill over the jagged crest like a sheet of gold.

But today, even that grand panoply of light couldn't keep her heart from hammering out an erratic drum finale.

She parked in the space next to Rhys's Jeep, feeling some comfort in being as close to him as she could for just a little longer. Checking her hair in the rearview mirror, she saw faint violet smudges under her eyes.

She'd lain awake most of the night, and when she finally drifted off, the night terrors she'd had as a kid returned like an old movie on fast forward: the tears, the awful screams, Morgan's tiny arms clutching, scratching at her legs, tormented faces—Morgan's, her mother's—the basement door thudding like the lid on a coffin and she couldn't see for the blackness. All black, so black, and cold, so cold, and she screamed and screamed until the back of her throat burned and she bolted upright, drenched and shaking in her bed.

She hadn't had that nightmare for a long time.

Rhys rose from his chair the instant he saw her come in. He didn't have to say a word for her to know he wanted to help. Ironically he thought her concern was about her mother.

He stood hesitantly behind the desk, then picked up a pencil, tapped it a couple of times on the stack of papers in front of him and smiled, that sweet sexy smile.

Probably the last one she'd ever see.

"Morning," he said softly.

Unable to give even the tiniest smile in return, Whitney said, "Rhys, I need to talk to you, and it's not about my mother."

Rhys came around the desk and laid his hands on her shoulders. Uncertainty flickered in his eyes. She stiffened, dread seeping through every cell in her body.

"Rhys, can we just talk?" Her voice sounded quavery and far away. She cleared her throat. "I have something to tell you and I just don't see any easy way to do it."

He looked puzzled at first. Then, after a moment, he took a deep breath, returned to his desk, sat and hoisted his feet up. As casual as he appeared, she knew better. She saw the hard line of his jaw, the jerky movement as he waved a hand toward her.

"Shoot. The floor is yours."

"It has to do with why I came here."

"You're moving on. Right?" He avoided her gaze. "Makes sense. Obviously you can't get all your research in one place."

Oh, God. He didn't have a clue. She wrung her hands.

"No, that's not what this is about. I want to talk about why I came here in the first place. It wasn't to do research."

Tears welled in her eyes, and she wanted more than anything to run away. She turned, stepped to the window, unable to bear his expression when she told him.

"I came here to find my sister's baby."

Feet thudded to the floor, the chair scraped, then a crash. She swung around and he was a fraction of an inch away, his face crimson, the veins in his neck throbbing.

"SaraJane is my niece," she said.

She waited, blood pounding in her ears, as she watched him fight for control. When he finally spoke, it was through clenched teeth.

"You'd better leave." His voice was deathly quiet, masking the anger she felt coming at her in waves. She felt it as deeply as if he'd shouted at the top of his lungs.

She wanted to explain, to tell him it wasn't just a simple lie, that it was complicated and that her intent wasn't to hurt anyone. Surely he could understand that.

But she knew the words wouldn't make any difference to him. Not now. Yet she had to say something.

"SaraJane's mother, my sister, is dead." Her voice trembled, but she went on. "Before she died, she asked me to find her baby. SaraJane has a right to know her mother's family."

It wasn't what she wanted to say at all, but she needed to stand back from her emotions. She needed to return to the safe world of not feeling, not caring. No love, no pain.

But it was much too late for that. She was in love with him. And that realization was as painful as seeing the contempt in his eyes.

He glared at her, his features like granite. "I said you'd better leave." He strode to the door, yanked it open and held it for her.

RHYS STARED OUT THE WINDOW in the shop without seeing a thing. He'd spent a long time moving parts around, restocking shelves, rereading blueprints. Anything to take his mind off the look on Whitney's face when she'd fled from his office.

Dammit, why did he care how she'd looked? She was the one who'd been dishonest. She'd come here under false pretenses, lied about who she was and what she wanted. And like a fool, he'd believed it all. He'd been taken in.

Duped.

Whitney Sheffield wasn't any different from his ex-wife.

The big difference was that Stephanie had told him up front what she wanted, and he'd been young and in love enough—stupid enough—to try to make her happy.

But he'd learned that happiness didn't come that way. All the money in the world wouldn't have made Stephanie happy. Hell, he'd spent most of his own life seeking that Holy Grail. For a long time he'd thought happiness would come with success, with living well from all the money he'd made.

But that wasn't how to achieve contentment of any kind. And he'd never realized it more than he did at this moment.

Whitney had out-and-out lied. Faked it all because she had an agenda. He'd been right about Whitney all along. But why the deceit?

If she'd come here to see SaraJane, why didn't she just say so? What was the point of all those lies? If SaraJane's mother was dead, what did Whitney want, other than to get to know her niece?

She'd said SaraJane had a right to know her mother's family, and he couldn't argue with that. It wasn't the fact that Whitney was SaraJane's aunt that bothered him.

It was the fact that she'd been dishonest with him from the minute they'd met.

Or was it because she'd made love to him—and stolen his heart? But she'd never said anything about love. Not one damn word. If he imagined she cared about him, it was his own doing—or rather his undoing.

Still, the pain in her eyes when she'd left had been real; he was sure of that. And dammit, so was his.

But he still couldn't get beyond wondering why. Why hadn't she told him who she was? Somehow, that seemed important.

He glanced at his watch. Noon. She'd been gone for an hour. If she'd packed up and left, he'd never know the answer.

He seized the phone. "Mabel, is Charley around? I need him to mind the shop for a bit."

"Nope. He's not here. Got some stuff to take to the assay office today," Mabel said excitedly. "Looks like all his dirt-digging is finally gonna pay off."

"Great, Mabel. Tell Charley that's great." Yeah, but not for him. He had other things on his mind.

"Where's Whitney? She coming for lunch?" Mabel demanded. "You didn't scare her off, did ya?"

Rhys sighed. "No, I didn't, Mabel. Listen, I'm going to close up for a few hours. If you see anyone around, can you please tell them to come back later or even tomorrow?"

"Everything okay? Anyone sick?"

"Fine, Mabel. Everything's fine. I just need to be…somewhere else, and Whitney's not here. If Charley comes back soon, maybe you can send him here till I get back."

"Sure thing. In the meantime, I'll keep an eye on the place. You better treat that young lady right," she added. "She's a keeper."

Yeah, he'd thought so, too—in moments of madness. "I treat everyone right, Mabel. You know that."

"Things ain't always what they seem, you know. Sometimes you gotta keep an open mind."

What the hell was that supposed to mean? Did Mabel know? In the short time Whitney'd been in Estrade, she and Mabel had become fast friends. An odd combination, but it seemed to work for both of them.

"I will. My mind's so open it's a sieve. And thanks, you're a doll."

A few minutes later the Sportster rumbled underneath him as he snaked down the switchbacks. The wind whipped his hair across his face, reminding him he'd forgotten his helmet. But there was no time to go back—not if he wanted to catch her.

When he'd asked her to leave, he'd acted impulsively out of his own hurt. He hadn't even allowed her to explain.

Regardless of what it meant to him personally, the whole situation could affect SaraJane's future. He needed to think straight—with his head, not his heart.

When he reached the inn, he saw her car still there. Thank heaven his folks had gone shopping in Flagstaff and taken SaraJane along. They didn't need to know. No one needed to know until he could ensure that SaraJane was safe.

He parked the bike, charged in and took the stairs two at a time. Her door was open.

A suitcase yawned across the bed, and Whitney stood with her back to him, dragging clothing from the drawers. Apparently she hadn't heard him come in, because when she turned to put something in her suitcase and saw him, she jumped.

Her eyes were red-rimmed and puffy. Her hair hung

loose, framing her face. He nearly crumpled at the sight of her, yet he kept his distance.

"I'm sorry I didn't let you explain." He crossed his arms and leaned against the door frame. "My head is clearer now."

She continued placing folded items neatly in the suitcase, pointedly ignoring him.

He stepped into the room, walked to the bed and slapped the suitcase shut.

"I said I'm sorry." He shoved his fingers through wind-snarled hair and tried to catch her gaze with his. "I'm sorry. I should have let you explain."

She looked away, then sank onto the bed, her shoulders slumped in defeat, hands folded on her lap. Her shoulders heaved upward as she drew a deep breath. Oh, man, it was all he could do to keep from dragging her into his arms.

But dammit, *he* was the one who'd been hurt. Why did he feel such a need to comfort her? Did he have no pride whatsoever?

"Do you want me to explain now?" she asked, turning to face him. Her pale hair fell across her forehead, and she brushed it away, staring at him with those limitless blue eyes—eyes seared with pain.

"Please," he said softly, sinking to the bed on the opposite side.

When she finished her last shaky sentence, there was nothing left of his tattered heart. If he'd been in the same situation, he would have done exactly the same thing. How could she tell him why she'd come when she'd been given a description of him that rivaled Jack the Ripper's?

He shook his head. He stood. He paced in front of the bay window. "So let me get this straight," he said, suddenly wanting more than anything to fix things between them.

"You came here thinking I was your sister's lover, SaraJane's father. You believed I was a drug dealer and that I'd kidnapped my own daughter to get her mother to come back. And before SaraJane's mother, your sister, died, you promised her you'd find SaraJane." He stopped to breathe, then continued.

"When you saw Luth give me money, you thought he was a part of some drug scheme I ran from the shop, but later when I told you that R.J. is SaraJane's father, you realized you were wrong. And everything else you told me, all the rest of it, is true? Your name. Your profession. The book, all that?"

She nodded and kept staring out the window beyond him.

"Exactly when did you decide I wasn't the Manuel Noriega of Estrade?" *What about when we made love?* Did she believe he was the scum of the earth then? "Why didn't you tell me the truth when I told you about R.J.?"

She stood, turned toward him and crossed her own arms. "Rhys, after a very short time, I knew something wasn't right. I knew you couldn't be the person Morgan had described—even before you told me about R.J. But I didn't know what to do."

She drew her bottom lip between her teeth. "When I thought you were SaraJane's father, I began to think Morgan must've lied about you. But I didn't know why. I needed time to figure it out. To see for myself.

"I also realized I wanted to get to know SaraJane, especially in case I couldn't stay once I told you who I was." She stopped again, her breath catching.

"And...and then I felt so terrible because I was at-

tracted to you. You see, I'd made Morgan a promise.''
She placed shaky fingers over her mouth.

"Oh, dear God. I'd made her so many promises that
I didn't keep. I felt so guilty. Guilty because I left her
with our parents when she was so young. I felt responsible for what happened to her.''

She took in a few jerky breaths, trying desperately to
gather her composure. "I still do. If I'd stuck around…''
Her voice cracked, and she waved a hand, pausing.
"Then, when you told me about R.J., I…I couldn't
think.'' She looked away.

"But none of it—'' she drew another breath ''—none
of it changed my feelings about you, Rhys.'' These last
words were barely a whisper. Her shoulders began to
shake and she covered her face with her hands.

In the next instant he was at her side, pulling her to
his chest, wrapping his arms around her, holding her,
soothing her, wanting more than anything to be as close
to her as he could.

He felt her relax against him, and he placed soft kisses
on her forehead, her eyelids, her tearstained cheeks and
lips. "Ah, Whitney, it's okay,'' he whispered. "Everything's gonna be okay. We'll work things out.''

"Oh, Rhys. I want that. I want to work things out so
very much.''

He did, too. He didn't know what he meant about
everything being okay, except that it was what he
wanted. Most of all, he couldn't stand to see her hurting
like this. He wanted her to be as she'd always been—
happy and excited about life, and desiring him as much
as he desired her.

His mouth sought hers and when she returned his kiss,
his whole body sprang to alertness. Realizing where they

were, he took her by the hand and whispered, "Let's go for a ride."

He placed his leather jacket around her shoulders and grabbed one of his father's for himself. "You okay without a helmet? I forgot mine but we won't go far. Okay?" She nodded. Outside, he got on the bike, extended a hand to help her on and put both her arms around his waist, holding his hands over hers for a moment before they took off.

THE WIND DRIED Whitney's tears as she held on to Rhys, her hands clamped around his hard stomach, her cheek flat against his back, her insides shaking. He took the curves with ease and in the bright afternoon sun, the fall air seemed almost warm. An Indian-summer day, perfect for a ride.

Her thoughts were on Rhys and what he'd said.

How would everything be okay? What was the solution? Did he forgive her for being dishonest with him, for lying and sneaking around behind his back?

How could he forgive that? She could hardly forgive herself. And what about his parents? She'd deceived them, too.

But he'd told her everything would be okay and she *needed* to believe him.

They climbed to the top of the crest and another road appeared to the right. She recognized it as the one they'd taken to Rhys's house. Rumbling into the drive, he pressed a button on the front of the bike, waited till the garage door slid open, then drove into the garage tucked underneath.

He pressed the button again and she heard the door slide down behind them. After helping her off the bike, he dropped the stand to secure it.

She glanced around. They were surrounded by motorcycles of all kinds, old, new, parts and pieces. But Rhys hustled her up the stairs, shrugging out of his coat along the way.

They stopped in the middle of the stairwell, and he pulled her to him to slowly slide the jacket off her shoulders and then he held her tightly, a captive in his embrace, and she felt the raw power in his body, saw the naked desire in his eyes.

Then everything vanished but her awareness of him. She was intoxicated—by his scent, his touch, his burning sexuality, and she wanted him. God, how she wanted him.

His breathing deepened and he pressed her closer, his body hot and hard against hers. She shuddered at the contact and a low moan tore from her throat. His mouth touched hers and irrepressible need exploded within her. She put her arms around his neck, and he scooped her up and carried her into his bedroom.

Gently placing her on the king-size bed, he bent over her, his mouth claiming hers, his tongue plunging, sending shivers of desire through her. He drew back, exhaling raggedly, stopping only long enough to remove his boots.

She reached for him, and he came to her. His hands cupped her face, his mouth sought hers, only this time slowly, tenderly, and she felt as if she were going to fly apart. Never had anyone touched her so deeply. Never had she wanted to give herself so completely.

Somehow, her whole world narrowed to this unequivocal moment in time, this supreme moment in Rhys's arms. Nothing else mattered.

AFTERWARD, AFTER THEIR lovemaking, Rhys held her, drawing his fingertips up and down her spine. He liked the way she curled into him, her face nestled at the base of his throat. He listened to her breathing grow slow and deep, a hypnotic contented sound that lulled him into slumber.

A short time later, he awoke and sat for a long time in the soft leather chair next to the bed, staring at her, wondering where they went from here.

He decided to let her sleep before he took her home and before he picked up SaraJane. They had to talk, he knew. But right now he was satisfied just to look at her.

She was so beautiful. So passionate, matching his nearly insatiable passion, move for move, with her own. And he'd loved every second.

But as much as he relished the passion, he'd felt something more. Need. *She needed him.*

She needed him as much as he needed her—whether she knew it or not. The thought made his chest expand with something he'd believed long dead.

No, he wasn't mistaking sex for love. He knew love when he saw it. He'd just been too goddamn bullheaded to admit it before.

What he didn't know was what to do about it.

He rubbed the late-afternoon stubble on his chin. She'd never once said she cared about him. And while he *hoped* he knew her feelings, he realized that it wasn't enough.

THE SCENT OF PINE was carried by the wind through the open window. Whitney hiked up the masculine sheets to cover her naked body. Outside, dark clouds scudded above the pines. It felt as though she'd only slept for a few minutes, but the encroaching darkness made her wonder.

Rhys had disappeared from the bed the way he had that night in Phoenix, but she knew he couldn't leave, he had to drive her back to the inn. Satisfied, she plumped the pillows behind her head, noticing her clothes neatly folded across the cedar chest in front of the footboard.

She happily remembered their urgency in removing those clothes only a short time ago.

Feeling a rush of warmth, she hugged herself, pulled the blankets close, wanting to savor the pleasures they'd shared.

She looked around Rhys's bedroom and saw heavy oak furniture with clean straight lines. It was like the rest of his home, warm and inviting, and she knew she could get very used to being here.

Her gaze fell to a photo on the dresser. She could tell even from a distance that it was like the one she'd seen earlier in his desk drawer. The one of Rhys and his son.

She couldn't imagine what Rhys must've gone through having a son whose mind had been poisoned against him. But the very thought of R.J. made her stomach lurch.

R.J. was SaraJane's father, and he was in jail for murder.

And Rhys believed in his son. He'd never give up on him—even if it resulted in his losing the business. She knew what his business meant to him and admired his strength.

Yet the possibility of R.J.'s being acquitted sent an icy shiver up her spine. What would happen to SaraJane then? Even if she and Rhys worked things out between them, that didn't solve the bigger problem.

Rhys had said everything would be okay, and she wanted to believe him. Wanted desperately.

"Hi." Rhys stood in the doorway, a steaming mug in his hands. He was barefoot and wore faded jeans and a plaid flannel shirt that hung unbuttoned in the front. A light dusting of dark hair on his chest tapered to a narrow V below his navel, and just looking at him started her pulse racing.

"I made some cocoa," he said, ambling over. He set the mug on the night table beside the empty foil packet, reminding her that in spite of their heated passion, they had indeed practiced safe sex. Rhys brushed the packet into the wastebasket.

"Marshmallow?" He drew out a tiny bag from the pocket of his flannel shirt.

"Only if they're miniatures." She held out her hand and he emptied the bag into it.

"SaraJane likes them, too," he said. "Guess I'll need to replenish the supply."

The mention of routine things brought a somber expression to Rhys's face. Had that small thought triggered another host of questions? Such as, *Where do we go from here?*

She didn't want to think about that right now. She didn't want any intrusions on their happiness, even if that happiness was momentary.

Which, she knew, all happiness was.

Maintaining the spell he had on her, Rhys sat on the bed, his hip touching hers. He leaned an arm on either side of her and brushed her lips with a velvety kiss.

Her pulse quickened further at his touch, and she knew it wouldn't take two seconds to send her into another frenzy of passion. She brought her arms up to circle his neck, and the sheet slipped down.

Rhys pulled back, swept her with a languid gaze, his

pupils dilated. He ran a fingertip over one nipple, then the other. She shivered.

"You're cold," he whispered, his voice low, sexy.

"I know a good way to warm us both up," she said, pressing her body against his, startled by the contact of her taut nipples and his bare chest.

His eyes sparkled as he bent forward to nibble on her lower lip and then her earlobe. "I never cooled down," he said huskily.

CHAPTER THIRTEEN

RHYS STOOD FOR A MOMENT at SaraJane's bedroom door, watching her sleep. So pure, so sweet, and innocent.

So vulnerable.

The first time he'd seen her, she was little more than a year old, all pink and pretty and smelling of wet diapers, and he'd been struck by an overwhelming surge of protectiveness. He had the same feeling right now, and it had never been more intense.

Man, what a day. He left the door ajar and went to the kitchen, where he chucked a couple of ice cubes into a glass and splashed some vodka on top. Drink in hand, he moved out onto the deck and leaned against the redwood railing.

The sky was pitch-black, with only a few stars winking above the treetops. The wind roared through the pines like a freight train, and he gave an involuntary shiver. A storm was brewing.

Damn, his muscles ached. He rolled his shoulders, easing the stiffness. Rhys had put off thinking about Whitney's revelation, but now that he'd taken her back to the inn and he was alone, he could no longer avoid it.

On one hand, he was relieved to know the reason for her recent withdrawal; on the other hand, he couldn't forget the lies. Realistically, he understood that she'd had no other choice. She'd believed her niece was living with a drug dealer, someone who abused her. Considering that, how could she tell him who she was?

But he should've recognized something wasn't right from the beginning, and now that he knew, it was as obvious as the resemblance between SaraJane and Whitney.

What wasn't obvious was whether the things Whitney had learned about his son and her sister were true. That R.J. was a drug dealer, that he'd treated her sister badly and kidnapped SaraJane. But regardless of everything, he had to give R.J. the benefit of the doubt.

And he had to get some distance. He should have done that immediately, but somehow Whitney had penetrated his barrier. Even though they'd planned to talk, to work things out, they'd made love instead. He'd allowed himself to get involved, and it had influenced his thinking.

He let out a snort.

After all these years, Gannon, you haven't changed. He was still trying for the brass ring—only this time it was platinum.

What exactly was she after? What was her plan now that she no longer saw him as the ultimate villain? He grinned, thinking about the afternoon, coming back into his bedroom and seeing Whitney stretched out on his bed as if that was where she'd always belonged.

The image was stamped indelibly in his mind—how she'd looked waiting for him, anticipating. And such fire inside. Who would've known?

He would have.

He'd known it every time his gaze caught hers and she looked back at him with those transparent blue eyes—eyes that told him there was more than lust in her heart. And he felt the same.

He loved her. Admitted it, for whatever good it might do.

He brought the glass to his lips, refusing to think about the obstacles. Problem was, he *had* to think about them if he wanted solutions.

The biggest difficulty, as he saw it, was that she had another life, a life that she intended to return to when she was finished with her research.

And he'd be the village idiot to think she'd want to give up that life to settle in a place like Estrade. If for some bizarre reason she'd even consider it, how long would it take before she was bored to death? How long before she'd try to get him to do something different?

Five years with Stephanie had pushed him to his limit. Wouldn't the same thing happen with Whitney?

A cold gust of wind forced him inside, where he tossed some logs into the fireplace. Whitney had said she liked his house, but he doubted she liked it enough to move in. He crouched in front of the hearth, poking newspapers under the logs to get the fire going.

You're dreaming, Gannon. Being compatible in bed didn't translate into a life together, and it was unrealistic to even entertain the thought.

After a couple of hours, the fire had died out. Rhys had sat there on the couch all that time, thinking about the situation, testing various scenarios. He sighed and pinched the bridge of his nose. He had no more insight than before. In fact, the more he contemplated, the more useless he felt.

He reached for the phone and punched in the area code for Chicago followed by Luth's number. "Hey, buddy, how's it going?" Rhys asked, attempting to jack up his enthusiasm.

"Got my bike ready?"

"No, it'll be a month or two. Got a part on order."

Luth laughed. "Guess I should've known you wouldn't be calling me after midnight to tell me my bike's ready."

"Right. You got a minute?"

"Hey, no problem, man. What's happening?"

Rhys held back, but after a little small talk, Luth asked about Whitney, and the whole damn thing came out.

Luth didn't see the problem.

"Do what you're always telling me to do," he said.

"Which is?"

"Meet in the middle. Way I see it, the two of you need to get together and talk. I mean, all ya gotta do is decide where you want to live, her place or yours, or maybe both. Man, I'd love an arrangement like that. Why does anyone have to give up anything?"

The muscles in Rhys's shoulders bunched. He had no interest in being a kept man. And with the state of his finances at the moment, that was virtually what he'd be.

"Oversimplification, old pal."

"Only if you want to make things difficult," Luth said. "But then, you always do."

What the hell did that mean? He had problems. The least of which was that he'd fallen in love with a woman he had no business even thinking about.

"Look at it this way," Luth added. "You've got nothing to lose."

Rhys filled his lungs. "Yeah," he said slowly. "Maybe that's true...."

When they finally ended the conversation, they'd decided Luth would come out in a few weeks to see the progress Rhys had made on his bike.

When Rhys's head finally hit the pillow somewhere around 4 a.m., he'd made a decision. Luth was right; he had nothing to lose. He doubted there was much he could do to change things, but he sure as hell was going to try.

TANYA'S PHONE CALL came on the heels of Rhys's early-morning call asking if she'd be interested in a Sunday picnic with him and SaraJane. Whitney had been euphoric; his understanding had taken her by surprise. She'd learned early on that if you screw up, you don't get a second chance. Why was fortune smiling on her now?

"So, Tanya—" she fluffed the pillows behind her head and brought her knees to her chest, tucking the down-filled quilt around her legs "—what are you doing up so early?" Whitney set her watch back on the table next to the bed.

"What do you mean? There's only an hour's difference between Mountain and Pacific time. It's seven already."

Whitney chuckled. She'd never known Tanya to rise that early in her life. "And why are you still in California?"

After college Tanya had become a workaholic. She'd never taken a vacation, never done much of anything other than work. In New York, they'd go to the occasional play, a movie or dinner, but Whitney knew that was the extent of Tanya's social life. The fact that she'd stayed in California for more than a week astonished Whitney.

"That's one of the things I wanted to talk to you about. I've decided to take a couple of extra days. You mind if I stay here? I need a little vacation."

Whitney gasped. "A *what?* Uh, pardon me for a minute." She held the phone out and whacked it a couple times with her hand, then returned it to her ear. "Okay. There was something wrong with the phone. I thought I heard you say 'vacation.'"

"Okay. I deserved that," Tanya said. "But yeah, I need a little time. Besides—" she seemed to be hedging "—I have some things I want to look into—business things. And, well, I just thought as long as I'm here, I could see a little more of the area. Al said he'd show me around."

"Al?"

"Yeah, Al. Your cousin."

"You're joking."

"No, really, I'm thinking of investing in something, and he's going to check it out."

"Okay. Now I get it. It's not a vacation at all." For the last few years, Tanya had talked about doing something different, starting a new career, and maybe this was it. "Fine, stay as long as you want. You know it's okay with me. Besides, I like having someone there."

"Good. Listen, Al tried to call you, but something was wrong with the connection. I think he might have some new information for you. And, oh, yeah, your mother's doctor called, trying to get in touch. She said it was important."

Whitney's fingers tightened involuntarily on the receiver. Important to whom? If her mother didn't care, why should she?

"It really did sound important."

Whitney heaved a sigh of resignation. "Yeah, okay. Thanks for telling me." She'd call the doctor later. Right now she didn't want anything to spoil the picnic with Rhys and SaraJane.

After saying her goodbye to Tanya, Whitney recalled the last meeting with her mother. It had ended in total disaster. In the ten minutes she and her mother were together, they'd had a fight and Whitney had run out, desperate to escape—just as she'd done twelve years ago. Her mother didn't want her help. She never had.

It was too late, just too damned late. And the only emotion Whitney could feel toward either of her parents was a deep abiding anger.

She threw off the quilt, got up and showered, then went to the closet. Rhys had said to dress in layers. It would be cool when they started out, but since they were going to a lower elevation, it would get warmer, especially later in the day. She pulled out a pair of faded jeans and a white tank top, her blue baggy V-neck sweater and tennis shoes.

When she'd dressed, she stood in front of the mirror to do her hair. As she studied her image, she couldn't resist a tiny grin. Her mother would be horrified. So would Brock.

The thought satisfied something perverse in her, and she hoped Brock had listened to the message she'd left on his voice mail last night, saying that she wasn't interested in financing his movie now or in the future and that he needn't worry about talking to Rhys because she'd already done so.

Working on a French braid, she walked to the door and opened it halfway, waiting for her coffee. Wanting to save time, she'd asked that it be brought to her room this morning. She went back to the mirror, wondering if Rhys had told his parents she was SaraJane's aunt. She hoped not, because she really wanted to sort things out with Rhys first.

"I hear you're going on a picnic," Johnny said as he wheeled the cart into her room. "Nice day for it. It's gonna be in the high seventies in Sedona."

Whitney turned around. "That's where we're going." She smiled brightly, covering her discomfort. "Rhys said he knows a perfect spot near some Anasazi ruins."

Johnny nodded. "Rhys is a pretty good tour guide. He spent a bit of time exploring the area when he first moved here. Kinda surprised me at first, how much he likes small-town life. Guess you never know someone as well as you think you do. Not even your own children."

Whitney's stomach plummeted, wondering if the comment was meant for her. But no, she'd noticed before how Johnny's face lit up every time he talked about Rhys, and she could see he meant what he said. He was truly happy Rhys had chosen to live in Estrade.

"You didn't think he'd like it here? What's not to like? It's beautiful and the people are wonderful." She stopped braiding her hair long enough to glance at him. "I felt at home immediately."

"Well, you know…" Johnny stood next to the cart and poured coffee into a delicate china cup.

She smiled, watching his large hands handle the fragile dishes with ease. Hands that were so much like Rhys's.

"I had my doubts for a while," Johnny continued. "Rhys lived in Chicago most of his life, and knowing the success he'd carved out for himself, I guess I figured it'd be kinda hard to go from all that excitement to such a quiet place."

He smiled. "But like I said, he's adapted really well. Loves those motorcycles, you know. But I think he had to experience the other things first to figure out what was important to him."

Johnny was talking about Rhys, yet he could have been talking about her. Finished with her hair, she sat at the small gateleg table and poured a little cream into her coffee. "Rhys seems happy with the choices he's made," she said as Johnny started for the door. *I wish I could say the same.*

Johnny turned with a knowing look. "Making the decision is what matters. It's the decisions that don't work out that help us recognize the right ones."

Whitney nodded. She had a decision to make and it had to be the right one. But how would she know—and who would she hurt?

SARAJANE PRIED a rock from the red-clay soil, using one of several sticks she'd collected, while Whitney relaxed on the patchwork quilt Rhys had spread on the ground. To Whitney's surprise, Rhys had brought all the picnic supplies, including some fried chicken he'd picked up from Gretta the night before.

It had been a wonderful day so far, filled with laughter and fun. They'd hiked and played at Slide Rock, and Whitney had taken dozens of photos, even a few on the timer so they could all be in them.

Finally Rhys had taken them to a place called Red Rock Crossing, and instead of settling in the most popular site, he'd led Whitney and SaraJane down a narrow path alongside the creek to a secluded area where an old mill stood, its giant paddle cracked and silent.

A verdant clearing next to the stream was the perfect spot for a picnic. Rhys had spread the blanket under a towering sycamore tree, near the creek bank where the crimson rock of twin buttes was reflected in the crystal-line water. Tired, Whitney had dropped to her knees on the quilt and that was where she'd stayed.

"Iron," Rhys said matter-of-factly, shoving up the

sleeves of his black knit shirt. "It's the iron in the soil that makes the rock red."

Whitney leaned on her elbows, feet stretched out in front of her. "Thanks, Mr. Geology. But if you don't mind, I think I'll just pretend some magic fairy painted them with her wand."

"I got more." SaraJane plopped a pile of rocks at Whitney's feet. "See?" she said proudly, her chubby fingers sorting through them. "A red one, a black one, and this little one's a geode." She held out a rock that resembled a clump of clay.

Whitney looked askance at Rhys, who lounged beside her on the quilt. Whitney held the clump between two fingers. "How can you tell?"

"'Cause it's round." SaraJane dazzled them with a smile, then skipped off, as happy as any child could be.

Rhys raised his hands, palms up, and shrugged. "Just thought she should know a little about what she's picking up. You never know. I've heard there's gold in them thar hills."

Whitney tossed one of the rocks at his booted feet. "So I hear. Or at least that's what Charley thinks."

"Y'know, speaking of Charley," Rhys said, brushing a red smudge from the knee of his jeans. "The other day, Mabel said he was going to the assayer's office. Maybe he did strike a vein." Rhys shook his head. "Wouldn't that be something after all these years?"

"Well, I have my own opinion about Charley." Whitney peeled a banana. Fruit salad, Rhys had called the bag of loose apples, oranges and bananas. "I think Charley just uses that as a reason to hang around Mabel."

"He really does work the mine, you know." Rhys hooked his hand around hers, brought the banana to his mouth and chomped off half of it. After swallowing, he rolled over to face her. "What if that old reprobate actually did strike the mother lode?" Rhys chuckled. "Maybe I should take lessons from Charley. I could use a strike about now."

His expression shifted from cheerful to pensive, and Whitney guessed he was thinking about the bank loan that had been refused. She'd been thinking about it, too, but she wasn't quite sure how to broach an idea she'd had. Now that he'd brought it up, however...

"You know, there are other ways to get money for your business," Whitney said. At last, the perfect opportunity to do something for Rhys.

"Right." He produced a sarcastic laugh. "Like rob a bank." He shifted to watch SaraJane as she sat on a rock poking at something near her feet.

"Really. I'm serious. There are other ways." She turned to look at him. "I could help."

His expression went cold. "SaraJane!" he called harshly. "Get back over here."

Whitney had never heard him use that tone with SaraJane, and it struck a note of discord within her. When he didn't respond to her suggestion, she decided he might not have understood what she meant, so she went on.

"I mean, *I* could make you a business loan—the money you need for expansion. I also had some ideas about a mail-order catalog—"

"SaraJane, c'mon over here." Rhys bolted to a standing position, hands on his hips. He cleared his throat. "You need more sunscreen." He knelt to pick up the bottle of lotion and glared at Whitney.

"I'm not a charity case, Whitney. I don't need your money."

Oh, jeez! His voice was controlled, but she knew by the set of his jaw that she'd said the wrong thing.

Lord, the man was proud—too proud for his own damn good. But given his change of mood, she didn't pursue her suggestion. She took a soda from the cooler and raised it as if making a toast. "Okay," she said. "But the offer remains open if you ever want to reconsider."

Still kneeling when SaraJane came over, Rhys pulled the little girl close and applied dabs of sunscreen to her nose and cheeks. His motions seemed sharper than usual, and Whitney knew that the festive mood had been broken.

After several minutes of silence, she said, "Talked to your father this morning. He reminds me a lot of you." She was hoping to redirect the conversation so he'd forget what upset him. "Or should I say you remind me of him."

SaraJane ran back to her rocks, but she remained within eyesight as Rhys had told her. He'd trained her well, Whitney thought, wondering how she would've done if she'd had the little girl since she was a year old.

"He said he's happy you've adjusted to life in a small town."

Rhys shrugged. "Yeah. I guess he was worried about that for a while." He gave a short wry laugh. "Frankly, so was I."

He sat down beside Whitney again. "I really respect my dad. My mom, too. Years ago, they made their plans and forged ahead. It took a long time, but they fulfilled their dreams."

Whitney saw a look of regret wash over his face. "Except for all the problems I've given them."

She reached out and gently placed her hand over his. "Your father is very proud of you. His face lights up like a football stadium on homecoming night every time he talks about you.''

Rhys's expression softened. ''Yeah, but I sure don't deserve it. As a kid, I couldn't wait to get away from the neighborhood. We were dirt-poor and I always vowed I'd make something of myself, that I'd do better than they had. I was pretty self-absorbed.''

He shook his head. ''What I didn't realize was that they had mountains of bills from their own parents' illnesses and deaths, and didn't believe in taking handouts. They worked hard for everything they have.'' He stopped for a breath.

''I didn't understand then, but I do now,'' he went on. ''I succeeded in getting out, but I really screwed things up otherwise.'' He hurled a rock into the stream.

''I don't think you should blame yourself for that. I mean, other people, other events, do influence our lives in ways that we don't even know at the time.''

''Maybe so. But ultimately the choices we make are our own. When I married Stephanie, I worked hard to build my career. I was so focused on that I forgot everything else.''

Whitney saw a flicker of pain in his eyes. He blamed himself for the failure of his marriage, and it hurt to talk about it.

But he *had* talked about it, and the fact that he'd opened up to her as much as he had made her spirits soar. He trusted her. In spite of everything, he trusted her enough to share his past, no matter how painful it was.

''I didn't know that Stephanie was having an affair, never even had a clue. I'd seen the relationship my parents had with each other, and it never occurred to me that mine would be any different." His eyes filled with remorse.

"Steph always wanted more. No matter what I did, it wasn't enough. Worse yet, I was blind. I didn't realize how vindictive she was, never imagined she'd turn R.J. against me. Guess I wasn't too bright there."

He snorted. "Hell, she was probably right. It probably *was* my fault. If I hadn't left, maybe R.J. wouldn't be in the trouble he is today." Rhys picked up another rock and flung it into the water.

Unbelievable. Rhys held himself responsible for the failure of his marriage *and* for the mess R.J. had made. "But you said she was having an affair, that she poisoned your son's mind."

"Yeah, but she didn't want the divorce. She was happy with the status quo. Only I couldn't live like that. It was my choice to leave. If I hadn't, if I'd stuck it out..." He stopped, as if he'd said enough.

"But..." Whitney started to say he'd made the right choice, then realized nothing she said would matter. He'd been beating himself up about it for years. No wonder he'd never wanted another serious involvement.

She also knew that, whether he realized or not, he saw SaraJane as his last shot at redemption.

"Poppy, look! It's a snake."

Rhys's head jerked up and his eyes flashed with fear. "SaraJane, don't move an inch. Stand perfectly still," he said in a calm even voice.

In one swift movement, he'd darted to SaraJane's side and plucked her up in his arms. He grabbed a stick of wood from the ground and stood completely still with the stick raised like a club. And Whitney just sat there, frozen in terror.

Then she saw him relax. "Aw, man." He set SaraJane

down and returned to the blanket, slightly short of breath and obviously shaken. "A lizard," he said sheepishly. "Quite common in Arizona and totally harmless."

When SaraJane came over with another load of rocks, she lay on the blanket between them and scrubbed her eyes with tiny fists.

"Getting to be about nap time," Rhys said affectionately.

Whitney watched as Rhys gently removed SaraJane's tennis shoes and socks. Then the little girl snuggled against him and within minutes fell asleep. He brushed the golden curls from her face, and Whitney's heart filled at the sweet poignancy.

SaraJane would never be without love, not if Rhys had anything to say about it.

"She's precious," Whitney said softly.

"Yeah," he agreed, "she sure is. I don't know what I'd do without her." His eyes grew dark.

Remembering her promise to Morgan, Whitney felt her stomach lurch. But things had changed considerably since she'd made that promise. All Morgan had really wanted was for SaraJane to be safe, to be loved. And Lord knows, she certainly was that.

But there was still R.J. A chill settled in Whitney's bones as she confronted the thought that had been half-hidden in the back of her mind, bothering her since Rhys had told her about R.J.

"Rhys," she said tentatively, hating to bring it up. "I'm worried about what'll happen to SaraJane if R.J. is acquitted on the appeal. What do you think he'll do?"

Rhys exhaled as if he'd been holding his breath. He bowed his head. "I don't know. I just don't know, and I've run through that scenario a million times."

"What if R.J. wants to take her away?"

He was silent. Then he shifted his position to move SaraJane onto the pillow beside him. He turned to Whitney, speaking low. "He has a right to do that. It's not what I want him to do, but then it's not my choice to make." He stared at Whitney and said bluntly, "He's her father."

The words were like a knife to the heart. There was no nice way to say it. "Do you think that under the circumstances, R.J. would be fit to take care of her?"

Rhys was slow to answer. "I understand why he got into trouble. I know it doesn't look good. But much of it was beyond his control. He's clean now and I believe he deserves a second chance." Rhys's tone was crisp. "So what's your point?"

"Have you ever considered filing for legal custody yourself?" God, she'd finally said it; now she had to continue. Regardless. "That's what my sister asked me to do."

Rhys looked beyond her as if she wasn't even there. He pressed his lips together, then slowly brought his gaze to hers. His eyes widened and he seemed to be seeing her for the first time.

"That's really why you're here, isn't it?" His tone was incredulous. But then, although his words were whisper-low, he practically spat them at her. "You didn't come *just* to find SaraJane or get to know her. You came to take her away."

He shook his head, his expression unbelieving. "Is that why you so generously offered to lend me money for the business? In payment? Or were the bedroom offerings supposed to suffice?" He shook his head again, his contempt clear. "Man, I should have known."

CHAPTER FOURTEEN

THE SHARP PAIN dead center in Whitney's chest increased as she once again flung clothes into her suitcase. She closed her eyes, reliving that final scene with Rhys. His bitter words echoed in her head, but it was the look on his face, the stark recognition of her betrayal that was embedded in her mind.

They'd driven home from Sedona in terrible silence, and it was clear she couldn't stay at the inn any longer. Thank God SaraJane had slept the whole way.

After the confrontation with Rhys, Whitney's emotions had shut down as if she'd had a lobotomy or a massive dose of novocaine. She'd been like that ever since, and when Albert called saying he wanted to meet her in Phoenix, that he had the birth certificate and some other information to give her, she barely heard a word he'd said.

In a fog, she closed the suitcase and locked it. Rhys's response had cut her to the quick, worse than anything she'd anticipated. It might've been easier to take if he hadn't been so understanding before, talking about how they'd work things out. For a little while, she'd actually believed...

But, good Lord, how could he believe his son would be a fit parent for SaraJane? What on earth was the man thinking? Even if R.J. was acquitted of murder, there were still the drugs. Not to mention his abusive treatment of Morgan.

Besides which, R.J. didn't give a damn about his daughter. It was obvious that Rhys's judgment was flawed where his son was concerned. Well, she wasn't about to leave it to chance. As long as she could draw breath, R.J. would never get his hands on SaraJane.

Rhys had accused her not only of dishonesty, but also of using her money and her body to manipulate him. She squeezed her eyelids shut. She'd never forget the contempt in his voice or the hatred in his eyes.

The room tilted and she placed a hand on the suitcase for support. *Maybe he's right.*

Why had she offered him the loan? She knew how stubborn he was, how proud.

Why had she made love with him when she knew that nothing could come of it? Was there some truth to what he'd said?

Her chin quivered and she fought back tears. If only she'd never grown fond of Rhys. And his family. God, how this was going to hurt them all.

She hauled her packed suitcases to the door, trying to be as quiet as possible. She couldn't face either Johnny or Gretta. She was a fraud—a fraud and a coward—and she couldn't bear to be around when they found out.

With her camera case over one side and her backpack over the other, she grabbed a suitcase and swung open the door. Gretta was coming up the stairs.

"Can I see you for a minute?"

Whitney nodded and set her bags down. She ached for Gretta and Johnny, ached for them all. If there was any other way, God knows, she'd do it. "I'm sorry, Gretta. I'm so sorry I came here under false pretenses—"

Gretta held up a hand. "You don't have to explain. Rhys already did."

Whitney could hardly stand it. Facing Gretta was as painful as telling Rhys. "I need to explain, Gretta, because…well, because I…" Turning her back to the woman, Whitney wrung her hands and blurted out the whole story.

She told Gretta what Morgan had said about Rhys, and that she'd believed him to be the scum of the earth, how she'd made a promise to Morgan, how she felt guilty about everything. She said she couldn't let SaraJane be subjected to the possibility of living with R.J.

When Gretta came up behind her and settled both hands on her shoulders, hot tears slipped silently down Whitney's cheeks.

"I have a confession to make, too," Gretta said, directing Whitney to sit on a chair while she sat across from her.

Whitney sniffed and brushed at her damp cheeks with her knuckles. Gretta didn't seem nearly as upset as Whitney had figured she'd be.

"When you went to Phoenix with Rhys, SaraJane and I brought flowers to your room. She found your journal—and when she handed it to me, it was open. I didn't mean to read it."

Gretta bowed her head in shame, twisting her silver-and-turquoise ring. "I glimpsed the names you'd written, and before I knew it, I'd read some of it. I told myself I was doing it for SaraJane's sake. You see, I've always been worried that her mother might come for her—or even send someone else.

"Anyway, I read only a couple of pages." Gretta

closed her eyes. "I know it was wrong and I've been agonizing about it ever since. So I'm sorry, too."

"I...I don't understand," Whitney mumbled. Was Gretta saying she'd found out Whitney was SaraJane's aunt? And now Gretta was apologizing to her?

"You knew why I was here and didn't say anything?"

Gretta nodded. "I realized it after I read your journal, but I think I knew in my heart before that." She heaved a sigh, as if finally glad to get it off her chest. "I saw how you and Rhys got along," she said softly. "I saw the way he looked at you and how much SaraJane loved you. I guess I hoped that because you and Rhys both love SaraJane, you might learn to love each other. I hoped that everything would work out."

The older woman released another resigned sigh. "I wanted it to be that way. So very much."

Whitney also mourned the loss of that dream. It was something she'd fantasized about more than she wanted to admit. Until Rhys... A dreadful thought struck her.

Maybe Gretta didn't know everything. "Did Rhys tell you I don't believe R.J. should have custody?"

Gretta nodded. "I think you're right." She stood up abruptly, twisted her ring again.

"I know this may sound terrible, but I don't believe my grandson is capable of taking care of SaraJane properly. Even if he gets off, he has too many other problems. I haven't said anything to Rhys, though. The whole situation with R.J. has already taken its toll on him."

Gretta sat on the chair again. "Both Rhys and his sister, Lisa, have seen hard times, and Johnny and I always believed we should do everything we could to help them and the grandchildren, including R.J. But I don't know what we'd do if he wanted to take SaraJane. I do know that Johnny would never fight Rhys on it. It's the one area that we don't talk about, because we disagree on how to handle it."

The words were a profound relief to Whitney. She wasn't as wrong as Rhys had made her feel. But her heart went out to the older woman; Gretta was visibly torn by the dilemma.

"Rhys can't see the whole picture," Gretta continued. "Right now he's hurt. He feels responsible because he wasn't there for R.J., and he believes that's the reason the boy turned out as he did. That's hogwash, of course. There comes a point when people have to take responsibility for their own actions. R.J. is responsible for what he's done. Not Rhys."

"But Rhys believes he is. He also believes that I betrayed him," Whitney said. "And he's right about me. No matter what my reasons were."

Gretta gathered Whitney into her arms, hugging her with warmth and love and forgiveness. "Maybe time will help," Gretta said softly. "If two people love each other, they should be able to solve most any problem."

Oh, how Whitney wanted to believe that. But she knew as well as she knew her way around a camera that forgiveness was the last thing on Rhys's mind.

THE SMALL PLANE was cramped and noisy, and the woman in front of Whitney kept turning around, raising her voice to be heard over the engines. It was an irritation Whitney could have done without.

She'd decided that driving the three hours to Phoenix would give her too much time to think about how she'd hurt Rhys, so she'd left the car at the rental company's office in Flagstaff and caught a shuttle plane. In her haste, she hadn't been able to say goodbye to SaraJane, and all she could think about was what Rhys would tell her niece. Would he tell her the truth? Or the truth as he saw it?

Initially, her promise to Morgan had been her only motivation. But somewhere along the way, she'd lost sight of it. She'd actually allowed herself to believe that maybe, just maybe, she and Rhys and SaraJane could be together. It would have been the perfect solution—one she'd known deep inside would never happen.

Because the truth of it was, marriage scared her to death. She'd seen her parents' example, and most of the families around her. For a while, though, she'd almost believed what Gretta had described.

It wasn't meant to be. She knew that now, and she had to get used to it. She had to be single-minded. She couldn't take the chance that R.J. would ever get custody of SaraJane, and she couldn't count on anyone else to prevent it.

After a rough flight with the four-seater Cessna bouncing in the sky like a Ping-Pong ball, she caught a cab to a hotel near Sky Harbor Airport and waited for Albert.

He'd said he had more information, and if Whitney's memory was correct, he'd gotten it from a girl who lived with R.J. after Morgan had left. But what was so compelling that he had to fly all the way to Phoenix to tell her?

When Albert finally arrived, he barreled into her hotel room waving his briefcase like a flag, then dropped it on the coffee table. He gave Whitney a perfunctory hug and held her at arm's length.

"Don't be offended, cousin, but you don't look so good."

Whitney shrugged away. "And I feel even worse."

She plodded to the phone. "I'll order room service. What would you like?"

"Not hungry," Albert said quickly. "Ate a cardboard sandwich and peanuts on the plane. But a drink would be good." He scanned the room, and spying the small refrigerator, he strode toward it. Whitney motioned that the key was on the bureau.

Although she didn't feel like eating, either, Whitney ordered, anyway. When she finished the call, she stood next to the phone, arms crossed, one hand cradling her chin.

Albert was stretched out on the couch, sipping a gin and tonic, his briefcase open on the table.

"You sure you're okay?" His eyes filled with concern.

Albert was thirty-five, but there was a boyishness about him. His classic all-American features were accented by sandy curls that sprung loose over his forehead.

She nodded. "I'll be fine. Do you know if Tanya's still at my place?" She couldn't bear the thought of being all alone.

"She is, but she's going home tomorrow. Which is why I'm heading back in a couple of hours."

Whitney's eyebrows shot up. "What's that all about?"

"I'm checking something out for her. A business venture we're considering—an Internet company, okay? And if you must know, cousin, we're having a good time in the process. In fact, if the business thing gets going, your friend might even make the break and move out here." As usual he paused for effect before he added, "with me."

Good grief, the last two people in the world she'd ever

imagined together! Tanya and Albert. Her friend was a
no-nonsense person who'd saved every penny she'd ever
made, and Albert was as laid-back as a siesta, and just
as relaxed about his money.

It was an impossible match on any level—yet both
Albert and Tanya seemed willing to try. Maybe she
didn't know either of them as well as she thought. Or
her own fear of personal risk colored everything. She
sighed. Maybe Tanya was right. ''You think that'll
work? You and Tanya, I mean.''

''Never know unless we do it.'' Albert smiled, handing her his drink. ''Here. I'll make another.'' He got up
and gave her a slight push in the direction of the couch.
When he finished making his drink, he sat beside her,
scrutinizing her again. ''You sure you're all right?
Maybe you want to wait with all this. Maybe after you
eat something?''

Whitney shook her head. Might as well get it over
with. Her life would never be the same, anyway, so what
did it matter? She'd wanted custody of SaraJane; now,
according to Albert, they had the evidence that would
clinch it.

According to Willie Atwater, her attorney, the evidence was good enough. He'd left her a message at the
hotel and she'd returned it immediately.

The birth certificate listed the father as ''unknown,''
and even though Morgan had used a phony last name,
she'd listed her correct birth date and used her own first
name and ''Sheffield'' as a middle name. The birth certificate was enough to establish the relationship between
SaraJane and Whitney, and the information Albert had
collected about R.J. was enough to convince any judge
he was an unfit parent. It was how all this would affect
Rhys that worried her.

"I called Atwater for you. Did he get back to you?"

Whitney nodded. "Uh-huh. Willie said he'd prepare the papers to petition the court for custody. Rhys and I will both be notified of the court date." Whitney gave Albert a sharp look. "Let's see the birth certificate."

He handed the copy to her and Whitney held it up, noting that SaraJane had been born in New Mexico. No wonder Albert had difficulty locating it. "Well, guess that's all we can do for now, huh?"

Albert sat back, one arm slung over the back of the couch.

"Pardon me, but I can't help noticing that you're not jumping up and down with excitement." His soft brown eyes questioned her. "Isn't this what we started out to do?"

Slumped bonelessly on the loose pillows, Whitney stretched out her legs on the coffee table and dropped her head to one side to look at him. "Yep. It sure is."

"Well? How come we're not ecstatic?"

There was a knock on the door and she got up to let the bellman in with the food. In less than two seconds, Albert was at her side.

"Smells good. Maybe I am a little hungry."

Whitney glared at him.

He backed off, holding up his hands. "Hey, I only said it smells good."

That coaxed a reluctant grin from her. Albert really was a sweetheart and she was glad he was here. Glad to have someone on her side. She sat at the table to remove the metal covers on the plates, then motioned for Albert to sit across from her. "Okay, help yourself," she said, pointing to the French fries. "I can't eat them all, anyway."

The phone rang. It was her attorney.

"Hi, Willie," she said, not making any effort to sound more cheerful than she felt. "What's going on?"

Atwater's low voice resonated through the phone wires. Usually she found it soothing. Not so today. Nothing could make her feel better.

"I filed the motion, but I wasn't the only one. Your guy in Estrade filed one, too."

Whitney froze. "I don't understand."

"Uh, let me see. Here it is. Rhys Gannon, who claims to be the baby's grandfather. Claims he's had physical custody since the child was little more than a year old. Abandonment by the mother and subsequent incarceration of the father."

Rhys filed for custody? He'd just told her he wouldn't do that to R.J. What on earth...?

"What does it mean? What do we have to do?" Moreover, what did she *want* to do?

A week ago she would've been deliriously happy if Rhys had even expressed an interest in gaining custody.

A glimmer of hope struggled for life inside her. Maybe there was still a chance? But remembering the hatred in his eyes, the bitterness in his words, she couldn't imagine anything of the sort.

And it wouldn't change the fact that if R.J. was acquitted, he could come for SaraJane and Rhys would let her go. If Rhys had custody, it would be the same as if his son did.

That had to be it. Rhys was filing to protect his son's rights.

"We continue," Willie said. "Don't know how much leverage we have at the moment. Guess I need to do a little more research. You know I haven't been involved in this kind of thing for years."

"I know, Willie, and I thank you for taking it on."

William Atwater was her contract lawyer, and she'd only used him for those purposes. When she'd asked him to help her out, it was because he was the only person she could think of on short notice. "What do you think?"

"We have the birth certificate and we can show relationship. Since the father's name is not listed, they'll have to establish paternity before they do anything else. If it's established, things'll be more difficult for us."

"How's that?"

"A grandparent with physical custody, one who's able to care for the child well, would be seen favorably by the court. It's a stable environment, and any judge will look at what's best for the child. We have to prove you're in a position to do it better, and that it's in the child's best interests to live with you.

"We'll have to show reason why Gannon *isn't* the best person to have custody."

Whitney's breath caught. "You mean...discredit Rhys."

"Whatever it takes. Got any ideas?"

"I couldn't do that. I couldn't say things against Rhys."

"Believe me, he'll do it to you. And to be very frank, he might have a pretty good case. Your life-style, with all your traveling, isn't exactly conducive to raising a child. Not only do we need to show chinks in his armor, we also need to show how much better you can make life for your niece."

But she planned to change her working schedule, at least cut back on the travel.

"What about the baby's maternal grandparents?" Willie asked. "Can they stand behind you to support the family unit?"

Whitney squeezed her eyes shut and clutched the

phone to her ear. Finally she said, "My father's a drunk. A very rich drunk, but a drunk nonetheless. Yeah, we've got a lot of support there," she said hollowly. "In fact, the last time I saw him was at Morgan's funeral, and he wasn't sober then, either." The irony of it all hit her, and she fought the urge to dissolve in a hysterical fit of laughter—or maybe tears. Instead, the pain of the past came tumbling out.

"And while we're at it, let's call my mother, too. She's in a substance-abuse center. After thirty years of pills and booze, she tried to off herself. My parents haven't had a real marriage since I was a baby, and I doubt whether they even had one then. Let's see, their child-rearing philosophy consists of shipping children off with the nanny, the maid, or to boarding school, anywhere out of sight.

"And if the children get in the way or, God forbid, act like children, well, that's taken care of by locking them in the basement or closet."

Her body started to shake. In a blur of pain and regret, Whitney barely felt Albert's hand on her shoulder as he pried the phone from her hand.

"Hi, Mr. Atwater, it's Albert Evans." He nodded. "Yes, we spoke yesterday. Listen, I think it might be better if Whitney called you back later."

He searched his pocket for a pen. "Okay, shoot." Albert sent Whitney an understanding glance as he scribbled a number on a hotel tablet and hung up.

Whitney wrenched herself from his hold, threw herself facedown on the bed and buried her head under a pillow. Albert sat next to her, rubbing her shoulders. She stayed like that for a long time, until she finally grew numb.

Sitting upright, she brushed the hair from her face and gave Albert an apologetic look. But she was unable to hide the hopelessness she felt. "I never summed it up quite so succinctly before," she said in a faint voice.

"Hey, sometimes it's good to get it all out. Then you can forget about it and go on with your life."

A strange urge to laugh bubbled up. "Yeah, I thought I'd done that when I left home twelve years ago. I made a life for myself, quite successfully, too." She shook her head. "Now look at me."

She bolted to her feet, stalked to the table and picked up the remains of her drink, tossing it back in one swallow.

"Hey, you look pretty good to me, and if we weren't related…" He clicked his tongue and gave her a thumbs up.

Grateful for Albert's light banter, she sank onto the couch, feeling as if she'd been torn apart and hastily glued back together—but the glue was still wet and one small nudge was enough to make her fall apart.

"I guess you're in love with him, huh?" Albert asked as he ate some cold French fries.

Whitney did a double take. "Why do you say that?"

"I saw the expression on your face when you thought you might have to testify against him."

"But it's the truth. I couldn't discredit him. He's a wonderful person, kind, affectionate, loving…" Her voice softened as she spoke. "And he's devoted to SaraJane. She couldn't ask for a better father."

Albert's grin broadened into a one-hundred-watt smile. Before taking a sip of his drink, he raised his glass. "Point made."

RHYS TUCKED SARAJANE into bed and headed toward the garage. On the way, he stopped at a window in the living room and listened to the wind howling outside like a coyote baying at the moon. It was an eerie lonely sound that reflected how he felt. Cold and alone. A few flakes of snow began to fall.

He allowed his mind to drift, fantasizing Whitney and SaraJane curled up with him under thick afghans in front of the fireplace on a snowy day, sipping cocoa with tiny marshmallows bobbing in their cups.

He willed the image away. It was pointless. The die was cast and no amount of wishing would change it.

Whitney had come to Estrade with one purpose. To gain custody, to take SaraJane away with her. And it appeared she was going to do everything she could to make that happen.

And dammit, he'd do whatever he could to stop her.

He flicked on the lights in the stairwell and descended to the garage. A week ago he'd had other plans for his collection of vintage motorcycles, plans that didn't include selling the bikes it had taken him years to accumulate.

At the bottom of the steps he switched on the garage lights. Now, instead of extending the shop to accommodate the collection, he'd need to sell some of the inventory to pay the attorney representing him in the custody suit.

His attorney had painted a grim picture of what would happen in court. With R.J.'s background, the boy wouldn't stand a chance in the custody battle against Whitney, and the attorney had recommended Rhys file for himself.

He'd tried to call R.J. a couple of times to see if he agreed, but as usual, his son hadn't been available. And because it all had to happen quickly, Rhys hadn't had time to think, much less okay it with R.J. Better that he see him face-to-face, anyway, to tell him what was going on.

R.J. would understand because there was no other choice. Rhys felt a jolt of anger, and he drew back a fist and punched the leather chaps hanging next to the door. Bitterness pumped through his veins.

Dammit! Dammit all to hell! He sent a flurry of punches into the wall.

Spent, his chest heaving, his knuckles throbbing, he sagged against the doorjamb, surveying the collection. How much did the attorney say he needed for a down payment? Was that one Norton or two?

He hated to sell any of these bikes. This was the only part of his old life he'd retained. The only good part.

But he couldn't think about any of that now. He had to stand by his family, and whatever it took would be worth it. He only wished he hadn't made such a fool of himself in the process.

THE NEXT DAY Rhys waited at the prison door for the guard to let him into the room where he could talk to R.J. Except during their last visit, R.J. hadn't been receptive to much of anything.

God, he hated this place, hated seeing his son locked up like an animal. Most of all, he couldn't fathom that R.J. might be here for the rest of his life.

When R.J. sauntered out, Rhys was struck by the resemblance between his son and how he himself had looked at that age. A carbon copy, and yet his son was a total stranger to him. He didn't even know the boy.

But he had only himself to blame. If he'd demanded custody, demanded visitation... True, he'd had to work seventy-hour weeks to establish himself, and there didn't seem to be much point in just leaving R.J. with a sitter.

And it was also true that Steph had dragged R.J. all over the globe, so Rhys didn't know where his son was most of the time, and yeah, he was young and stupid—but that didn't make it any less his fault.

If he'd hauled Stephanie's ass into court back then, maybe R.J. wouldn't be in the trouble he was today.

R.J. sat opposite him, slumped on the straight-backed chair. His cobalt-blue eyes were shuttered by long black lashes, and as usual, Rhys couldn't tell what was going on inside the boy.

"Something major happened since I was here last." Rhys didn't think he could stand replaying the scenario; it hurt too much. He moved on. "Whitney, the woman I told you about before? I found out she's SaraJane's aunt."

R.J. perked up.

Good. He'd hit a nerve. Maybe it would make his son take an interest in his own life again. "The baby's mother, Morgan, is Whitney's sister." Correcting himself, he added, "I'm sorry. *Was* her sister. Morgan died a few months ago."

R.J. pinned him with a gaze as hard as marble, emitting no emotion whatsoever. Nothing. No trace of feeling for the mother of his child.

"Where's the kid now?"

"Still with me," Rhys said, a little relieved. For the first time since he'd been incarcerated, R.J. had asked about his child. "And I intend to keep her there. Which is why I came down to see you. I need you to consent to blood tests."

R.J. was silent. The news about Morgan must've finally sunk in, Rhys decided. He wished he could comfort him, but he knew R.J. would reject that, too. "I'm sorr—"

"Blood tests! What for?"

Okay. R.J. didn't need condolences. Maybe he already knew. "Whitney promised SaraJane's mother that she'd find the girl and raise her." R.J. made no visible response, so Rhys cut to the chase. "She's filing for custody."

Nothing. Not even a blink.

"Uh, anyway, I talked to an attorney and we figured the only way around it is for me to file for custody—because I'm the grandfather and SaraJane has been with me for two years. It needs to be done quickly, so the attorney has already petitioned the court on my behalf."

R.J. bolted to his feet and the metal chair flipped backward. "You already did this? You hired an attorney?" he spat out the words. "I thought you didn't have the money to spring me from this dung hole, but now you have enough money to hire someone to get custody of the brat."

Rhys flinched. He'd seen R.J. like this before, when he'd been found guilty. He'd excused his behavior then, because he had good reason to be angry and bitter.

But this was different. Way different.

Rhys glanced at the guard, who was already on his way over, and motioned for R.J. to sit so they could finish. R.J. yanked the chair back to the counter and held his hands up to the guard, indicating he'd make no more disturbances.

Rhys's blood surged through his veins like water from a burst dam. He'd forgiven R.J. many things, blaming himself for much of it, but where SaraJane was concerned, no one, *no one,* was going to hurt her.

Clenching his fists, Rhys said through gritted teeth, "I don't have the damn money. I still have to sell some things to get it. Now, sit your ass down and listen. You need to have a blood test to show paternity. Without it, we'll lose custody.''

R.J. drummed his fingers on the counter, his gaze cold and calculating. Finally he leaned toward Rhys. ''Well, tell you what, Daddy dearest,'' he said in a menacingly low voice, ''after you left the last time, I did a little research.''

He paused, drawing out his words. ''The prison has a great library, you know. Anyway, since you'd talked about your photographer friend being famous and all, I checked her out. *People* magazine did a story on her about a year ago. Did ya know that?''

Rhys stared blankly. R.J.'s words were filled with so much venom.

''Yeah, nice story about her jet-set life—the celebrity photographer who does all these photos of the rich and famous. Nice story about her wealthy family, too. So I got to thinking.'' He paused to lean in, speaking low. ''Let me tell you something. For a little blow, I can get any information I want. Some dudes here have connections and they'll do anything for some primo—or cash.'' He gave a contemptuous laugh, his voice rising. ''D'ya know your girlfriend's parents are drunks? Did ya know that?'' His eyes sparkled with excitement. ''And now I find out that little whore Izzy had a fortune behind her and never said a word. Hah!''

R.J. stopped. A thin smile appeared as he waited for Rhys's reaction.

Rhys steeled himself against R.J.'s outburst. He was a kid, a kid whose whole life was in the trash. The boy's response was defensive, self-protective. That had to be it.

''What's your point?'' Rhys finally asked, struggling to maintain what tiny shred of control he had left.

"The point, Daddy dearest, is that your little Ms. Whitney and her family have tons of bucks I'm sure they'd be willing to part with in order to get custody of that brat."

The smile became a malevolent grin. "Probably enough to get me out of this hole and enough to start a new life in another country." He paused. "Maybe Mexico or Brazil?" He slapped a hand on the counter. "Better yet, the French Riviera."

Rhys launched himself to his feet, stumbling back as he did so. His face burned and his gut ached. He felt as if he'd just been kicked in the groin. He couldn't draw a full breath.

"What's the matter, Pops? I think it's a pretty good exchange. The kid'll have a good life and so will I. I'd even repay you for the lousy attorney you hired."

R.J. rose to face Rhys, leaning forward, hands spread on the counter, his face as close to the glass as he could get.

"So, no blood tests," he hissed through clenched teeth. "Just tell the broad that for the right amount of money, she can have the kid." He rolled his eyes. "Say we start with a mill. Yeah," he said. "Kinda like a settlement. My attorney fees and a million bucks oughtta do it."

R.J. motioned for the guard. "Get back to me on it, Pops." His mouth twisted into a mocking grin. "I'll be waiting."

CHAPTER FIFTEEN

TWO DAYS LATER Rhys still hadn't heard from his attorney. So far he'd found nothing they could use to cement their case. All they had was Rhys's unsupported statement that he was the paternal grandfather and that he'd had physical custody of SaraJane for two years.

He was tired. Damn tired. He hadn't slept more than a few hours each night. He hated that he wasn't in control and all he could do was wait. Unless they came up with something, the outlook was bleak.

And to complicate matters, every time he looked at SaraJane, he saw Whitney. Doubt consumed him. When he wasn't thinking of Whitney, he was remembering R.J.'s words—and the contemptuous look on his face. Whitney had been right. Even if R.J. was acquitted, he wasn't capable of taking care of SaraJane.

But he, the child's grandfather, damn well was!

Whitney had left immediately after their last meeting, then she'd called the inn with a Phoenix hotel number in case anything came up involving SaraJane.

At first he'd been furious at her deceit, but when he'd finally managed to really think about it, he couldn't deny she had every right to see SaraJane, every right to be concerned about her welfare. And it would be unfair to keep SaraJane from being part of her mother's family.

The child had grown to love Whitney, and his heart stopped every time SaraJane asked when she was coming back. But his feelings were so raw he couldn't an-swer her.

Whitney had led him down the garden path, and like a besotted fool, he'd willingly followed.

She'd used him. But what really galled him was that he'd trusted her. The lady was hell-bent on getting cus-tody, no matter who she hurt in the process. And he hadn't even seen it coming.

He poked absently at the fire. He had to do something; he couldn't just sit around and let the attorneys make all the decisions.

He'd never felt so ineffective.

He laughed hollowly. The joke was on him. He'd been protecting R.J.'s interests, and all his son cared about was money. Only a cold-blooded monster would sell his own child.

A new fear replaced the old. What if R.J. contacted Whitney with his offer? Would she take him up on it?

What would Rhys's options be then? Right now, he had no options. Without blood tests, without a birth cer-tificate or marriage license, he couldn't even prove he was SaraJane's grandfather.

Despair threatened, but in the middle of that despair, an idea struck. He dragged himself to the phone and punched the number for the inn. He wasn't going to *let* things happen, he had to *make* them happen. Allowing Stephanie to take charge of R.J.'s life was a mistake he couldn't correct now, but he could make a difference where SaraJane was concerned.

''Mom, hi. Sorry to call so late. Thanks for watching SaraJane last night, I really needed the time to think.'' He paused, hoping his parents didn't have plans. ''I have to go into Phoenix tomorrow and I wondered if you could keep her there for another night.''

"Of course," Gretta answered. "Is anything wrong?"

His mother sounded tired. Both his parents had been through so much with him and R.J., and now this. Yet they never complained. They carried on, doing whatever was necessary to support their family. A lump of gratitude formed in his throat.

"No, Mom. I just need to work some things out. Do you have the number for the hotel where Whitney's staying?"

He waited while his mother put the phone down and came back with the number, no questions asked.

"Mom..." Rhys paused. He wanted to let her know how much he loved her, appreciated all she'd done for him, but he couldn't get words around the tightness in his throat. "Thanks."

Ten minutes later he was out the door, and two and a half hours later he was at Whitney's hotel. It was midnight.

STARTLED FROM SLEEP by a knock at her door, Whitney glanced at the clock on the nightstand. What the...? Who on earth would show up at this hour? Albert had returned to California and she didn't know another soul in Phoenix. Maybe her cousin had forgotten something or missed his flight.

She rolled off the bed and threw on her blue satin robe. Peering through the peephole, she was astounded to see Rhys standing on the other side. She ran her hands through her hair once before she pulled open the door.

He stood for a moment, uneasy, his eyes avoiding hers. She gestured for him to come in, then moved aside and closed the door. She couldn't imagine why he was here—unless something had happened to her niece.

"Is SaraJane okay?" she asked urgently.

"She's fine. She's staying with the folks tonight."

Worry was etched in his face, and he looked as if he hadn't slept for days. But why was he here?

"Can I take your jacket?" she asked perfunctorily, not having any idea what to do next. What she *wanted* to do was rush into his arms and tell him everything was going to be okay, just as he'd said to her last week.

But everything hadn't been okay then, and it wouldn't be now—not for any of them.

He hesitated, his expression uncertain. Finally he shrugged out of his leather jacket and handed it to her.

"Whitney. I don't know where to begin, even though I've been over everything a hundred times." He stalked to the minibar and yanked out a bottle of mineral water. He held it up. "D'you mind?"

Hanging his jacket in the closet, she turned to him and shook her head. "Sorry, I should've offered."

Rhys unscrewed the cap, put the bottle to his lips and drank half the contents. Then he set the bottle on the coffee table, took Whitney's hand and led her to the couch, where he tugged her down next to him. "We need to talk."

His pain was evident, and in the darkness of his eyes, she saw something else. Fear. A deep and desperate fear.

He clasped both her hands between his, tension vibrating between them. "I've had some time in the past few days to think about what's happened, and I've concluded that, as two adults, we should be able to talk things over and arrive at some solutions." His voice was firm, as if he'd practiced what he wanted to say.

Anguish seared Whitney's soul to see him like this. But she kept coming back to the same conclusion—she had to separate her feelings about Rhys from her need to gain custody of SaraJane.

But the two were inextricably entwined. Did Rhys feel the same? The way he touched her hand, the tenderness in his eyes when he looked at her, said he did. But perhaps that was only her wishful thinking.

She waited, her heart in her throat, for him to continue. *Please, please love me like I love you. Tell me something I need to hear.*

"I realize you had a reason for doing what you did. I guess if I'd been in your shoes, I might have done the same thing." He withdrew his hand, as if it was too painful to continue touching her.

"I can't say I'm proud of the fact that I didn't see it coming. I guess I was too concerned with my own needs at the time." He raked a hand through his hair, stood, grabbed the mineral water and guzzled the rest.

He began to pace, talking slowly and precisely. "I realize that as SaraJane's aunt, you have a right to see her, and she has a right to know her mother's family. It would be completely selfish on my part not to acknowledge that. Most importantly, it would be unfair to SaraJane."

"Rhys—" Whitney wanted to tell him how sorry she was. She wanted to tell him that her feelings for him were real, despite the circumstances that had brought them together.

"Please." He held up a hand, then laughed nervously. "I'm having a tough time saying this as it is." He dropped into the armchair across from her and leaned forward.

"We both love SaraJane and want the best for her. Therefore we should be able to work things out. So I propose we agree to a method that will be satisfactory to all of us."

He gazed warily at her. "I now believe you're right

about R.J. I don't think he'd be the best person to raise SaraJane. Even if he's acquitted.''

Whitney listened in shock. Good Lord, did he really believe that? Was there hope for them, after all?

''I don't intend for him to ever have the option of custody.''

He hesitated and her heart went out to him. What had it cost him to admit that?

''But I still believe it would be wrong to take SaraJane from the people she loves and the only life she's ever known, just because you made a promise to her mother. Her mother couldn't know what kind of life she has with me.''

His eyes pleaded his case. ''You said yourself that Morgan thought SaraJane was with R.J. And I can understand her concern and yours. But now that you know she's with family who love her and would allow you whatever visitation you wanted, it would be cruel to take her away.''

Whitney's heart bottomed out. ''Visitation?''

''Yes,'' Rhys answered, a spark of hope in his eyes. ''You could see her whenever you chose. We could work out a visitation schedule, whatever's best for SaraJane.''

Whitney felt the blood drain from her face. She sprang to her feet and turned away. God, what had she thought? That he'd say he loved her? That he'd suggest they get married and live happily ever after?

It was ridiculous, a fantasy.

So why did she feel such a letdown?

Facing him, she saw the expectant look, the hope, and it hit her that any disappointment she'd had was minuscule compared to what he must be going through. He'd cared for SaraJane since she was little more than a year old; he'd been both father and mother to her, changed his life to accommodate raising her in the best way he could. And that included Gretta and Johnny, who thought the sun rose and set on their great granddaughter.

What did she have to equal that? Love, yes. Money, yes. And that was about the extent of it.

Still, there was no guarantee that Rhys wouldn't turn SaraJane over to R.J. if he was released. The only fool-proof way to prevent it was to gain custody herself. Just as she'd promised Morgan.

"I'll have to discuss it with my attorney," she said, fighting to stay detached, or at least appear detached.

Rhys's face fell into hard lines.

"I really couldn't make a decision like that without legal consultation."

"Then there's always the option of joint custody," he said.

Whitney stared blankly, her mind putting words into his mouth, wanting desperately to hear him say, *And then there's always the option that you and I admit we're in love and we raise SaraJane together.*

"You know. Two families have equal time." He poked at the rug with the toe of his boot, then removed a tiny piece of lint from his black turtleneck sweater, his eyes avoiding hers as he said, "I don't believe that's best for SaraJane, though. And I think we all want what's best for her."

"Of course we do, Rhys," Whitney practically whispered. "I'll talk to my attorney and he'll get back to you."

Rhys was silent, and when he didn't make any move to leave, she asked, "Is there something else?"

"Yes. How long will you be at the hotel?"

"I'm leaving for California tomorrow at noon."

"I'll wait to hear from you, then. I'm in room 227."
And then he was gone.

For a long time afterward, Whitney paced the room, her nerves stretched to the breaking point. Rhys's scent still lingered, reminding her that he'd forgotten the jacket that she'd hung in the closet. He'd come back for it, she was sure, and if not, she'd ask the desk clerk to give it to him the next day.

She reached into the closet, took the jacket from the hanger and slowly brought it to her chest. She inhaled deeply. Her stomach pitched. Tears threatened. Forcing them back, she sank onto the couch. What was the answer?

Maybe she *should* drop her bid for custody and arrange some kind of visitation with Rhys. If she did that, she could at least hold on to a thin thread of hope that things might work out between them. But every time she thought about spending her life with Rhys, fear of another kind crowded in.

Cradling the jacket as if it were a baby, she went to her suitcase and pulled out a photograph she'd taken of SaraJane and Rhys together. She stared at it. She loved them both.

Her own life was empty by comparison. The wealth of love in Rhys's family was something she'd longed for but had never believed in. It existed only in stories, only in the movies. It wasn't real life for her—she'd never known anything like it.

But it was real for them. And she was about to destroy it.

How could she think about tearing them apart? If Rhys had custody of SaraJane, shouldn't she be comfortable with that? Why did she have to pursue custody herself?

Because she could give SaraJane a mother's love. She could watch her grow and be part of her life, giving her the love and support every child needs.

The love she and Morgan had never had.

But so could Rhys.

The difference was, he'd been doing it all along.

She flashed on the times they'd been together. Remembered the happiness, the adoration in Rhys's eyes when SaraJane ran to him, the raw fear when he thought SaraJane was in danger. And she'd frozen. If it had been up to her and there really had been a snake that day, she wouldn't have been able to protect the child.

Oh, God. Pain welled in her chest for Rhys and in that instant she knew. She couldn't do it.

No matter how much it hurt her to leave SaraJane with Rhys, that was the only answer. The tears she'd been holding back began to fall at the thought of losing both of them—and at the thought of being alone.

She would probably always be alone, she realized. But she couldn't tear others' lives apart to assuage her own loneliness. She set the jacket aside, then placed the photo on the nightstand and sat down on the bed to read the notes Albert had left her.

THE NEXT THING she knew, the ringing phone jarred her from sleep, and it took a minute to orient herself. She wasn't in her comfortable room at the Estrade Inn and she wasn't at home.

Groggy, she threw off the papers lying across her chest and reached for the receiver. Her senses went on alert when she remembered it could be Rhys wanting his jacket.

"Yes? I mean, hello," she answered, her voice husky with sleep.

"Whitney, Willie here. Hope you're up for good news this morning."

She wrestled herself to a sitting position against the headboard. "Right now I could use some good news," she said, greatly disappointed that it wasn't Rhys on the line. She glanced at the clock. Maybe he'd still come for the jacket—if he hadn't already gone back to Estrade.

"You may know this already if you've read the papers Albert brought you."

Albert had said the information in the papers might be important and that he'd faxed copies to Willie. "I started reading them last night but didn't finish. I fell asleep. What should I know?" she asked, attempting to rouse herself.

Albert's scrawled notes were difficult to read. Most were disjointed summaries concerning the two years of Morgan's life, including an interview with R.J.'s next girlfriend. Another entry was about how Morgan had tried to get her mother to help her; apparently Kathryn never did. Which was no surprise. But why, oh, why hadn't Morgan called Whitney? She would've dropped everything to help her.

"So far, I haven't read anything pertinent."

"It's toward the end," Willie said. "What it says may be just what we need to dispute Gannon's paternity."

Whitney's back went rigid. "What're you saying?"

"When you have a minute, look at the entries about three-fourths of the way through. The dates are right around the time when your niece would have been conceived. Apparently your sister and this Gannon guy weren't sleeping together anymore."

He paused and she heard him drag deeply on a cigarette. Willie thrived on coffee and cigarettes.

"Then there are two entries detailing how he convinced her to sleep with other guys to finance his habit. The woman didn't know who the baby's father is, but said she was pretty certain it wasn't R.J."

Whoa... Whitney felt as if the breath had been knocked out of her. Stunned, she gathered the papers into her lap and leafed through the part Willie had mentioned. "I still don't know what it means, Willie. What if this woman doesn't know what she's talking about?"

"What it means is that we can get a court order to do blood tests. DNA if necessary. We'll do whatever it takes. If we're lucky, this guy R.J. won't prove to be the father. That will cinch custody for you, and it shouldn't take too long to do it."

"And if it proves that he is?"

"We'll be no worse off than we are now. The fact that he forced her to sleep with other guys will prove he's unfit to have custody, anyway."

"But it's SaraJane's grandfather who's filing for custody."

"Right. And to hedge our bets, we're getting some background on him, too. Looks like he might've been involved in that junk-bond scandal in Phoenix a few years back."

Whitney felt as if she was on a speeding train with no hope of getting off. "I don't think so," she said. "He told me he left his job when he suspected something wasn't right."

"Doesn't matter. If we can create doubt about his character, that's going to help."

Her head swam. "So what's next?" she asked, still trying to sort it out. It was near impossible to get beyond the fact that SaraJane's father might be some nameless stranger who'd paid for sex with Morgan. Or that her sister had deliberately gone to her grave with such a secret. Yeah, Whitney found it tough to be elated at Willie's so-called good news.

"What's next is you get what you want. Custody. Instantly."

RHYS HAD SPENT half the night wearing down the floor in his hotel room. At 4 a.m. he'd decided a walk outside might clear his head, and then discovered he didn't have his jacket.

But he couldn't disturb Whitney that early in the morning and remembering her plane didn't leave till noon, decided he'd get the jacket later. And he could see her again.

By six he'd been to the hotel restaurant for breakfast and was back half an hour later. He resumed his pacing. He'd spent the entire night trying to figure out how to make things work out for all of them.

Shared custody and/or visitation seemed reasonable, and he assumed Whitney would eventually agree. It was the only logical thing to do. Except that Whitney had to consult her attorney.

But that wasn't what was eating at him. They should be able to work something out with SaraJane easily enough. What bothered him was that whatever arrangement he came up with still didn't seem satisfactory.

That Whitney would go back to California or New York and he'd only see her when she came to get SaraJane, or when he did likewise, wasn't good enough. Last night he'd forced himself to face it: he wanted Whitney *in* his life. Not just passing through.

Last night when he'd looked into her eyes, he couldn't

find the words for what he wanted to say. He kept hearing the voice inside telling him he had nothing to offer her, nothing that would make her want to spend her life with him. He couldn't expect her to give up a life filled with luxury and excitement. And not once had she said she loved him.

What would she think if he went to her now and professed his love? For all he knew, she always operated in the same way. Another assignment, another love affair. Except that he didn't believe it, not for one second.

He knew what kind of person Whitney was, and she wasn't the kind to fall into bed with just anyone. He'd known it from the beginning. Just maybe her feelings went deeper than she was willing to admit.

In ten minutes he'd showered and shaved. Not much of an improvement, he decided, seeing the dark circles under his eyes. He combed his wet hair straight back and debated whether to call first or just go to her room and blurt it all out.

Surely the lack of sleep had affected his brain. Right now it seemed even the simplest decision was hard to make. But it had been that way ever since she'd come into his life.

What would happen if he told her his feelings? If she rejected him, he'd be in the same situation he was now—only with a bruised ego. Was that what he was protecting? His damned ego? Was that what his reluctance was all about?

The truth was there, staring him in the face. An ugly reflection in the mirror. He was a coward. Because love was all about risk. And about trust.

If he wanted a future with Whitney, he'd have to take the risk. He'd have to trust his heart to another one more time.

If she cared about him as he did for her, they could work out the rest of it. Luth was right—no one had to give up anything. Maybe together they *could* have it all. One thing was certain. He'd never know if he didn't talk to her.

He was out the door. Impatience overtook him as he waited for the elevator, so he bolted up the fire stairs and, four floors later, stood at the door to her room, sweating and out of breath, his heart hammering.

Damn, he was nervous and excited, both at once.

He glanced at his watch, then rapped, lightly at first. Then harder.

Nothing.

Nine o'clock. She couldn't have gone yet. He headed to the phone at the end of the hall next to the elevator and called her room number. No answer. He left a voice mail message and hung up.

Maybe she was in the shower. He marched to the elevator, deciding to leave a message at the front desk as well, asking her to call his room as soon as possible.

With that done, he walked back to his room and waited.

And waited.

At ten he called her again and let it ring. Finally an answer. His heart leaped.

''This is the housekeeper. I'm sorry, no one's here now. They checked out and we're just here cleaning.''

When? When had she checked out? Had she even received his message? Immediately he called the desk.

''Yes, Mr. Gannon, I was about to call to tell you there's something for you at the desk. It's a jacket on a hanger. You can pick it up anytime.''

''Did Ms. Sheffield in room 625 check out?''

''I'm sorry, sir, I can't give you that information.''

"Damn." He banged the wall with the flat of his hand.

"Sir, that's the policy."

"Sorry, I wasn't swearing at you." Rhys gathered his composure. "I left a message for Ms. Sheffield earlier. Can you tell me if she got it?" A silence ensued, as if there might be some question about giving out *that* information, too. Finally the clerk said he'd look.

"There are no messages from you in the box for room 625, Mr. Gannon."

Rhys lowered the phone, his energy drained. She'd gotten his message and left, anyway. He hung up, then waited, letting the disappointment settle before he called the inn.

After the perfunctory hellos and asking about Sara-Jane, he told his mother he'd be home in a couple of hours. "Tell Dad I'll go right to the shop, so he can plan to go home then."

"Oh, one other thing before you hang up, honey."

Rhys hoped she wasn't going to ask about Whitney, because he didn't have it in him to even talk about her.

"You had a call this morning from your attorney, and he asked that you get back to him as soon as you can."

Rhys released a deep sigh. God, he was tired.

"Is everything okay, honey?"

For his mother's sake, he feigned a cheerful tone. "Things are fine, Mom. I'll tell you more when I get back."

But things weren't fine. Not at all. Not with Whitney gone. He called his attorney.

"Court-ordered blood tests?" Rhys was dumbfounded.

"It was inevitable, anyway, in order to establish your son's paternity."

"I know that. But what's *their* purpose?"

"Apparently paternity is being disputed."

Rhys scoffed. It was ludicrous. What did they hope to prove now? Paternity was something he'd never questioned. Even if Morgan hadn't willingly given R.J. the baby, there'd never been any question about paternity.

Good God, R.J. didn't want his own kid, much less someone else's. Then he remembered R.J.'s face—and his last words.

A stab of pure unadulterated fear sliced through Rhys. In that finite moment, he knew the dark truth.

CHAPTER SIXTEEN

"IF YOU CAN MEET ME for coffee at Goldberg's in ten minutes, I'd appreciate it. It's right around the corner. I have to talk to my attorney about a few things and then I'll be right there."

Coffee? Whitney's invitation rang in Rhys's ears. At this moment, hate was not a strong enough word.

Whitney had waltzed into his world and made him love her, then she'd ripped his heart to shreds and stolen the only thing that had any meaning in his life.

They stood outside the chambers where it had taken the judge mere minutes to issue the order. Rhys didn't need to be there, but he'd felt compelled. Even in his emotional distress, he couldn't stay away.

The blood tests had proved R.J. was not SaraJane's biological father. And the news had rocked him to the core. That was two days ago and he was still reeling from the impact, unable to function normally. Shell shock was the only thing he could compare it with.

The anguish was beyond pain, beyond tears.

"Sure," he said, willing his voice to remain even. If nothing else, he'd see what he could work out to spend time with SaraJane once in a while.

Whitney looked wonderful. Despite everything, he still appreciated her beauty. And he hated himself for even noticing. He forced a thin smile and nodded.

Feeling as hollow as a gutted deer, he went to the

coffee shop and requested the booth in the back. He sat on the side facing the door so he could see her when she came in. He ordered black coffee for himself.

Whitney, no doubt, wanted to make arrangements to pick up SaraJane. The judge's flat emotionless words awarding custody to the natural mother's sister, Whitney Sheffield, still pounded in Rhys's head.

Whitney's being awarded custody wasn't a shock to anyone. After the blood tests, it was inevitable. She'd been kind enough to request the court to let SaraJane stay with him and his folks until the legalities were finished.

He blinked back the burning wetness behind his eyes. He swallowed the steaming coffee and scalded his tongue. All too soon, it would be over and he'd be left to pick up the pieces of his worthless life.

Somehow he couldn't get past the feeling that he'd failed them all. He didn't know what he could have done to stop any of it from happening, but it just seemed there should've been a way.

All he could do now was continue to help his son and hope for the best. All he could do now was hope to see SaraJane from time to time.

Whitney entered the coffee shop, her gaze seeking him out. He'd never seen her dressed as she was today, in a pale-yellow business suit, her hair swept into some kind of twist with golden wisps framing her face. He'd only seen her in the casual clothes she'd worn in the shop, except for that one night at the convention—that one memorable night.

He remembered how she'd appeared in the doorway of Smoky Joe's, all long legs and floaty hair and dressed in witch-black. She'd cast her spell over him—and every other guy in the room.

But the way she looked today only served to remind him just how far out of her league he was.

In the few seconds it took her to walk to the booth, his mind played over the past weeks, their days together in the shop, the nights together at dinner, with and without SaraJane, the camaraderie and the lovemaking. Ah, the lovemaking.

They were in the same league then.

If nothing else, he had some good memories. If he could think of them, instead of his losses, he might get through this. But right now, even those memories felt like losses.

"Sorry to keep you waiting." She stood in that casual confident way that made his blood rush. Was there a hint of pity in her eyes? He sure as hell didn't need her pity.

He straightened in his chair.

"No problem. I've got all the time in the world."

Her soft eyes held his. Quickly he took another sip of coffee and shored his reserves. He wasn't a kid fighting neighborhood bullies anymore. He had to learn when to give up. He was a big boy—and big boys don't cry when they lose.

EVEN BEFORE WHITNEY SAT DOWN, she felt the wall between them. She literally ached with regret, although there'd been no alternative once the tests had determined that R.J. wasn't SaraJane's father.

Rhys knew it, too. And he'd finally given up, apparently realizing his case was hopeless. He could sell off all his assets and he'd still lose in the end.

She bit her lip. How in God's name would she ever get through this? She touched the waitress's sleeve as she bustled by. "Coffee, please." She placed her hands in her lap and looked directly across the table.

"I'm sorry, Rhys. I'm truly sorry things worked out the way they have for you." Damn, she knew it wasn't going to come out right. "But I need to talk to you about SaraJane and how to go about this whole transition process."

His forehead furrowed, eyebrows clamped together. He waited for her to continue, and she knew she was going to do it badly. She pulled in a deep breath and forged ahead.

"I realize it would be very hard on SaraJane if I just came in one day and whisked her away from the only family she's ever known. So I was hoping that you could help me with this."

Rhys's eyes widened. He must've thought she was stark raving mad to expect his help in any way.

"What I mean is, it'll be harder on her if she knows you don't want her to leave."

He leaned back against the booth with a derisive laugh.

"What would you like me to do—send her away thinking I don't want her?"

"No. I'm simply asking you to make it easier for her by not letting her know how *much* you want her to stay." She glanced down, twisting the napkin in her lap. She looked up again and found herself staring into eyes that glittered with pain. She bit her lip, forcing back her own tears.

"I would never do anything to hurt SaraJane," Rhys whispered, his voice cracking with emotion. His knuckles whitened around the cup.

Whitney saw the muscle on one side of his jaw twitch violently. A moment later, when he'd obviously reined himself in, he said evenly, "How do you want to do this?"

She exhaled, unaware till then that she'd been holding her breath. God, she admired his strength—and she loved him more at this moment than ever before. She glanced down, then back to him again.

"I...I've been thinking about that. If it's okay with you, that is," she stammered. "I have some things to organize to get ready for having a child in the house. I think it might take me a week or two. And I hoped SaraJane could stay where she is—with you—during that time."

He nodded for her to go on.

"Then maybe we could get her used to the idea that she's coming to live with me. To be truthful, I really don't know how any of this will work without your co-operation. Please say you'll help make this easy for her."

Lord, she was asking a lot. Here she was, ready to rip away the light of his life and asking for his help to do it. "I think," she added, "you should be the one to tell her."

Rhys had an elbow on the table, his chin cupped firmly in the palm of his hand. Whitney felt his enormous restraint—and suspected his courage.

Then he took a sip of coffee and said, "You're right. I'll tell her. I'll do whatever you want, keep her however long you need to get ready. Just let me know what you think is best and I'll do it."

She swallowed hard, feeling his pain because she knew what it had taken to tell her that. And she had no doubt whatsoever that he meant every word.

"Good," she said, finishing the conversation. "I trust

you'll know when the time is right to talk to her, so I'll leave that to you. I'll be in touch with you both.''

Raw emotion flared between them. He nodded, then put his hand over hers. ''I'm so very sorry about your sister, Whitney,'' he said softly. ''I didn't know. Truly I didn't.'' He inhaled shakily. ''I know there's no way I can make amends for R.J.'s part in that…''

His voice cracked again and he shook his head, as if nothing he could say would ever be enough. ''I'm sorry.''

She squeezed his hand, got up, turned, then walked away. The few yards to the door felt like a thousand miles, and she wanted more than anything to hear him call her back. But he didn't, and she couldn't see a thing through her tears.

RHYS PARKED next to his dad's white Blazer. He sat for a minute trying to decide what to say to his parents. He felt physically ill thinking how losing SaraJane was going to affect them. They loved her as much as he did.

Although Whitney's attorney had assured him that she wanted them all to continue to be part of SaraJane's life, he knew how those things went. Especially when they lived in different places, far apart.

And SaraJane was so very young she'd soon forget all about the life they'd had together. Just as R.J. had.

''Hi, son.'' Johnny greeted him at the door.

Rhys could tell his dad was making every effort to act normally, even down to his cheery smile.

Rhys knew his parents would put up a good front for both his sake and SaraJane's. ''How'd things go at the shop?''

''Great, but I don't think I'm going to give up inn-keeping for motorcycles. Two guys came in looking like

Marlon Brando in *The Wild One,* took one look at me and left. Don't think I'd be much good for business.'' Johnny clapped Rhys on the shoulder.

"Nonsense. We'll just have to get you some different duds.'' Rhys tried desperately to keep up the small talk they both knew wasn't going to work. Finally Rhys broached the subject because he knew his dad wouldn't.

"It's done,'' he said, while hanging up his jacket. "I'll tell SaraJane as soon as I can.'' He dropped his briefcase onto the desk and opened it. "I really don't know how she'll react.''

"She's sturdy. I guess if you approach it in the right way, she'll be okay. She's been asking about both you and Whitney.''

Weary, Rhys thumbed through the papers he'd thrown into his briefcase. He found the one with Whitney's phone number in California and handed it to his father after writing it down for himself.

"Here, this is Whitney's number in case anything comes up during the day that you want to tell her about. I'm not sure when she'll be ready for SaraJane, probably in a week or two. Apparently she has some things to take care of first.''

A query appeared in Johnny's eyes. "Really? What could be more important? It's what she's wanted all along, isn't it?''

Rhys had been slightly puzzled, too. Whitney got what she'd wanted, and now she'd asked him to keep SaraJane even longer. Maybe she was feeling guilty about the whole thing and just offering him some compensation?

From his perspective, it was just prolonging the inevitable. If he had only himself to worry about, he'd want it over and done with.

Maybe then he could get on with his life—without SaraJane. Without Whitney. Funny how he couldn't think of one without the other. How long, he wondered, would it take him to stop expecting SaraJane to run into his arms when he came home, to stop seeing her smile, hearing her laughter? How long would it take him to forget how Whitney felt in his arms?

Never, he suspected. He didn't think he'd ever forget any of it—nor did he want to.

"Yeah. It's what she wanted. And she has every right," Rhys admitted, surprisingly protective of Whitney's status. "SaraJane is her niece. That's more than I can say."

Johnny cocked his chin toward Rhys and took off his bifocals. He pulled a clean hanky from his pocket and started wiping the lenses. "Yep," he said, and wiped some more. "But somehow I got the impression that the two of you…"

"That the two of us what?" Rhys said defensively. "The two of us were at cross-purposes. Two storm fronts moving against each other."

Johnny shook his head. "Nope. Uh-uh. That's not what I saw. And I'm pretty darn good at people-watching."

"And what exactly did you see?" Rhys hated to ask, but again, hope flickered.

"I saw two people who should be spending the rest of their lives together. Two people in love."

Rhys scoffed. "Thanks, Dad. But I don't think so. I think this is one time wishful thinking took over."

Johnny shrugged. "I saw it."

"Okay. Fine." Rhys's face went somber. "But I can only speak for myself, Dad."

"And have you?"

Lamely, he shook his head.

"Then why don't you? What do you have to lose by approaching her?"

Rhys cracked his knuckles. He had nothing and everything to lose. His self-respect for one. Sure, he could go to her, tell her what was in his heart, and what would she think? She'd think he was making a last-ditch effort to keep SaraJane in his life, that was what.

"It wouldn't work, Dad. She's got her life and I've got mine. They're not even remotely the same. Let's just leave it at that."

Slow and easy, Johnny returned his glasses to the bridge of his nose. "You hear about Charley?"

Rhys nodded, relieved at the change of subject. "Last I heard, he was headed to the assay office. Did that ol' grizzly finally hit the mother lode?"

"Enough to ask Mabel for her hand in marriage." Johnny gave a huge grin.

"Why, that old rogue." Rhys had to grin, too. "After all these years. What's he been waiting for?"

Johnny ambled into the office and Rhys followed. "Guess he thought that since Mabel owned the restaurant and all and he didn't have a dime of his own, she wouldn't want him."

Rhys laughed. "So he wasted all that time? Anyone could see they were crazy about each other."

Plucking up some papers from Rhys's desk, Johnny studied them and without looking at Rhys said, "Guess he was wearing blinders. Believed she was too rich for him or some such nonsense."

Rhys tagged his dad on the shoulder. "You're so subtle."

Johnny cleared his throat. "Subtle, hell. I'm right. Nothing subtle about that."

"The situation is different."

"She loves you, boy," Johnny said affectionately. He took his jacket from the closet and walked to the door. "Anyone can see that."

Later that night, when he brought SaraJane home and after she'd asked about Whitney for the hundredth time, Rhys told her she could go and stay with Whitney for a while. Then, tucking her into bed, he'd asked her what she'd think if he told her he'd just found out that Whitney was her aunt.

SaraJane beamed. "Chrissy has a aunt. Am I going to have a aunt like Chrissy?"

"Well, sweetheart…" Rhys sat on the side of the bed, facing her. He reached over and tucked a golden strand of hair behind her ear, then cupped her tiny chin in his hand. "Yes, you are."

SaraJane's eyes rounded like saucers, and a dimpled smile lit her perfect little face. "Can I get a mommy, too? Like Chrissy and Jennifer?" she asked excitedly.

Rhys's heart split.

"If you want that, sweetheart. I'm sure Whitney would like nothing better than to be your mommy. She loves you, you know."

SaraJane's dimples deepened. "I love her, too, Poppy. I *want* her to be my mommy."

Rhys lightly brushed her cheek with a kiss, touched the tip of her nose and then her eyelids to close them. "Well, you have sweet dreams, punkin. We'll see what we can work out."

SaraJane was still smiling when he tiptoed from the room. He'd tell her in bits and pieces. That seemed best.

SHE COULDN'T WAIT. She absolutely couldn't wait. Whitney glanced around SaraJane's room, making sure everything was there. A Pooh bear, another doll that looked as if she could be Miss Agatha's sister, the small stove and table and chairs—everything SaraJane was used to, the things she had at home—at Rhys's parents' home.

Lord, she was so ready for SaraJane she was sure she'd burst. Though her happiness came with an ache of regret, Whitney felt happier than she had since…well, she couldn't remember ever feeling so good. In addition to readying the house, she'd sold her apartment in New York and also made some decisions about her mother.

After seeing Rhys's unwavering support for his son, the way the whole family stuck together, she'd realized she'd never free herself from the anger and bitterness she felt toward her parents unless she made an effort to understand. And that would never happen if she ran away again.

Surprisingly, she'd gained new insight about her mom after talking with the clinic psychiatrist and decided, for her own sake, as well as her mother's, that they both deserved another chance.

She'd arranged to be Kathryn's partner and vowed to do whatever she needed to get her through the program. By no stretch of the imagination was it the solution to their problems, nor would it wipe away their history. She had no illusions about the toll it might take.

But she knew now that she could do what the psychiatrist had said—take it one day at a time.

It was a start, and she felt better about herself for trying. Even a tiny bit hopeful. She could thank Rhys for making her see it was possible.

He'd stood by R.J. and so had his parents. The last time she'd heard from Gretta, the boy had started therapy in prison. Gretta sounded positive and said he was making progress. Whether it was true or not didn't matter. Whitney hoped for Rhys's sake that it was.

She'd learned so much from Rhys and his parents she felt overwhelmed with gratitude. Most importantly, though, she'd realized that to help herself, she had to open her heart.

She had to risk getting hurt again. And she had to learn to forgive—not only her parents but herself. She had to forgive herself for not being there for Morgan. She hadn't been in charge of Morgan's life; she'd barely been able to salvage her own.

Knowing that and making the decision to try with her parents had brought her a new inner peace. If supporting her mother did any good at all, then maybe her father would see it and make some decisions of his own. It was all she could do; the rest was up to them.

She glanced around the room again, her excitement building. SaraJane's room was ready, the house was childproof, and Maddie had already moved into her quarters. Thank heaven for Maddie. Whitney had interviewed more nannies than she cared to see in a lifetime and had finally found the perfect one.

Yes, she was ready. Now all she had to do was wait for SaraJane. When she'd called Rhys and told him she could fly out to get her niece, he'd insisted he needed to come to California for business and he would bring SaraJane then.

Whitney had agreed because it might ease his mind to see where SaraJane would live and what her room looked like. That way, when he talked with SaraJane on the phone, he could picture it in his mind.

All Rhys wanted was to assure himself that his little girl would be okay.

His little girl. The thought sent a shiver up Whitney's

spine. Would she always think of SaraJane as his little girl? Would she always jump when the phone rang, hoping it might be Rhys? Would she always hope for something more? Or would those feelings fade with time?

She doubted it, doubted it very much. She'd never experienced such deep emotions about any man. And even though she knew he hated her now, Rhys Gannon would not be easy to forget.

RHYS DROVE THE RENTAL CAR around the corner of the narrow street, taking in the homes lining the coast. Palatial homes, some hidden in lush coves, some right out there on the beach.

"Poppy," SaraJane gushed excitedly from her car seat in the back. "Look! Lots and lots of water. Can I go swimming?"

"I don't think this is the right time of year for swimming, kiddo, not in the ocean. It's too cold, and besides, it's going to get dark in an hour."

And you'll have the rest of your life to swim in the ocean. His heart ached. Damn, he'd hoped he'd have more control. He'd thought it would be easier for him to bring SaraJane here than it would be to watch her leave with Whitney.

In the past two weeks he'd thought of every conceivable way to prevent this from happening—even down to leaving the country with SaraJane. He'd also thought of declaring his love for Whitney. Because he knew now that anything worth having was worth more than his stupid pride.

He'd tried out a slew of scenarios about how it might work—how they could maintain their careers, live in one place or both. She'd had some great ideas about his business, ideas he could implement with her help—if she was willing. If she wasn't traveling the world. Which was an important part of her work, her life. And he knew how much her work meant to her.

In the end it came down to doing what was best for SaraJane. That was all that really mattered. And he'd only recently begun to realize that she needed something he couldn't give her. A mother. A little girl needed a mommy.

Once he saw SaraJane's excitement, he couldn't have kept her from Whitney no matter what he'd wanted for himself. He couldn't deny SaraJane what she deserved, what was rightfully hers.

Fact was, *he* had no rights whatsoever. Even if Whitney kept her word about allowing SaraJane to visit, it was all at her own discretion. He had no rights. Period. The end. And he wasn't about to do anything to screw things up for his little girl.

He drove into a circular drive, his gaze drawn upward. The two-story white stucco home was magnificent. Even in his imaginings, he hadn't pictured it quite like this. SaraJane would certainly have the best.

When he stepped from the car, the humid salt air enveloped him. It was almost balmy for late October, he decided, remembering the times he'd been in Southern California on business.

He lifted SaraJane from her car seat, and she wriggled down from his arms, then waited for him to hand her the small backpack she'd insisted on carrying because Whitney carried one.

He'd convinced her to leave most of her things in Estrade, saying she'd be coming back. Or he could send them later. The resilience of a child, he thought ruefully. Would that he had some of it.

Rhys held SaraJane's hand as she bounced excitedly

waiting for the front door to open. She rang the bell again and he gently held her back. "Patience is a virtue," he said, trying to lighten the moment.

The door opened and a pleasant fiftyish woman stood before them. Rhys started to ask for Whitney when the woman knelt down to SaraJane's level.

"Well, hello, sweetheart. You must be SaraJane. I'm Maddie and we've been expecting you." Her warmth seemed genuine.

SaraJane said, "Hi. I've been 'specting to be here, too."

The woman laughed and stood up, smiling at Rhys.

"Hello, I'm Maddie Harrison," she repeated. "You must be Rhys. Please come in."

Following the woman into the foyer and through the living room, Rhys saw Whitney coming through a sliding door in a wall of windows that led directly to the ocean.

The sight of her took his breath away. She wore gauzy vanilla-colored pants and a flowing matching top that was slit up the middle to the waist. Her pale hair hung loose, exactly the way he liked it.

Hurrying toward them, she reached down and in one quick motion scooped SaraJane into her arms. Whitney whirled around and smiled over her shoulder at Rhys, and something warm and wonderful unfolded in his chest just watching them.

Yeah, SaraJane would be just fine. What more could he ask?

Whitney set the child down, then hugged Rhys as if they were old friends and there'd never been anything between them. He'd wondered how he'd feel seeing her again—wondered what he'd say.

And now he knew. They'd act like friends. Even though he wanted her, loved her.

Moments later they sat at a table on the deck sipping coffee and making small talk while SaraJane drank milk and chomped on one of the chocolate-chip cookies Whitney had baked.

"Go ahead," Whitney said, seeing him eye the platter. "But just remember, I don't know the Heimlich maneuver."

Rhys snatched a cookie and took a bite. "Not bad," he said after swallowing. "I'm surprised. I didn't know you could bake."

"Lots of things you don't know about me, I guess." Her tone was sexy, challenging.

"Oh, you're probably right. But I know the important things." His eyes searched hers for a connection, and almost instantly he was lost in those transparent blue eyes that said she still felt something for him, still wanted him.

Jeez, Gannon, get a grip. Are you losing your mind? Hallucinating? He shoved the cup away. "I think I'd better go now." He wasn't going to let himself believe that this was anything more than the simple thing it was.

His palms started to sweat. He got up and motioned SaraJane over, then knelt next to her.

"Listen, punkin..." His voice broke. SaraJane threw her arms around him in a fierce hug. He hugged her back, holding on longer than he should have, until she wriggled away.

WHITNEY'S HEART constricted. She clutched her throat, then touched fingertips to her lips as she watched the two of them. Still crouched, Rhys began again, his chin quivering just the tiniest bit. She saw the shine of tears in his eyes.

"I think it's about time..." He cleared his throat. "About time for me to go."

Whitney felt her own chin begin to quiver.

"We'll see each other soon, sweetheart, and you be..." His shoulders heaved upward as he drew in a calming breath, his voice almost a whisper. "You be a good girl for Whitney, okay?"

"Poppy, don't go!" SaraJane ran at him and flung both arms around his neck again. "I don't want you to go. Stay with us," she demanded.

Rhys hugged her and Whitney saw him struggle to win the battle of emotions warring within him. He smoothed SaraJane's hair from her face and held her at arm's length, looking deeply into her eyes. When he spoke, the tears were in his voice.

"Hey, remember what we talked about? Remember our pact?"

SaraJane nodded, her curls bouncing.

"And you have all the phone numbers so you can call me collect whenever you want."

SaraJane nodded again and he tweaked her nose.

"See, no problems. And remember..." He cleared his throat a second time. "Remember how much Poppy loves you." He looked at Whitney and his voice broke again as he finished. "And how much Whitney loves you, too."

"Yes," SaraJane whispered.

"So give Poppy one last hug and then go play." It was a hug he put his heart and soul into, burying his face in his little girl's shoulder.

CHAPTER SEVENTEEN

OH, GOD. HOW COULD she do this? How could she be so cruel? Rhys's controlled despair tore great chunks from Whitney's heart, and it took every ounce of strength she possessed to hold back her tears.

When Rhys loosened his grip on SaraJane and pried the chubby fingers from around his neck, Whitney interrupted, her voice choked with emotion. "Rhys, please." She touched his shoulder as he stood up. "Please, I need to talk to you for a minute."

She glanced at SaraJane, who looked up at her with all the love and trust in the world. "SaraJane, sweetheart, maybe Maddie can show you around for a few minutes while I talk to Poppy, okay?" Whitney nodded at Maddie, who instantly took over, taking the child by the hand, chattering as they disappeared down the hallway.

"I have something to ask you, Rhys." She looked at him, groping for words. Trying to work out her thoughts, she frowned at the floor, swiping away the hair that fell in front of her face. *Control. Stay in control. Smooth easy voice. Breathe...and for God's sake, slow down.*

"I feel really foolish about this," she said, waving a hand. "I just got this offer for an incredible shoot in Europe, and—" she laughed nervously "—wouldn't you know, it was an offer I couldn't refuse."

She whirled around in a circle, feigning excitement—and indifference to the stunned look on Rhys's face.

Rhys stared. Finally he murmured, "I think I got lost somewhere in the middle. What are you trying to say?"

"Well, it was too late to reach you, but I thought you might want to keep SaraJane for a while longer—as long as I'm away."

He eyed her suspiciously. She looked away, focused somewhere off in the distance, toward the ocean. It was all she could do to keep her voice calm, keep him from seeing her hands shake—and her heart break.

At this moment she didn't know which of them hurt worse. She had to get either him or herself out of there.

"What do you say? Is it a deal? I go on the shoot and you take SaraJane back with you while I'm gone? Maybe she can stay even longer?"

Rhys's expression was incredulous. "I wouldn't do that to her. Good God, Whitney! I've already prepared her for this. She's ready to be here. How long do you plan to be gone?"

Whitney used every mental tactic she knew to steady her voice. "Don't know," she replied crisply. "Hopefully, not more than a month or so."

Rhys's mouth dropped open. "You…you expect a small child to come here and be with a nanny, a virtual stranger, for a month or more while you're out taking pictures on the Riviera?"

His voice rose by the end of his sentence, and she saw the cords in his neck stand out, his face growing a deeper crimson with every word. Anger seethed from every pore.

"That's why I hoped you might want to take her back with you," she stammered. Her heart pounded so hard she was sure he could see it. "You can stay the night.

I wouldn't expect you to go back right away. Besides, I'll be out this evening and won't be here to bother you.''

She just kept babbling and he just stood there watching her. When she couldn't stand it any longer, she opened the sliding door to the beach. ''I think I'll go for a walk to make things easier for you. If you'll take SaraJane out for dinner, I won't be here when you return. Maddie will let you in.''

Saying that, she fled down the steps and onto the beach—out of Rhys's sight.

Rhys stood, mouth gaping, taking tentative steps in one direction, then the other. What the *hell* had just happened?

The woman was crazy. What was she thinking? He'd brought SaraJane here to live. It was all planned.

Then Whitney up and decides to go on a photo shoot when she has a child to care for? Goddamn, what a mess. He raked his fingers through his hair, scanning the room to see where Maddie had taken SaraJane.

''SaraJane?'' he called. Something wasn't right. ''SaraJane!'' he hollered.

''Up here, Poppy. In my new room with Maddie.''

Suddenly it didn't matter to him if Whitney had custody or not. He was taking his little girl home for good, and Whitney would have to get her over his dead body. He flew up the stairs.

Several poster-size photographs on a table in the upstairs hallway caught his eye. He glanced peripherally while advancing down the hall to where he heard SaraJane's giggles.

When he reached the room, he saw it was decorated like something out of a home-decorating magazine. Frilly, but not too frilly, just enough for a precious little girl. As he gazed around the room, noticing the great care Whitney had taken, he was even more confused.

The Pooh bears, the dolls, the same tea set and oven SaraJane had at home, the dollhouse she'd been wanting forever—all the things SaraJane knew and loved.

His heart lurched when he saw his own face on the wall, framed in white ceramic. And there were others, several of him, his parents—all of them, alone and together.

Something definitely wasn't right. Why would Whitney go to all this trouble and then...

He looked at SaraJane, who was playing with the dollhouse; she and Maddie were laughing. ''It's okay, honey,'' he said. ''Just wondering where you were.''

Confused, he backed away. ''Just go ahead and keep playing. I'll be back in a little while.''

What the hell? Why would Whitney go to all the trouble of fixing everything up for SaraJane, hire a nanny and then decide to take a job in Europe? It just didn't make sense.

Slowly he descended the stairs, looking around, searching for some clue to figure out what was going on. The interior of the house was beautiful, which he hadn't paid any attention to when he'd come in. The decor was casually elegant, just what he'd expect Whitney to choose. Just like Whitney herself.

The home wasn't overdone with gilded mirrors and elaborate furniture; it was simple and uncomplicated. If anything, it tended toward the spare, but it was definitely warm and homey, with lots of windows to let the sunshine in.

In the family room, two supple white-leather couches flanked a full-wall entertainment unit with built-in bookcases. The tables were mostly distressed mission-style, mixed with some antiques. The walls were conspicuously bare, but he saw several large framed photographs vertically stacked against the wall behind one of the couches.

He walked over, deciding he wasn't leaving until he found out exactly what Whitney was doing. He held up the first photograph. The girl was young and beautiful, almost more beautiful than Whitney, if that was possible.

He deduced from the *M* on her gold necklace that this must be Morgan, Whitney's sister. SaraJane's mother.

Sadness filled him as he thumbed through the rest of the photographs. Pictures of Whitney and Morgan as children, hugging, laughing, Whitney as a teenager holding a toddler on her knee—probably Morgan. He was struck by how much the little girl looked like SaraJane.

After his visit to R.J. in prison, Rhys had read the *People* magazine article about Whitney and her family. It had given him insight into the relationship between Whitney and Morgan, and in these photographs, he saw it even more clearly.

Whitney had been the one to watch out for her little sister, protecting her from the trauma of living with alcoholic parents—but who, he wondered, had been there to protect Whitney? Who had been there to dry her tears?

The last two photographs shocked him. They were of him, Whitney and SaraJane, the three of them on their picnic. He remembered the fun they'd had setting the timer on her camera, and Whitney, laughing and scrambling to get into position before the shutter went off.

These were photographs she'd cared enough about to enlarge and frame.

She loves you, boy. He heard his dad's words as if Johnny was right there in the room. Rhys drew air into his lungs, hoping a blast of oxygen would clear his head.

Despite all they'd been through, he still loved her. He charged back up the stairs to SaraJane's room, stopping at the doorway.

"Maddie. Do you know anything about a photo shoot in Europe?"

The woman said, "I sure do, Mr. Gannon. Ms. Sheffield turned it down straight away. She said nothing's more important than being here with this little gal." She ruffled SaraJane's hair. "Said she was only doing local assignments now."

The pieces began to fall into place. How did he miss all the signals? What an idiot! An absolute dolt!

He bolted from the room, calling upstairs as he went, "I'll be right back, Maddie. I'm going to the beach for a minute."

He hit the deck running, down to the beach, scanning right and left to see which way she'd gone. Empty. His heart raced. Where would she go?

He glanced out to sea. The sun glowed low on the horizon, and soon it would be too dark to look for her, since there were no lights or piers along this stretch of beach. Pure fear pounded through him, and he started to jog in the direction of some faint footprints.

He came around an outcrop of rock and saw her walking slowly, head bowed, arms crossed over her chest.

Relief flooded him, but the fear, the thought of losing her, had hit him like a sledgehammer.

"Whitney!" he yelled. "Wait!" Running, he caught up with her. "C'mon back to the house. We need to talk."

Obviously surprised that he'd come after her, she hesitated. He grabbed her arm more roughly than he'd intended and swung her around toward the house.

"C'mon, we need to talk."

She shrugged him off. "Excuse me. I'm not in the mood for being manhandled today." She glared at him through moist eyes, rubbing her arm where he'd grabbed her. "Or ever, for that matter." But she started walking back with him, anyway—in silence.

"Whitney, tell me again why you're accepting this assignment."

Nothing.

"Do you think you can just flip everyone's life upside down and then run off?" He had to say something to get her to talk—even if it made her mad. "Is it that easy for you to do whatever you want, regardless of who you hurt? Is that your usual mode of operation?"

Nearing the house, she turned on him. "I *will not* make a scene in front of SaraJane. I had enough of that in my own childhood, and I don't intend to subject her to the same. If you have something to say about my decision to continue my career, do it now and be done with it. If you don't want SaraJane with you, you'd better let me know that, too."

Rhys caught his breath. Half angry, half excited, he blurted, "Dammit. Yes, I do have something to say." He latched on to her again, only gently this time, and stared directly into her eyes.

"I love you. That's what I have to say."

WHITNEY FROWNED. Was she really hearing him say, *I love you?* Hope grew within her. His face came closer and closer until she felt the warmth of his breath on her own parted lips.

"I said, I love you," he whispered huskily. "And I'll keep saying it until you believe me."

Her heart danced crazily in her chest. In the last half hour she'd despaired of ever feeling whole again, and now, all at once, Rhys was standing there saying the words she'd ached to hear. Words from the man she loved, the man who said he loved her, too. Was that possible—in spite of everything?

Rhys cracked the quirky little smile she'd always found irresistible. Her pulse raced. Her mind spun.

"It took your going away to make me realize I don't want to spend the rest of my life without you." His expression sobered and his eyes glistened. "Whitney, I want to marry you. I want that more than anything I've ever wanted in my life."

Marriage. The word, with all its implications, sent a jolt of fear through her. She stiffened, drawing back.

"Whitney don't do that to me." Rhys tightened his grip on her arm. "I know what you're thinking and I won't let you shut me out. This is about us, only us. It's you and me and what we're going to do with the rest of our lives." He paused for breath. "I love you, Whitney Sheffield, and I don't intend to stop."

He drew her into his arms, his body pressed close to hers. She was sure he could feel the violent thudding of her heart. Could she believe?

"Whether you're in Arizona or California or Europe," he said lovingly. "Whether SaraJane is with me or with you, whether you want me to or not. I'll still love you."

Whitney melted from the inside out, a spark of hope flickering, struggling to ignite. Could it actually work for them?

"Oh, Rhys, you don't know what you're saying," she whispered, her mouth so close to his she could almost feel the softness of his lips.

"The hell I don't." He locked his gaze with hers. Abruptly he tipped his head back and laughed out loud.

Then he raised his arms high and shouted to the heavens, "Yes!"

A fraction of a second later, he embraced her, saying, "God, Whitney. For the first time in my life, I know exactly what I'm saying. I know exactly what I want. I love you and I want to marry you. Yes, in spite of any problems we might have. We can work together. I can help you and you can help me. We can make it work." He paused for a breath.

"You, me and SaraJane—we can be a family."

Whitney's heart stopped completely. *A family.*

"All I know—" Rhys's pupils dilated and his voice became a soft caress against her cheek "—is that we were meant to be together for the rest of our lives. Trust me to love you, Whitney. Always."

He pressed gentle kisses on her cheeks, lifting away the wetness, and then his mouth claimed hers, hungry, needy, and she tasted the saltiness of her own tears on his lips.

Trust me. Trust me to love you. A surge of warmth infused her. Oh…she did trust him. She knew she did. Because she'd never have left SaraJane with him if she didn't.

Her heart swelled and suddenly she felt dizzy with love and joy, and she kissed him back and knew her heart was his forever.

When finally they broke the kiss, she said, "I love you, too, Rhys, and I will for the rest of my life." It sounded—and felt—like a vow.

A giggle erupted from the dunes behind them, and SaraJane ran out, tugging off her shoes as she went. A slightly frazzled Maddie plunked down on the sparse tufts of salt grass, hands raised in exasperation.

SaraJane dashed over to them, grabbing Whitney

around the knees. "See. You can't get away now," he said.

SaraJane let go of Whitney and stared at her with round-eyed innocence. "Please don't go away. I promise to be good."

Whitney gasped with a shiver of recollection and a fleeting vision of her own past. She quickly reached down and scooped SaraJane into her arms, holding the child tightly between her and Rhys.

Oh, Lord, what had she almost done? She'd almost pushed the two most important people in the world out of her life. Her throat seized up and she said in a whisper, "No, sweetheart. I'm not going anywhere. I love you very much, both you and Poppy. And I'm not going anywhere without either of you."

SaraJane stuffed a finger in her mouth. "Promise?"

Whitney had come full circle. It was the same promise she'd made to Morgan so many years before.

But seeing the love and trust in SaraJane's eyes, and the same love and trust in Rhys's, she knew. Whatever it took, it was a promise she had to keep.

She rubbed SaraJane's nose with her own and said tenderly, "I promise, angel."

And SaraJane, satisfied, wriggled down and planted her feet squarely in the sand. Placing one chubby hand on her hip, she cocked her head, looking up at both of them. Her blue eyes sparkled impishly. "Are you gonna stay, too, Poppy? 'Cause I want you *and* a mommy."

Rhys looked at Whitney, his expression solemn. "I will, if you will."

Whitney's heart soared. "Promise?"

"Forever," Rhys whispered. "I promise forever."

HARLEQUIN® SUPERROMANCE®

You are now entering

WELCOME TO RIVERBEND
POPULATION 8793

Riverbend...the kind of place where everyone knows your name—and your business. Riverbend...home of the River Rats—a group of small-town sons and daughters who've been friends since high school.

The Rats are all grown up now. Living their lives and learning that some days are good and some days aren't—and that you can get through anything as long as you have your friends.

Starting in July 2000, Harlequin Superromance brings you Riverbend—six books about the River Rats and the Midwest town they live in.

BIRTHRIGHT by Judith Arnold (July 2000)
THAT SUMMER THING by Pamela Bauer (August 2000)
HOMECOMING by Laura Abbot (September 2000)
LAST-MINUTE MARRIAGE by Marisa Carroll (October 2000)
A CHRISTMAS LEGACY by Kathryn Shay (November 2000)

Available wherever Harlequin books are sold.

HARLEQUIN®
Makes any time special™

Visit us at www.eHarlequin.com

HSRIVER

Back by popular demand are

DEBBIE MACOMBER's

MIDNIGHT SONS

Hard Luck, Alaska, is a town that needs women!
And the O'Halloran brothers are just
the fellows to fly them in.

Starting in March 2000 this beloved series returns
in special 2-in-1 collector's editions:

MAIL-ORDER MARRIAGES, featuring
Brides for Brothers and *The Marriage Risk*
On sale March 2000

FAMILY MEN, featuring
Daddy's Little Helper and *Because of the Baby*
On sale May 2000

THE LAST TWO BACHELORS, featuring
Falling for Him and *Ending in Marriage*
On sale July 2000

Collect and enjoy each MIDNIGHT SONS story!

Available at your favorite retail outlet.

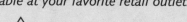

HARLEQUIN®
Makes any time special ™

Your Romantic Books—find them at

www.eHarlequin.com

Visit the *Author's Alcove*

➤ Find the most complete information anywhere on your favorite author.

➤ Try your hand in the Writing Round Robin— contribute a chapter to an online book in the making.

Enter the *Reading Room*

➤ Experience an interactive novel—help determine the fate of a story being created now by one of your favorite authors.

➤ Join one of our reading groups and discuss your favorite book.

Drop into *Shop eHarlequin*

➤ Find the latest releases—read an excerpt or write a review for this month's Harlequin top sellers.

➤ Try out our amazing search feature—tell us your favorite theme, setting or time period and we'll find a book that's perfect for you.

All this and more available at

www.eHarlequin.com
on Women.com Networks

HARLEQUIN®
SUPERROMANCE®

*Pregnant and alone—
these stories follow women
from the heartache of
betrayal to finding true love
and starting a family.*

THE FOURTH CHILD by C.J. Carmichael.
When Claire's marriage is in trouble, she tries to
save it—although she's not sure she can forgive her
husband's betrayal.
On sale May 2000.

AND BABY MAKES SIX by Linda Markowiak.
Jenny suddenly finds herself jobless and pregnant by
a man who doesn't want their child.
On sale June 2000.

MOM'S THE WORD by Roz Denny Fox.
After her feckless husband steals her inheritance and
leaves town with another woman, Hayley discovers she's
pregnant.
On sale July 2000.

Available wherever Harlequin books are sold.

HARLEQUIN®
Makes any time special ™

HARLEQUIN®
SUPERROMANCE

COMING NEXT MONTH

#924 BIRTHRIGHT • Judith Arnold
Riverbend

Aaron Mazerik is back. He isn't the town's bad boy anymore, but some people still don't think he's good enough—especially not for Riverbend's golden girl, Lily Holden. Which is fine with Aaron, since he's convinced there's even *more* reason he and Lily shouldn't be together.

Riverbend, Indiana: Home of the River Rats—small-town sons and daughters who've been friends since high school. These are their stories.

#925 FULL RECOVERY • Bobby Hutchinson
Emergency!

Spence Mathews, former RCMP officer and now handling security at St. Joe's Hospital, helps Dr. Joanne Duncan deliver a baby in the E.R. After the infant mysteriously disappears a few hours later, Spence and Joanne work closely together to solve the abduction and in the process recover the baby girl—and much more!

#926 MOM'S THE WORD • Roz Denny Fox
9 Months Later

Hayley Ryan is pregnant and alone. Her no-good ex—the baby's father—abandoned her for another woman; her beloved grandfather is dead, leaving her nothing but a mining claim in southern Arizona. Hayley is cast upon her own resources, trying to work the claim, worrying about herself and her baby.... And then rancher Zack Cooper shows up.

#927 THE REAL FATHER • Kathleen O'Brien
Twins

Ten years ago, Molly Lorring left Demery, South Carolina, with a secret. She was pregnant with Beau Forrest's baby, but Beau died in a car crash before he could marry her. For all that time, Beau's identical twin, Jackson, has carried his own secret. Beau *isn't* the father of Molly's baby....

#928 CONSEQUENCES • Margot Dalton
Crystal Creek

Principal Lucia Osborne knows the consequences of hiring cowboy Jim Whitely to teach the difficult seventh graders. Especially when Jim deliberately flouts the rules in order to help the kids. Certain members of the board may vote to fire Lucia and close the school. But Lucia has even graver consequences to worry about. She's falling in love with Jim...and she's expecting another man's child.

#929 THE BABY BARGAIN • Peggy Nicholson
Marriage of Inconvenience

Rafe Montana's sixteen-year-old daughter, Zoe, and Dana Kershaw's teenage son, Sean, have made a baby. *Now what?* Rafe's solution—or rather, proposal—has Zoe ecstatic, but it leaves Dana aghast and Sean confused. Even Rafe wonders whether he's out of his mind.